THE GALLUS ULTIMATUM

Brian A. Hawkins

Chapter 1

Ceres paced back and forth in anguish and frustration. Her watery eyes twitched nervously in response to her inner torment. Her large head jerked in awkward little movements that signaled the brooding desperation within her.

She now lived a hopeless life in cold gray confinement, caged inside two square feet of wooden bars in a damp concrete cellar. Cooped up in this cruel detention, she was cheated from the taste and texture of the good earth, imprisoned away from the warm brilliance of the sun, and deprived from seeing the blueness of the sky. She knew it existed out there, above these dark cellar walls. Sometimes she imagined she could even smell its airy sweetness. But now she had a sickening premonition that she was near her end: that she could soon be executed. Butchered. Ripped apart and devoured.

She had to quell this gruesome vision: to suppress it in her mind, but her palpitating heart would not quit racing. It went its own way in frightening exertion, pounding and pumping her blood through her veins. She could feel her life thrashing and coursing around inside her in a vain attempt to escape an impending death.

Gradually she forced her mind to become calmly detached, separating it from her panicky body to reason out the unknown fearful fate that she sensed. Ceres had been given a mission. She had been given a reason for living that was far greater than her own life. From the billions of chickens on this earth, only she and four thousand other Plymouth Rock hens shared this awesome responsibility to make "The

Connection": to deliver an ultimatum that would shock and change man's world forever. She must be the first to do it. The need to fulfill this mission now crowded all else aside. It dominated her will. She didn't know why she had been chosen, but now she was honor bound and couldn't allow death to rob her of this sacred obligation.

Her heavy body shivered as she settled down in the filthy cage, reeking with the smells of countless other victims. Dirty dried fecal matter mottled the scratched and splintered floor: a gruesome reminder of those that had gone before her, leaving an ugly pattern of soiled feather remnants and the tattered tuffs of past plumage stuccoed to the floor by the excrement of past avian life.

Ceres's sharp eyes had lost their frightened stare as she stoically accepted the crushing confinement of her prison, for she possessed intelligence, will, and the ability to reason. She was a white Plymouth Rock chicken now in the third year of her life. Her great obese body pushed down on her thighs and overburdened legs, causing her tail feathers to drag and splay across the dirty floor boards. Several broken feathers from her rump bent and spread to stretch out through the doweled prison bars.

Ceres weighed almost eight pounds. She was well past her peak laying period and during her life had pushed and strained exactly 762 large light brown eggs out of her fertile body for greedy humans to consume. None of her embryos had reproduced her image. Motherhood had been denied her. Those round oval miracles of life that emerged regularly from her body were taken from her to become omelet, mayonnaise, wedding cake, and endless other foods for her human oppressors. Now she was getting old and tough, destined eventually to be slaughtered as so much stewing meat. It was a common fate of chickens her age.

Small splotches of her yellow skin now poked through her molting feathers. Her hackle feathers were matted and hung from her neck, shredding away in chalky clusters. Her comb sat forward on her head, a dull red scalloped fin above her yellow beak. Her wattles drooped from either side of her beak: great ruddy blobs of misery like two crimson tears of despair.

She was a product of man, her body reluctantly complying to endless generations of genetic breeding, molded and influenced by man's needs and his selection. For countless centuries, man had employed "selective breeding"; the deliberate crossbreeding of animals to exploit and engineer desired and particular traits in domesticated animals.

Her true origins lay in Asia – probably in the Indus Valley – where the beginning of her species (Gallus gallus) still run wild and free, their red plumage dashing through the dark jungles of that continent.

Like all bird life, she is a direct and distant descendent from the dinosaur. Over 5,000 years ago, man first imposed his slavery, breeding her captive forefathers and giving her species the disturbing distinction of possibly being the first animal to be "domesticated".

Ancient records have revealed that the Chinese were raising an early variation of Ceres as early as 1400 BC. Over time, her Asian heritage spread throughout the world, enslaved to the relentless progress of man.

Through the centuries, "the bird that gives birth every day" has been worshipped, mythologized, ritually sacrificed, and eaten in a thousand different ways by endless cults and cultures that have come and gone. Chicken bones found by anthropologists in Chile give hard proof to the theory that Polynesian seafarers brought pre-Columbian chickens to the shores of South America as early as 1350 AD.

Columbus brought her European ancestors to the New World on his second trip in 1493, but Ceres was a very American chicken. A part of her DNA could be traced back to Jamestown, Virginia, where in the early 1600s; the practical British colonists had brought over 500 chickens, and were raising them for their eggs and their meat.

Ceres's deformed shape and her gross size were too heavy to be lifted into flight by her tiny wings. She represented the most recent genetic manipulation by man in America. In 1849 in Plymouth, Massachusetts, he had performed this unnatural experiment, creating a hardy, dual-purpose chicken that he found tasty to eat and excelled in its egg-laying ability. He christened his latest mutation *Plymouth Rock* to commemorate with flesh and feathers the Pilgrim's landing on the shores of Massachusetts in 1620. Yet in spite of this cruel genetic joke, the true strains of her ancient ancestry still survived within her.

Her quiet agony was suddenly interrupted by the rough lifting of her caged cell. She was tossed on end, scrambling to right herself as her prison cage was taken out of the cellar into the bright sunlight, and then ruthlessly heaved – with a jarring force – into the back of a battered white delivery van. The doors slammed shut and she was plunged into a deep darkness. Fear filled her heart as the engine started and nauseous fumes began to seep through the floorboards to attack her eyes and throat. With a violent lurch, the van began to move. It would take her to the city, there to be sold unlawfully at an open market.

For Ceres, it was not to be the end of her life but the beginning of her sacred mission; however she was not to know that as the truck rattled down the highway to her destiny.

Chapter 2

The city sweltered under the broiling summer sun. It hammered down relentlessly between the glass-box canyons, heating the toxic fumes from a thousand cars. Between the buildings, slim slivers of shade offered little relief to the sweltering pedestrians treading on the scorching sidewalks.

A million air conditioners sat on window ledges, thumping and pumping their cooling breath into the innards of the baking buildings. Inside the glassy facades of the high-rise condos and office towers, temperatures swung the other way, keeping its occupants' freezer-cool. By the middle of the day, the blazing heat was at its full intensity, steaming out rivulets of human perspiration, defeating deodorants and soaring the sales of beer, ice cream and soft drinks. It was enough to make a hundred brand mangers weep with happiness in their air-conditioned offices.

The sticky humidity only added to Trent Marshall's increasing feeling of remorse. He'd had a hell of an argument with Janice, brought about by her stubborn unwillingness to accept that his after-hours office relationships with some of his staff were strictly platonic. He insisted that he was only acting as a compassionate employer – soothing and smoothing away office tensions between some of his firm's younger female staff. He liked to socialize with the firm's young women, and while he might occasionally flirt – and fantasize amorous adventures of the flesh – that's where it stopped, for he was much too savvy to have one-night stands or affairs with office candy. He knew his defense was a feeble line of logic; still it annoyed him that her anger and his response had got so vocal. Worse still, it had attracted attention and embarrassment to both of them, happening as it did in the sedate and sophisticated Cafe Boulud, their favorite restaurant for a Saturday brunch. It reached its temper crescendo when Janice abruptly got up from the table and walked out. Avoiding eye contact with the other patrons, Trent had sat there for five minutes and then got up, paid the bill, and took a cab to his downtown lakeshore condo.

He had met Janice two years ago in Mexico, at the Museo Mural Diego Rivera in front of the great Mexican artist's masterpiece, *A Dream of a Sunday Afternoon in the Alameda Park*. Their mutual awe of this painting had brought them together in admiration and they shared her guidebook, walking slowly past the fifty-foot mural, discovering a great work of art and a little bit of each other.

Drinks and lunch followed. She was witty and intelligent and they hit it off quite naturally. He was in Mexico City for the first time, tying up the loose ends of a legal contract. She had attended an international product design convention and was alone. By that evening – knowing there was nothing urgent back home – Trent decided to suddenly take a few days off and Janice decided to extend her stay.

Small and delicate, she had a beautifully proportioned figure that made her appear taller than her actual height. Her best feature was her hair. It was golden blonde, softly framing her enormous blue eyes. She had a tiny nose and full lips that shaped a sensuous mouth which was perhaps a little too generous for her face. At twenty-seven, she easily passed for twenty, and sometimes looked even younger, depending on how she dressed.

For three days they shared the fresh adventure of Mexico City, doing all the normal things tourists do. Each day they discovered more of each other. He learned of her frog collecting fetish and bought her a little buff clay Mixtec frog: a copy of one unearthed in Oaxaca She bought him a traditional Mexican Guayabera shirt. They discovered Chapultepec Park, *The Ballet Folklòrico de Mèxico*, and La Lagunilla, the city's largest flea market, where they seemed to sell everything. They dined together, danced together and in the Hotel Lumina, they slept together.

There was also the serendipity surprise of discovering that they both lived in Toronto. This had allowed them to nurture their Mexico City encounter into a comfortable relationship – now in its second year – that was compatible and intimately satisfying.

Janice Carkson was an American, born in Palos Park, an affluent southwest suburb of Chicago. The only child of Phillis and Jack Carkson, as a child she had shown a natural artistic talent which her mother had encouraged and nourished with art lessons and books. This was her first venture in living outside the United States. A graduate of Chicago's IIT Institute of Design, with a Master's Degree in Product Design, Janice was now an Assistant Professor of Product Design at OCAD University in Toronto. She was popular with her students, many of them her age or older, some of whom had a crush on their attractive professor.

Wallowing in a sea of self-remorse and ashamed of himself, Trent left his condo and walked a short block down to the city's lakeshore park. He often came here to look out at the lake and passing ships and to quietly ponder about life. He had changed into a pair of white summer pants, the Mexican shirt Janice bought him, and Asolo leather sandals. Sitting on a bench gazing out at the lake, it occurred to him that he had never been to the Toronto Islands, though there they were just in front on him. It's got to be cooler over there, he reasoned. He got up, ambled down to the ferryboat dock and bought a round-trip ticket. It was lucky timing. He was among the last to board before the ferry pulled away from the dock.

The Toronto Islands were once a peninsula before the great storm of 1858 split the "islands" from the mainland. Only fifteen minutes by ferry, now they were a walkabout picnic park of bicycle paths, eateries and family-friendly attractions. The ferryboat he was on – named *The Trillium* – was over one-hundred years old. A side wheeler paddle steamer, its double- decks were crammed with city families seeking some escape from the hot and hectic city. *The Trillium* was headed for Center Island, sailing into a light breeze off the lake, and the short voyage had refreshed him. Once there however, the oppressive heat returned, giving young possessive couples the excuse to flaunt their near-nude bodies through the park, which only added to Trent's depression. He envied their youth: even resented it.

Ted Marshall, the adopted son of a distinguished Toronto family, had received a private schooling in Switzerland that smoothed his path to a law degree and eventually an MBA from the Harvard Business School. His upbringing and education made him a reasoned and rational thinker, overly considerate of others, and not given to impulsive anger: qualities that made him all the more remorseful over his quarrel with Janice

He was tall and slim, almost skinny. At age thirty-four, he still had all his own teeth and did not have to wear glasses. It was his thinning hair that worried him. It required studied combing and on the ferry the wind was its enemy. In addition, it was beginning to be peppered with gray. He was not Hollywood handsome, but there was a certain sculptured attractiveness to his strong English features. His eyes were brown and deep. Like most slim men, he walked loosely, his limbs moving with a casualness that women found attractive.

Wandering along a path where the grass had long ago given up its green to the bleaching sun, he rounded a small brown hedge to suddenly find himself looking at a group of wooden buildings. They were painted in red, and crisscrossed and trimmed with white painted sideboard. He could make out animal pens, what looked like a chicken coop, and rustic fences meandering between the buildings. In the foreground, several bright red farm implements and a tractor were being poked and pried by chattering children, while others – accompanied by their parents – were exploring the animal pens. Walking closer, he read the entrance sign: *Far Enough Farm*. What the hell did that mean?

It was obviously a petting farm, created to provide urban high-rise children with a touch of rural reality, and maybe at mating times, a "birds-and-the-bees" lesson. It was the home to about sixty animals; mostly donkeys, horses, sheep, pigs, lambs and rabbits. The duck, geese and chicken population changed with the seasons. An emu, llama and peacock had been added to confuse the children about the heritage barnyard animals of North America. The buildings seemed built on a miniature scale, and there was a washed-out Disneyland look about them. Joyful kids, with yellow boxes of popcorn, scampered down the farm paths, kicking up dust and spilling their popcorn as they searched for the penned animals. None were to be seen, for they had sensibly retreated into the dark private coolness of the buildings.

Through the maze of fenced pens, Trent spotted a little red barn, striped with white boarding which framed the cheerful lettering, *Little Red Barn* on its side wall. The path he was now on wound past an empty chicken coop and led him directly to the open door of the barn. He peered in and could see nothing. Stepping inside, he was immediately hit by the power of its barnyard smell. It was the smell of his youthful summers at his uncle's farm: hay and horse manure blending together to perfume his nostrils with a whiff of teenage nostalgia.

He felt the barn's inner coolness through his damp shirt as his eyes adjusted to its darkness. He could make out the interior beams and what looked like a hayloft and animal stalls. The stalls had been built to lead the public through the barn past the animals and out the open door at the other end. As Trent walked past these he found that each stall was empty.

When he came to the last stall, his eye caught the soft luminous glow of a light in the corner. It was a warm light inside some kind of windowed enclosure. He moved toward it and peered through the window. It was an incubator, and within it were two trays alive with small balls of newborn chicks stumbling and rolling in their own broken egg shells. They looked blind and senseless, their high peeping and cheeping sounding like radio static to Trent. He moved closer to look at this downy confusion of new life, and in that action seemed to sense something behind him.

Turning around, he found himself staring at a large jet-black Cochin rooster. It was like nothing he had ever seen before. The bird looked old but powerful, and seemed to be too top heavy for its full-feathered legs and feet. It was so covered in black fluffy plumage that it looked like it was wearing an overcoat. Its long sharp sickle-tail feathers curved out, covering its rump, and an enormous cluster of hackle feathers cascaded down over its wide breast. It did not look friendly.

It was its head and eyes that startled Trent. The rooster's head was crowned with a large bright crimson comb standing above hard beady eyes that glared defiantly at him. Its wattles and earlobes, long, round and also bright crimson, added to its fierce look. As the rooster did a defiant step toward him, the bird's head snapped back-and-forth in an excited manner, wobbling its crimson wattles and angrily vibrating its comb. As it moved closer, he could see that the bird's eyes were blood-red and they pierced him with a scary, spine-chilling stare.

Trent could now hear the bird making low menacing crowing and clucking sounds – then something impossible happened! Pushing through its cackling, his innermost brain was receiving patterns of words! His mind was suddenly throbbing to the beat of the rooster's cackling – buzzing with some sort of paranormal thought transference – a telepathic transmission of whole sentences! It was frightening! The shock of it paralyzed him. The rooster was speaking in an inner voice to him – inside his head – each statement coming in perfect syncopation to the odd rhythm of its angry squawking. A shiver went through him. He was dumbstruck with fear as he stood staring transfixed at the bird.

"What the hell are you looking at? Waiting for new life to grow big enough so you can eat it? How'd you like something to eat your children, you chicken-eating Bastard! If you were my size, I'd rip you to shreds! Chicken-eating, yolk-eating murderous Bastard – that's what you are! Your bloody hands –".

With a loud slam of a stall door, the rooster's cackling and the words inside Trent's head suddenly stopped when two young boys raced past him. At the same instant, the rooster jumped aside in a black blur of feathers, landing about two feet from the nearest stall. The boys continued their race through the barn, yelling and slamming every empty stall door as they ran.

The rooster had landed with its feathered rear facing Trent. The bird turned to look at him. For a moment it held its position in a frozen posture of silence, and then fluttered out its wings, slowly settling its weight firmly on both its feathered legs. Now it began to nonchalantly peck at a popcorn kernel on the dusty floor as if nothing had happened and that Trent did not exist. The bird's pecking took it around the nearest open stall door and it disappeared. Trent looked at his hands and they were trembling.

Jesus, he thought, this heat's making him lose his mind. It must have been a figment of his imagination. The mind plays terrible tricks when you're under emotional stress. He'd better get a hold of himself, calm down, swallow his ego, and make peace with Janice. Damn! When he was changing his clothes, he'd left his Blackberry at the condo. He glanced at his Rolex. It was almost three o'clock. He stepped out of the barn, back into the reality of the blazing sunlight, to go hunting for a pay phone and a cold drink.

Chapter 3

Jimmy Wong wheeled his van into the narrow alley that ran behind the row of shops. The potholed alley was lined with ramshackle garages, sheds, and cardboard boxes that were the backstage workings of the row of shops that faced the street. He drove halfway down the alley, stopping and backing into a small parking space. It was a tight fit, but he had done it a thousand times before, and he maneuvered the van in one sweeping movement, bringing it to an abrupt stop about two feet from the door at the rear of the building.

Inside the van, Ceres stood up in her cage. The long rocky ride into the city had been roaster hot and she was panting and fluttering her throat to expel her rising body heat. The van had stopped several times to pick up other caged chickens, and throughout the drive, the terrified birds had all sat inside the van's inky black interior, shaking and silent.

Jimmy got out of the van and opened the rear doors, suddenly piercing the pitch-dark interior with shafts of bright sunlight. He took the petrified caged birds out one by one and stacked all four of them atop one another, concealing them inside a lean-to shed that was hidden behind two large bins. Ceres was at the bottom of the stacked cages, staring at the dusty rear wheel of the van.

These four old birds would provide Jimmy with some easy pocket money – at seventy-five dollars a bird – 300 hundred dollars that didn't go through the shop's cash register.

Slamming the van's rear doors shut, Jimmy went into the building through a door with a crudely lettered sign reading, *Lucky Chicken Poultry – Delivery Only*. It was a cruelly ironic name for the thousands of dead chickens that had passed through this door in the past sixty-one years.

He strode through the kitchen where three women were busy glazing and roasting plump broiler chickens in two commercial ovens. Flashing them his best "Jimmy" smile, he went into the front shop. It was packed with the usual Saturday customers: a cosmopolitan mixture of trendy couples, young city professionals and local residents. They were of all ages and races, noisy, good-natured, and happily jostling for a place at a long refrigerated counter displaying dressed and roast chickens of all sizes, along with every other edible part of the bird's body. Jimmy's father was behind the counter serving the customers, along with Jimmy's two cousins. Roasted Lucky Chickens were practically dancing out the door and the cash register was singing its familiar Saturday song as Jimmy put on an apron and joined his father and cousins behind the counter, keeping his eye on the door for his special black customers to turn up.

Lucky Chicken Poultry was in the colorful heart of Kensington Market, a distinctive multicultural neighborhood situated in one of the oldest parts of the city. For the better part of ninety years, it had welcomed wave after wave of new immigrants, constantly evolving, yet always remaining the same. In the 1930s, eighty percent of the city's Jewish community lived in Kensington Market. The Portuguese began arriving in the early 1950s, then came the Italians, Jamaicans, Vietnamese, Chinese, Ethiopians, and now new waves of fresh faces from Mexico, Cuba, and Central and South America. The diversity of its shops and people represented generations of racial and ethnic harmony.

Wong Chan sat in the corner of the shop, nodding and smiling at the customers. Every Saturday this frail little man was brought down from upstairs for several hours to watch the action. He was Jimmy's grandfather. He was ninety-five years of age and had come to Canada in 1938 as a youth. Born on a small chicken farm near the city of Zijin in the Chinese southern province of Guangdong, he arrived with fifty dollars in his pocket and his mother's secret recipe for braised roast chicken, Dezhou style. It was an ancient Chinese recipe that combined five spices, honey and eleven other ingredients to create a glazed roasted chicken of crispy, crunchy skin and succulent meat that fell off the bone just by looking at it.

Starting from nothing but an outdoor stall, he had built a business on his mother's recipe. In 1944. with money borrowed from an uncle in Vancouver, he bought a ramshackle Victorian house that is today's Lucky Chicken shop. In the 1940s and 50s, most of Wong's customers were Orthodox Jews, and they loved his chicken. A kindly Rabbi suggested that if they were sold as Kosher chickens – prepared in accordance with Jewish dietary law – he could double his business. He did, and the business took off; he was on his way to becoming a local legend. In 1946, in the city's old Chinatown, he met and married a young girl from Zijin and they had three sons, one of them Jimmy's father.

In most of the homes in the area, the first floor was the shop and the shop owners lived above them. The Wong dynasty multiplied in the two floors above the shop, converting the gabled attic into a cramped bedroom for Wong's three grandsons. Jimmy's two older brothers went to university and moved on to pursue professional careers, but not Jimmy: Kensington Market was his world and he knew every inch of it.

After high school, he went to work for his dad in Lucky Chicken Poultry, knowing that one day he would own the business. He figured that in good times or bad, people would always be eating chicken. He was street-smart and fancied himself a killer with the local ladies, who came in all shades of colors and races. He was also smart in business, signing up over a dozen sports bars to sell his *Wing-Wongs* – chicken wings coated with a Dezhou type honey-glazed sauce. Most of Toronto's better restaurants now bought their dressed chickens through him, and he promoted roast chicken takeout dinners. He knew everybody and everything that happened in his multicultural community. And because of this, he never missed an opportunity to make a buck.

Toronto's black community had grown to be over 240,000, many of them from the Caribbean. They added to the vibrancy of the city – and to Kensington Market – with their carnivals, customs and cuisine. Within the black Caribbean community, there was a small, but unknown number of Cubans and Puerto Ricans who practiced the Santeria religion. Originally a Cuban and Caribbean faith of the Yoruba people of West Africa – to be later influenced by Roman Catholic Christianity – it was a closed religious sect practiced in "house temples", and part of its ceremonies involved sacred drumming, dance and ritualized animal sacrifices – most often with chickens.

Since the mid-80s, the city had legally banned the selling, breeding or keeping of live chickens within the city limits. Breaking the law was costly. The fine was stiff and the law was rigorously enforced. Santerians had to drive to a farm to buy a live chicken, and the farmer would want to question why a black guy from the inner city would drive all the way into the country to buy just one old live bird. Jimmy had found a need and he was just the man to fill it. He didn't know what they did with the chickens and he didn't care.

A large black man pushed his way into the shop, caught Jimmy's eye and casually ran his index finger across his throat, then left the shop. Jimmy slipped away from the counter, through the kitchen and out the back door to find a blue Ford parked in the alley with its motor running. Behind the driver's seat was a plump black woman. She smiled at him but said nothing. Stepping out of her sight into the lean-too shed, Jimmy took the top caged bird down, deftly removed it and put it in a square cardboard box. The bird offered no resistance and made no sounds. He closed the box and slid it into the back seat of the car, shutting the door just as the large black man came around from the street and up the alley. When he got up to Jimmy he handed him seventy-five dollars. Not a word was exchanged between them. The black man got into the car and Jimmy went back into the shop. During the afternoon this same silent exchange in the alley was repeated two more times until there was only one live chicken left. When that chicken was sold, Jimmy would put the empty chicken cages back in the van. Sitting there, thirsty and terrified, Ceres knew she was now alone.

Chapter 4

The farmer stepped out onto the back porch off the kitchen. He stood there for a moment, his eyes squinting into the early morning sun, examining the familiar stillness of the scene before him. Then he finished off the carton of milk in one long gulping action, tossing the empty container into the garbage drum as he descended the back stairs. As he crossed his yard he watched the tail of a jet's contrail cut the porcelain-blue sky in a straight white furrow, on route to a hill of clouds. He had never been in a plane.

He walked toward his hen house. It wasn't large compared with others in the county, but he was proud of it. It represented the combined efforts of Frank, his brother-in-law, and three helpful neighbors, and it was a structure he knew and loved down to the last nail. It was good and real to build something in this age of prefabrication: somehow more solid and more yours. His hen house was a long, low wooden building squatting on the top of a slight hill. Painted in a dull green with yellow trim, it had been environmentally constructed to withstand the changing seasons of Southern Ontario, and provide housing for his flock of two-hundred black Leghorn hens. A large outdoor chicken wire pen was abutted to the back of it with an opening that allowed the hens additional access to water and feed.

Though he didn't know it, his Leghorn chicken ancestors originated in rural Tuscany in the central part of Italy, arriving in North America in the 1820s. Most Leghorns were white and the big commercial operations had them by the tens of thousands, but he fancied the black ones. Black or white, they were "egg-laying machines", averaging one egg every twenty-five hours and laying anywhere from 280 to 300 eggs per year. Last year, his wife sold over 400 dozen eggs at the local Farmers Market.

His main farming was from the soil: tomatoes, squash, some corn, and cherries and apples from a small orchard, but he loved his "girls" for they were living things – predictable and dependable – that never failed to produce large white eggs.

His "girls" only delivered the goods in the daylight hours, so he had series of halogen lamps on a timer – strung up in the ceiling – to keep the "sun" shining down on his flock for fourteen hours a day. Leghorn hens are a nervous, noisy and flighty breed, and he could always hear them before he entered the hen house. When he reached its door he stopped, suddenly aware of an inner, unnatural silence. It was seven-thirty in the morning. He leaned his head against his shadow on the door and listened. In the silence he became aware of his breathing and felt uneasy when he couldn't detect the familiar sounds of the hens inside. For a brief moment he thought someone had stolen his chickens. Slowly he unlocked and opened the door, allowing the early sun's rays to join the inner halogen light.

He stepped inside. Not a single bird was moving. They sat in long rows in their nesting boxes like products on a store shelf. At first he feared they were dead. He shut the door and moved quietly towards the nearest birds. Still the hens did not move, but now he could see that they were alive by the slight heaving of their bodies and a sly shifting of their eyes.

He bent down and gently stroked the first hen with his right hand. Slowly his other hand slid under her feathery body into the warmness of the nest. The hen did not resist his fondling, her head moving slowly from side to side in rhythm with his stroking, her beady eyes never leaving his face. Her look was penetrating and for some unknown reason it made him apprehensive. His hand groped around under her soft fluffy-feathered body, feeling into every corner of the nesting box. He could find no egg. He lifted the hen up and looked down into the straw nest. It was empty. The hen offered no resistance to his actions, her plump body was strangely limp and her scrawny legs dangled down between his fingers like loose strands of rope. He examined the bird, turning it in his hands as it continued to stare at him with eyes that burned with a withering look that was almost human. The other birds continued to remain still and silent. Something was oddly wrong. He gently placed the hen back into her nest.

Moving to the next hen, he slid his hand under her ruffled body. His fingers felt the warm sticky fluid of a broken egg. Now he moved quickly down the first row of nesting boxes, feeling under the hens to discover that most had laid no eggs at all. Those few that had were sitting on smashed shells, their feathered underbellies sticky with yolk.

He spent the next hour checking his hens with a rising sense of disbelief. During his examination not a single bird had made the slightest sound or offered any normal reaction to his handling. Something dreadful that he couldn't understand had happened to his choice egg-laying flock. He walked cautiously past the mute and motionless lines of birds and out of the hen house. He closed the door, locked it, and hurried down the hill back towards the farm house.

He was half way up the porch stairs when he heard it. It was a low muffled thundering sound that grew into one screaming cackle from two-hundred feathered throats. It was a roar of triumph and jeering laughter, and it boomed through the early morning silence like a rumbling and distant explosion. It scared the hell out of him.

That morning the frightened farmer neither knew or cared that he was not alone in his panic. The same alarming discovery was shocking and challenging the reasoning of 273 other farmers across southern Ontario. With minor variations, poultry farmers were finding their flocks sitting in mute rebellion on smashed eggs or empty nests. Most farmers had been loudly heckled by the hens when they left their coops, and one farmer had been attacked by his birds and only escaped by tearing out a screen window.

Hundreds of frantic cell phone calls crackled through the air and e-mails surged through the internet as frightened farmers sought help and information from their veterinarians, the Ontario Egg Marketing Board, feed suppliers, even each other. As the panic and pandemonium grew, the web site of the Ontario Ministry of Agriculture, Food and Rural Affairs, crashed, and MPP's – the elected members of the Provincial parliament – were inundated with e-mails and phone calls from their farm constituents. They had no answers.

By ten o'clock, the chicken crisis had reached the campus City of Guelph, sixty-two miles west of Toronto. Home of the University of Guelph, it was the birthplace of the Ontario Agricultural College and home to the Ontario Veterinary College, the oldest veterinary college in North America.

By noon the Department of Animal and Poultry Science was in a state of total disruption. Things were made worse when an overwhelming requests for connection caused their web site to crash, just as overburdened cell phone communications in the Guelph area suddenly seized up. Veterinarians and nearby farmers were now driving onto the campus with chickens, roosters, broken eggs, nesting boxes and feed samples. Their nervous, worried actions presented a strange surreal contrast to the silent calm of the birds they lugged through the campus buildings. One farmer walked the corridors of the Veterinary College with a small plastic bag of bird droppings, convinced that the crippling cause of his flock's barren performance could be unlocked through examination of their collective excrement, and demanding that it be put under a microscope.

The chaotic confusion intensified when the students left their classes and mingled with the distraught farmers and their chickens, asking questions and offering imaginative theories. Bewildered professors tried to reason with both groups in what was quickly becoming a disorderly Campus Happening. Wild rumors began to spread amongst the farmers milling through the college corridors: feed suppliers were held responsible for an enormous and bumbling incompetence in their formulas. A new type of flock hysteria, brought about by climate changes, was alleged to be the cause of the radical change in the bird's social behavior. Some heard that a tropical avian disease was said to have been brought into the country in the feathers of a rare Amazon bird imported by a pet shop in Toronto. Some hatchery farmers argued that the roosters were to blame, having suddenly gone sterile through radiation fallout from nuclear tests in North Korea. There were even rumors that cows were not giving milk.

By one o'clock the Ontario chicken disaster had reached the federal attention of the Ministry of Agriculture and Agri-Food in Ottawa. From their lofty and distant perspective, they assessed the situation, and the Deputy-Minister decided that it did not warrant disturbing the Minister of Agriculture. He was a former CEO of a large agrochemical corporation, was not popular with farmers, and did not like to get involved in the daily dilemmas of his ministry. He was currently in Rome attending a World Food Conference on grain distribution – and because of the time difference – was at that very moment dining in Restaurant Trattoria Monti on *Pollo alla Cacciatora* with his frumpy wife and France's popular and urbane Ministre de Agriculture, accompanied by his sedate secretary, who magically morphed into his chic and gorgeous mistress at 6:00 p.m. every night.

This would have horrified Ottawa, but the French don't mind infidelity in its popular politicians – actually they like it – as long as it is carried out after-hours with élan and discretion. In contrast, most Canadians and Americans wouldn't know who was their Minister or Secretary of Agriculture.

The two politicians and their ladies ended the evening in a spirit of culinary concord, the cost for their diplomatic dining equally shared between the taxpayers of France and Canada.

Canada's Deputy-Minister – a farmer's daughter – with doctorate degrees in animal science and agronomy from the Ontario College of Agriculture and Edinburgh's famed Royal School of Veterinary Studies – had held her ministerial management position through three different governments and five different agricultural ministers. Her professional mantra was "Eating is an agricultural act" – a sage statement by the American farmer and author Wendell Berry. She constantly quoted it to her staff and to the minister of the day. Practical and hardheaded, she knew the importance of agriculture to Canada's domestic and export economy, and could usually spot a crisis "three fields away" before it happened.

She quickly put together a team of Associate Deputy-Ministers and the Chief Information Officer. By mid-afternoon they were winging their way to the Guelph Airport to find out what the hell was happening. Earlier, Canadian Press had picked up rumors of a developing chicken-and-egg story and had given it three lines in an updated online news release. The radio station in Guelph – CJOY – sensing a breaking local story, dispatched its mobile unit to the campus.

Chaos was now reigning in the buildings and on the campus parking lots: a mad mixture of docile hens and excited humans that had compelled the harried administration to urgently request city police assistance to help control the disorder.

About the same time, in Lancaster County, Pennsylvania, owners and operators of poultry farms noticed that some two million egg-laying chickens were behaving strangely, standing upright and silent. Oddly incidental to this, bird watchers across America were baffled by the unusual sighting of mass groups of flying starling – called murmurations. Hundreds – or even thousands – of starlings were flying together in a swirling crowd of tight formation patterns, simultaneously changing directions, twisting and turning through the sky, then breaking into triangular formations and flying low and fast over the countryside in different directions.

Meanwhile, in more than 900 hen and poultry farms in Ontario, over eight million hens sat motionless and mute amid their own droppings and smashed eggs.

Chapter 5

It had been years since Trent had used a pay phone. They were now as rare as windup watches in an age of cell phones and smartphones. He finally found one nailed to the wall next to the public wash rooms in a restaurant at the other end of Center Island. When he called Janice, she answered it on the first ring: a promising sign. They talked for more than thirty minutes as he kept feeding coins into the pay phone. He apologized first, filled with remorse for what he had said and the way he had said it. Then she apologized, bemoaning how terrible she had acted. Finally, they both agreed that what happened that morning was silly and stupid on both their parts. His end of their telephone tête-à-tête was a standing performance against the wall, whispered over the background clatter of the restaurant and the traffic to and from the washrooms.

Their phone reconciliation was "forgive and forget" and let's kiss and make up, and he would make it up to her by cooking up what he called "Tacos for Two", a Mexican memory that she loved, and one of the few cooking skills that he had mastered. He would pick her up in half-an-hour outside her condo, and they would buy everything they needed at Perola's, a Latin American grocery store in the heart of Kensington Market that had a range of Mexican products, including the best corn tortillas in town.

He hung up the phone with a sense of relief, and then suddenly remembered he told her he would be there in a half-hour's time and he was still on this damn island. Dashing back to the ferry landing, luck was with him again as he boarded the ferry just as it was about to leave for the city.

Getting back to his condo and car was a race against the clock and he pulled up in front of her condo ten minutes late. She'd been waiting for him inside the building's entrance and she came out smiling. She was carrying her small and familiar overnight bag, another good sign that all was really forgiven. She slipped into the car and kissed him lightly on the cheek. Trent wheeled the car into a U-turn and forced his way into a line of slow-moving vehicles.

"It's just getting worse. This bloody traffic – "He left his curse unfinished as he tried to ease his Lexus into the inner lane. The large taxi beside him was having no part of it and its scars and battered fenders told him that it had won many street battles.

"Where did you phone from? It sounded like you were in a bar," said Janice. He moved into the inner lane after the bullish taxi had rammed ahead – easing his way in front of an unsure woman driver – and guided the Lexus around the corner before he replied.

"It was a restaurant on the island."

"What island?"

"Center Island. I was so damn mad at myself and the way that I acted that I just couldn't go home. It was hot so I walked down to the lakeshore for the breeze and saw the ferry. I'd never been over to the Islands, so I took the ferry over, walked around a bit and ended up in a petting farm and then phoned you."

"A petting farm?"

Trent looked over at her. "Yes, a petting farm. Sort of a kid's farm the City has there for children to explain Mother Nature, the-birds-and-the-bees, and where does milk come from."

"Where does milk come from?"

Trent ignored her. "Except that the strangest thing happened to me in the barn."

"I thought that was the farmer's daughter's line," quipped Janice.

"No – I mean seriously. There was an incubator in the barn."

"Yes."

"And I was looking at it when a chicken came up to me from behind and –"

"Is this a chicken joke?"

"No really. It came up to me and – well you're not going to believe this – I don't believe it myself – but so help me God, for a moment I swear it talked to me."

"Oh, come on now Trent?" said Janice, rolling her eyes.

"Really!" said Trent.

Janice decided to play along with him. "Okay, I'll bite. What did the chicken say?"

"Well, as I remember it, it screamed at me. Called me a dirty chicken eating bastard." Trent felt a sudden surge of embarrassment, like the kind that comes after the poor telling of a bad joke. It caused him to avoid her eyes. He wished he had not allowed their conversation to take such a inane turn. He could feel her staring at him, waiting for his next line.

"If that's some sort of nonsensical joke, it's the worse one you've ever made. If that's a lawyer's sense of humor, no wonder you lose so many cases." Her voice softened. "Anyway, you phoned. Here we are, and that's all the matters." She settled back in the seat, dismissing his chicken parody as one of those few times when his sense of humor had laid an egg.

He drove through the heavy late afternoon traffic and made for the Kensington Market. It was a drive of stops-and-starts, hitting every red light along the way. Finally, they turned into a narrow street, made even narrower by the parked cars strung out along one side. The center of the street and the sidewalks were packed with a cheerful confusion of people. The market was a colorful and random collection of street stalls and shops all jumbled together and confined within several small city blocks. The air was perfumed with whiffs of spicy cooking that mingled with the jabber of over a dozen different languages. People were carefree and merry. It was a miniature mosaic of the world and its natural offerings.

Trent drove slowly past Perola's. There was no place to park. "So near and yet so far. We'll just have to keep going around the block until someone pulls out." He turned the corner, slowly driving down another street. "Keep your eye out for blinking back-up lights. It means someone's leaving. Parking here is like playing Russian roulette in reverse."

"There's one!" trilled Janice.

When the car pulled out from the curb, Trent quickly maneuvered his Lexus into the space. "How's that for luck," boasted Trent as he helped Janice out of the car and locked it. They set off into the crowds for the long walk back and around the block to Perola's. They had walked only a few yards when Trent stopped. "Hold on. Isn't this an alley between these two buildings? Look, it goes straight through to where we're going. If I'm right, Perola's should be just at the end of this alley, just on the left. Let's take it. It's faster and we won't have to battle the crowds."

Trent took Janice's arm and guided her into the alley. The sun had baked the alley's earth hard and it was graveled and rutted in places, but it was fun to see the back of these old buildings and what went on in back-alley life.

They had gone about a hundred yards down the alley when Trent suddenly stopped. A great cackling sound rumbled from his right to pierce his ears. It was happening again! Inside his mind, somewhere near, the screams of a chicken were forming words and thoughts. They hammered into his head, vibrating his skull like a dentist's drill.

"Someone Understand Me! Someone Understand!"

The anguished pleading sound was coming from his right. He saw the rear of a parked white van lettered "Lucky Chicken Poultry" with Chinese lettering below it. The van looked pretty beat up and was parked next to a lean-to shed. The cackling sounds seemed to becoming from the shed. Ted moved along the van towards the shed, dragging Janice by the hand with a grip too strong for her liking.

Inside the shed he saw a stack of four cages; in the bottom one was a lone chicken, staring at him with moist eyes. He bent down on his knees and looked at its frightened face.

"I understand you," he said quietly.

Janice looked at him as if he'd lost his mind. "Who in the hell are you talking to?"

"Thank God!" The chicken's words exploded inside Trent's head.

"Buy me! Get me out of here. You are 'The Connection!' Thank God! Thank God!"

Janice stared at the bird, fascinated yet frightened by Trent's sudden obsession with this chicken.

"I must buy this chicken," snapped Trent.

"Why in God's name would you buy this chicken? We came down here for Mexican groceries. Trent, will you answer me? What are you going to do with that poor live thing?"

Just then, Jimmy Wong came out the back door of Lucky Chicken and saw Trent, "What are you doing?"

"I want to buy this live chicken."

"You want chicken, go around front to the store – all kinds, all parts, roasted, barbecued –"

"I want to buy this chicken!" interrupted Trent in a harsh tone that meant business.

"This is not an eating chicken. Special Chicken. Very expensive," was Jimmy's reply.

"I don't care. I want this chicken. How much?" The bird watched intently, moving its head back and forth as it followed their squabbling words. Janice was startled by Trent's sudden sharp response and didn't like the way the Chinese guy was looking at her. There was something "slippery" about him.

"Hundred dollars," said Wong.

Trent glared at him but said nothing, removing two fifty-dollar bills from his wallet and slapping them in Wong's outstretched hand. Wong smiled and bent down, taking the chicken from its cage.

"Why do you want this live chicken?" asked Wong as he put the compliant bird in a large square cardboard box and closed the lid.

"Personal," replied Trent.

As he handed the box to Trent, Wong nodded toward Janice – who was now standing in the alley – and with a smirk on his face, whispered, "Oh I see. Different strokes for different folks eh." Wong could almost feel the heat from the sudden anger in Trent's eyes. He said nothing, turning away from Wong to join Janice in the alley. Then he turned back to look at Wong who was standing there with the money in his hand, and in his best legal baritone voice said, "I'm a lawyer. You just broke a strict City bylaw by selling me this live chicken in Kensington Market. You could lose your license and there's a stiff fine. I think you're going to need that money to pay it." With that, he and Janice walked back down the alley toward the street. Wong just stood there, nervously fondling the money in his hands.

"What did he say to you that made you so suddenly angry?"

"Never mind. It doesn't matter."

"Where are we going now?" Janice gently inquired, her eyes glued to the silent box in Trent's hands.

"Home. Back to the car".

"What about Perola's?"

"Forget it honey. We're going back to my place,"

Trent, looking down at the box holding a grateful bird inside it, and spoke to it. "You don't have to say anything."

"You don't have to say anything? Are you crazy?"

"Janice – something freaky happened to me at the island. It just happened again. I can understand this goddamn bird inside my head. Do you understand what I'm saying? I can't explain it. I'm not crazy, but I can understand this bird – and it can understand me".

"You're out of your mind!"

"You'll see. I'll prove it to you."

They reached the car and Trent unlocked the doors and gently placed the box on the rear seat. They pulled away and headed back to his condo. This whole mind-boggling incident had happened in just ten minutes in an alley. Janice, in the front seat beside him, could only believe that for some weird reason, he was putting her on.

From the box in the back seat she could hear the chicken beginning to coo and gurgle and Trent started to speak aloud, mimicking the pauses, phrasing and monotone inflections of an interpreter. During the ride back, Trent did an ad-lib monologue, supposedly from the chicken. Janice settled back to enjoy his spoof and found that he could invent a story line in amazing rhythm to the back-seat chicken's clucking. The effect was quite impressive.

As Trent told the story, chickens have no names but this chicken was given the name Ceres by a human that once owned her. She had been picked up in the country, along with three other caged chickens, and driven to the alley where all four had been stacked in the lean-to shed. During the morning the other three had been bought and taken away. Throughout the day Ceres had wailed her plea, desperate to make "The Connection". Only once had she contacted with a human being. He was a small Indian boy about seven-years old who had stood and talked with the chicken before his angry mother found him, cuffed him, and dragged him away in tears and protest. Janice thought the storyline was imaginative but absurdly silly, and told Trent that he had missed his calling; He should have been a fantasy writer instead of a corporate lawyer.

They arrived at Trent's building and he parked the Lexus in the underground garage, taking Janice and the chicken up the elevator to his condo on the seventeenth floor. When they got inside, he placed the box in the middle of the living room area, took off the cover and pulled Janice down beside him onto the couch to watch what would happen.

The chicken slowly stretched its neck, lifting its head out of the box and surveyed its surroundings in one swiveling movement. It repeated this action several times before looking at Trent and Janice. Satisfied with what it saw, it suddenly fluttered its wings to land beside the box and then settled down to silently stare at them.

"Honey, something funny and strange is happening."

"You're telling me?" said Janice as she stared transfixed at the chicken.

"No really. Did you hear the radio this morning? What happened in Guelph? Chickens are not laying eggs – they're acting strange." He pointed his finger at the bird. "This chicken – how come I can understand it when it makes cackling sounds? Why can I read its thoughts and feelings inside my head? You don't believe me, do you?"

Janice stared at him wide-eyed. "Listen. Just watch. I'll prove it." The bird sat there watching them with its flashing eyes. "Ask it to do something," he challenged.

"Lay an egg," she commanded.

Ceres stood up, feet wide apart, her bottom feathers spread out and her back feathers upright. The moist egg emerged a little further each time she strained her body until it suddenly popped out. She stepped back, her beak opened and panting. It was amazing.

"There! There! Now do you believe me!" said Trent.

"Darling, it's just a crazy coincidence."

"Coincidence like hell. Ask it again. Ask it anything."

She wrinkled her brow in thought. "Okay, here's one – break the egg!"

On command, the bird eyed her egg, took aim and gave it three sharp raps with its beak. The egg neatly cracked into two parts, the sticky, wet yolk oozing over the carpet. Janice stared in stunned amazement at the broken egg.

"Now that's not a coincidence!" exclaimed Trent. "You just proved it. Go ahead; ask it to perform some other tasks."

Rattled by what she had just witnessed, Janice timidly asked the chicken to perform a series of aimless acts throughout the room, some involving Trent. In every instance the bird performed to her requests, racing across the floor to sit on a chair or picking up a necktie and dropping it at her feet when asked. After more than a twenty minutes of testing, the chicken was visibly exhausted – and Janice was converted into a believer.

As she looked in silent wonder at the bird, Trent asked why Ceres could understand Janice but she could not receive Ceres's thoughts. Ceres explained that it was a complicated and random act. In the brief unnatural of life billions of chickens around the world, many thousands have a telepathic genetic gift to communicate to humans, but they cannot sustain it for more than a minute or two. Those very few that could, where often slaughtered before they could communicate, and no chicken would ever attempt to communicate with any human in the business of breeding or murdering them. Right now there was only 4,000 hens that had evolved far enough to communicate endlessly, and Ceres had no idea where the other 3,999 were in the world, but all of them had been laboriously tutored and trained to deliver the same message. With humans there could be thousands who unknowingly had the brain patterns to receive communication from one of these hens, but the odds against it were astronomical: over seven billion humans and just 4,000 hens. Ceres and Trent had incredibly beaten those odds.

They brought Ceres a bowl of cold water and a dish of Cheerios and listened intently as the bird confirmed the uprising of the chickens, stating that she brought word, warning that it could grow worse and spread beyond Canada and the United States to eventually encompass the entire earth.

"I am only a messenger. You are 'The Connection' for this message."

"I don't understand."

"To humans we are a 'species', capable of interbreeding and

producing offspring: a species that you call chickens and roosters. You humans think you know all about us; how we communicate; how we live; how we feel; how you can shape us to your needs. But you are wrong: dead wrong.

"We both live on one earth but in different worlds. It will surprise you to learn that we are capable of uniting together in a common cause by our collective will–a property of the mind you humans arrogantly believe only you possess. What you call 'avian species' can communicate in ways that humans do not know of and will never understand.

"So to communicate with humans we created 'The World Council of Chickens'. But there is no such thing; there is no powerful assembly of chickens or roosters in session somewhere on our earth. It is not our natural way. We do not need your cabinets or parliaments to speak as one. It's just that our wiser roosters felt we should make ourselves known in terms that humans understand, and so the idea of 'The World Council of Chickens' was hatched, so to speak – speaking through 'The Connection'–and that is you."

Ted looked at Janice but said nothing. He was about to speak when Ceres added that the poultry revolution could be reversed, but only if humans made drastic changes to their relationship with chickens. It was imperative that the bird deliver his message to someone in power. Time was running out.

Trent and Janice thought first of their Member of Parliament, but he was a backbencher of little political influence. Neither could think of any important politician they knew.

Suddenly it came to Trent like a bolt of lightning. His uncle! Senator Andrew Morriston. He could be the perfect man. He was a fixture in Ottawa. He knew every power politician in the capital and surely could have access to the Prime Minister's office.

Canadian Senators were not elected in the American sense, but appointed by the Prime Minister of the day. There were 105 of them. It was a cushy, well-paying patronage appointment: a reward filled with perks and privileges – guaranteed until one was 75 years of age – to be followed by a generous pension. Some had abused these entitlements and because of this, senators were not popular with most Canadians.

Trent's uncle was a Senator of power in charge of the party's coffers, and he filled it to bursting year-after-year by methods both fair and foul. For his fund-raising services, two years ago he was appointed a Senator by the current Prime Minister – and he could get directly to him.

Trent raced into the bedroom to place a call to Ottawa. It was late Saturday evening and the Senate doesn't sit on Saturday, so he called the Senator's home in Rockcliffe, an Ottawa suburb where the Senator maintained a luxurious home. His call was picked up on the second ring and the gruff voice of Senator Morriston floridly announced himself in the third person. Ted could picture him at the other end, a whiskey in his hand with a Havana cigar smoldering in a reachable ashtray. He could visualize him with his signature butterfly bow tie smothered under his sagging jowls, and his thick gold-framed eyeglasses straddling the end of his bulbous nose. He was sixty-three but looked older due to his weight and baldness. He was every political cartoonist's dream.

At the sound of his nephew's voice, the Senator's tone suddenly smoothed and softened. While the Senator had heard Ottawa rumors about some sort of chicken nonsense, it took a long time of persuasive conversation to convince the Senator that his nephew wasn't mad, drunk or joking, and that it was a matter of national urgency that Trent see him on Sunday. Trent had refrained from telling the Senator the full story, realizing that only the presence of this amazing bird would persuade his uncle to take it to the Prime Minister.

Janice was feeding Ceres more corn niblets when Trent came out of the bedroom, a wide smile on his face. "Well Ceres, we're going to Ottawa tomorrow."

"What did your uncle say?" asked Janice.

"Not much. He'll see me. I didn't tell him the whole story. All he knows is that it's about the chicken crisis." The chicken looked up at Trent and nodded its head in response to his news.

"If Ceres is going to Ottawa, I think we should clean her up. Make her pretty," said Janice.

"Good thinking," replied Trent. "How do we do that?"

"There must be something on the internet. Let me check on your iPad." Her first search on *How to clean a Chicken* turned out to be on how to gut its innards for cooking. She looked over at Ceres before refining her question, and came up with three items on cleaning and preening prize chickens for showing at Poultry Fairs.

"Trent, listen to this. Chickens clean and preen themselves with a dust bath, rolling around in the soil to clean their feathers, but you can wash them with warm water if you do it gently."

They decided to clean up the bird in the kitchen sink, first lightly washing her feathers and head in warm water, followed by a soft blow-dry using Trent's hand hair dryer. Janice took command of the styling, fluffing up the bird's naturally loose-lying plumage on her broad back and breast. When delicately cleaned, Ceres's bottom feathers were as soft and downy as a baby chick's. Trent cleaned the bird's yellow legs and feet and gently rubbed a soothing lotion on them. It was obvious that the bird was enjoying its bath and beauty treatment by its soft cooing. It was a new sensation for Ceres, and at one point she was so relaxed while being washed that she actually fell asleep. Then she began to cluck and cackle, her soft bay-colored eyes looking tenderly up at Trent.

"What's she saying?"

Trent listened for a moment before replying "She says that she feels like a show bird again. She once won first prize at the Royal Agricultural Winter Fair for her owner. She says that he was a nice man with dark skin, white hair and always smiling. He had four birds that he raised for showing. He was old and they were his pleasure. He would feed them grain from his hand, pet them and look after them. He had named her Ceres."

"Does Ceres mean anything? It's a strange name,"

The chicken began to cackle again, quick little sounds that rang around the room. Trent nodded and then turned to Janice. "The old man's grandchildren often visited and would pet the chickens. He named her Ceres since she was the biggest and their favorite. He told them that Ceres was the name of an ancient Roman goddess who is the mother of agriculture and the source of all grain in the universe. Then one day he died and his sons came and took everything away and gave his chickens to a neighbor."

"How sad," said Janice.

Ceres turned to look at Janice as Trent interpreted her cackling word for word. "He was a terrible human. He had a dirty farm and didn't care for us. He killed and cooked all but me. Then the human with the white van came and bought me and threw me into the back of his van. He bought others during the ride to the city and we ended up where you found me."

Janice reached down and petted the chicken. She went strangely silent and they continued to finish preening the bird.

They spent two hours cleaning and grooming the docile hen and Trent found a large wicker picnic basket that he bedded with paper strips from his shredder to serve as a dignified method of transporting her to Ottawa.

It was decided that Janice should remain in Toronto. He would drive like hell tomorrow morning and spend the day in the capital presenting the bird to his uncle and hopefully to the Prime Minister. They bedded Ceres for the night in the kitchen and provided her with fresh water and more Cheerios and corn niblets before taking themselves to bed. The unbelievable events of the day had smothered any desire to order in Chinese food or make love, and they finally fell asleep cuddled together, talking about Ceres and wondering what tomorrow would bring.

Early Sunday morning, after a quick breakfast and promising to phone Janice the moment he arrived at his uncle's home, Trent went down the elevator to the basement garage with the chicken in the basket. He unlocked his car and placed the basket on the passenger seat next to him, then drove up the ramp. The garage doors automatically rolled up and he wheeled out into the sunlight.

The Lexus roared down the street. Ceres was on her way to Ottawa and into history.

Chapter 6

The Deputy-Minister of Agriculture stared at the bird, her large blue eyes barely concealing her growing suspicions of the feathered animal. This must be some kind of ventriloquist trick, she thought. She had just gone through hell in Guelph with this chicken madness and now here she was – called out on a Sunday – to hear a lecture from a chicken? It was preposterous!

She had every reason to resent chickens. Chickens were becoming the bane of her life. Not just this crisis but the disaster of eleven months ago. The Minister of Agriculture – in Italy, and probably dining his way through Rome – had been tarred and feathered by the press, the public and the Opposition Parties for what was now called "The Great Scrambled Egg Scandal".

An estimated twenty-four million processed eggs – in liquid, frozen and dried form – stored as a national food reserve by the Ministry of Agriculture, had, through bureaucratic blundering, rotted beyond any possible use, even as fertilizer. The beefy Agricultural Minister, known for his international travels, had dropped himself, his Ministry and his government into political hot water which was still simmering. Now the poultry crisis sweeping through Ontario would only add to his misery when he got back from Europe. The Deputy-Minister always had to pick up the pieces. God, how she come to hate eggs and chickens and chickens and eggs.

Sitting in the Senator's home, she nursed a stiff rye and water and listened as the young man told his incredible story of how he came upon this amazing bird sitting in front of her. Trent had been hard pressed to convince his uncle and had an even tougher time getting through to the skeptical Deputy-Minister of Agriculture. Still the events were on his side. The antics of the chicken were like something she had never seen before, and there was no doubt that it was definitely addressing them with its clucking and cackling. The Deputy- Minister listened to this strange, implausible chicken that – through the bizarre interpreter talents of Trent – was putting forth its demands in forceful and compelling terms as it strutted back and forth across the Senator's priceless Persian carpet, often stopping to point an accusing wing at her. And always, always watching and observing the humans with a piercing look of intelligence and intensity that radiated a riveting charismatic authority over the bewildered humans.

The chicken's position was hard and simple: the unforgivable waste of millions of processed eggs was the last indignation chickens would permit. This incident, along with worse murderous ones in the United States, had taken an already smoldering resentful condition and pushed the chickens past the brink to a place of no return or compromise. This wasteful spoilage at a cost of so many deaths had only angrily advanced their inevitable action. Chickens would no longer produce or comply to man's insatiable needs for their flesh and their eggs until radical changes were made in their relationship.

The chicken's words were backed up by the actions of millions of egg-laying hens in Canada and now, tens of millions more in the United States. The Deputy-Minister knew to this be true for the American Embassy's Agricultural Minister-Councilor had been in constant touch with her and had confirmed that the same disastrous phenomenon seemed to be spreading across the US. He was receiving reports from Washington that in the last twenty-four hours, over nineteen million egg-laying hens in California had not laid a single egg. The same horror reports were coming in from Florida, Iowa and Arkansas.

Finally – as Trent had hoped – his uncle called the Prime Minister on his private line at the PM's residence. The Senator briefly outlined the urgency of the situation–both in Canada and the States – and then passed his cell phone over to the Deputy-Minister to fill in the alarming details. It was the first time she had ever spoken directly to the PM and it was an uneasy conversation. In her briefing, she avoided giving the PM the full story of the chicken, but she convinced him that the growing poultry crisis demanded the immediate involvement of the American Ambassador. The PM, aware of the situation in Ontario and its possible implications with the United States, had agreed and would dispatch one of his younger Executive Assistants to search out the Ambassador on the authority of the Prime Minister.

The chicken's insistence on now meeting only with the President of the United States had suddenly introduced a new complication into this frightening nightmare. When Trent told Ceres that they were trying to get a hold of the American Ambassador, the chicken stared at him but said nothing. They sat there in the Senator's front room, watching the summer sun play shifting patterns on the now mute bird and waited hopefully for the American Ambassador to turn up.

Opened in 1999, the American Embassy, known locally as "The Battleship", is a large brutish building built on a small hill that causes it to overshadow the historic market below it. Its architectural form is less than inspiring and some local citizens have complained that the extra protective barriers around it have impacted normal traffic flow and changed the nature of the market. Closed on Sundays, it nevertheless knows where the Ambassador is at all times. Since the attempted kidnapping of three American diplomats in Europe, all American Ambassadors were now protected by at least two security guards whenever they stepped out of their official residence or their embassy.

. . .

The exclusive White Sands Golf and Country Club is just outside Ottawa. Here the PM's Executive Assistant – now in league with the US Embassy's Minister-Counselor for Agricultural Services – found the American Ambassador. He was on the eleventh hole with two California State politicians who, between strokes and putts, were floating the idea of a Great Lakes freshwater pipeline from Lake Michigan to water the worst drought areas of their state.

In a sand trap, the PM's Executive Assistant quickly briefed the Ambassador with the urgent importance the Prime Minister gave to his involvement. Hurried apologies were given to the two freshwater lobbyists and the three men left, driving out to the Senator's home in the Minister-Counselor's Ford, followed by the two security guards in the Ambassador's Lincoln MKS. The Ford was a good career move on the part of the Minister-Counselor, for the affable American Ambassador was a former senior vice-president of Ford. His Detroit background, family summer cottage in the Muskoka lakes of Ontario, and his French-speaking wife made him a shrewd yet sensible ambassador choice by the President. Like Senator Moriston's appointment, his ambassadorial appointment was also his reward for his backroom ability to raise money for the coming election campaign of the President.

. . .

The Ambassador stared dumbfounded at the bird, hardly believing what he had been told to him about this chicken looking directly at him. The Senator's small den was now crowded with six human beings grouped around a Plymouth Rock hen that held its ground in the middle of the Persian carpet. The bird hopped two steps toward the Ambassador and started to cackle. Ted began his monotone translating.

"Believe as you will, but you cannot deny that my movements and the intelligence in my eyes underlines the words of my human interpreter." The chicken turned to look back at Trent before continuing. "I'm telling you again that this 'crisis in poultry' as you put it, is a deliberate, concerted effort on our part. It is a determined, premeditated action resulting from the final degradation of our species that we will no longer tolerate." Ceres jerked her head around to give a withering glare at the Deputy-Minister before addressing the American Ambassador. "The final solution to this unacceptable nature of things lies not in Canada but in the United States with your President."

"I can't ask my President to meet with a chicken!" the Ambassador blurted out, almost choking on his own indignation.

"You'd better!" screamed back the chicken, "Or your President and millions of Americans will never break an egg or taste chicken again!"

"This whole thing is preposterous," exclaimed the Deputy-Minister of Agriculture as she shook her head in disbelief.

"So is twenty-four million spoiled eggs!" shot back the angry chicken. The Ambassador suddenly sighed in resignation, wishing he was back in Detroit. "I'll see what I can do, but I can't promise anything. I'll have to go through State with this request. There's usually nobody senior there on a Sunday. They'll think me completely mad." The PM's Executive Assistant spoke up. "Sir, perhaps if you were to contact your President through the Prime Minister – with the Prime Minister – would that solve your protocol problem, Mr. Ambassador?"

The Ambassador pursed his lips before answering. "The president might think we're both mad. But you're right, it's the fastest way."

The Prime Minister's Executive Assistant knew that his boss was a measured and methodical man who would be in his library, still writing his book on *The Canadian Canoe*; it was his only passion in life, that and tinkering with his stamp collection. The PM was an economist and backroom policy wonk, an emotional cypher with blank facial features that frustrated political cartoonists. He gave few interviews; only three press conferences a year, rarely addressed the nation on television, and was so formal in his dress that Ottawa wits swore he wore a tie when he took a sauna. Distant from voters and disdained by many, he nevertheless had won two elections with a healthy majority both times. Pundits attributed his election landslides to his deliberate low profile that allowed him to govern overbearingly below the public radar, plus keeping the nation economically sane and stable during a decade of global economic tsunamis.

Without seeing the chicken, the PM's Executive Assistant knew it would need a tough and persuasive argument to get him to call the President of the United States, and only the American Ambassador could make the case. He stepped out of the room into the hall, took a deep breath and then called the Prime Minister and explained the urgency of a meeting requested by the American Ambassador, not mentioning the chicken.

The Executive assistant came back into the room, still holding his Blackberry and looked over at the Ambassador, "He can see us now." The Ambassador, the Executive Assistant and the American Agricultural Minister-Councilor got up, ready to leave. It was agreed that the rest of the group would wait in the Senator's den for the outcome from the Prime Minister's call to the President. The chicken sat in the middle of the room, her eyes moving as she listened to every word.

Later, sandwiches were made by the Senator and they poured themselves another drink. It was Trent that first noticed that the chicken had been neglected. A bowl of water and a packet of sunflower seeds were hastily brought in. They sat in silence, sipping their drinks, eating their sandwiches and watching the chicken peck away at the seeds scattered on the Senator's Persian carpet.

Two hours later a call from the PM to the Senator confirmed that a meeting with the President had been arranged. Both the President and the Prime Minister had ordered that everyone in the Senator's home were not to say a single word to anyone about the chicken and a meeting with the President, as it was now a matter on national security in both nations.

A US government aircraft would arrive in Ottawa Monday afternoon to fly Trent and the chicken to Washington. Trent told the news to Ceres and watched her do a triumphant jig across the carpet, spilling the water and knocking over a small magazine rack.

It was decided that Trent and the chicken would remain as overnight guests of the Senator until travel arrangements were finalized. As promised, later that evening from the Senator's kitchen, Trent called Janice on his cell phone, telling her what was happening and asking her to pack a suitcase for him and send it by priority FedEx to the Senator's address, otherwise he would be meeting the President of the United States in a turtleneck sweater. She said little but he could sense the excitement in her voice. He promised to call her from Washington and cautioned her to not say anything to anyone about Ceres and his trip to Washington. When he returned to the den, he found the chicken watching television and the wary Senator pouring himself another stiff drink.

. . .

That evening the PM's Executive Assistant teased his attractive wife before telling her of the incredible events of his day. Like most young and self-important men, he bragged and confided in his wife, basking in the pleasure of her admiration. At first she wouldn't believe him, but gradually, through his persistence, she accepted the essential facts of his surreal experience. He told of the search for the Ambassador and the secret meeting at the Senator's home; the unimaginable chicken and the priority call to the President by the Prime Minister. His eyes sparkled and the excitement in his voice confirmed the truth of his chicken story to her. She had already heard on radio and on television the conflicting rumors of some sort of chicken disaster, and she knew it would probably be the topic of insider gossip at her book club that evening.

They put their two children to bed and he resigned himself to acting as a baby-sitter for the evening. It was her girl's night out and she was already running late. She promised to drive carefully and hurried off to motor over to the home of the wife of the Minister of Finance, who was the hostess that evening for twelve politician's wives.

Halfway there she pulled the car over and stopped in a public parking area at one of the many parks that graced the city. Jiao was her name, and as her Chinese name suggested, she was indeed "dainty and lovely".

Born and schooled in Shanghai, she had met her husband in Hong Kong when he was attached to the Canadian Consulate and she was a translator in the visa section. That was six years ago. In the five years of marriage she had never cheated on him, except in inner cabinet matters that he told her in confidence. She did so because she was an imbedded agent of China's MSS (Ministry of State Security), a slender thread in the vast web of agents who were "the eyes and ears of the Dragon".

CSIS (Canadian Security Intelligence Service) estimated that within Canada's Chinese population of over 1.4 million, there were at least sixty agents under deep cover like Jiao.

She took out a stylish eyeglass case and opened it to remove a small black clamshell cell phone and punched in a number. The cell call was answered on the fourth ring. She identified herself by code name and spoke quickly in Mandarin. She couldn't be too late for the book club.

That night the startling chicken intelligence was put into Mandarin plain text, transposed into a complicated chain-addition cipher code, and transmitted from the Embassy halfway around the world to MSS's powerful receiving dishes atop the Jin Mao Tower in Shanghai.

The enciphered message was immediately snatched out of the Ottawa ether by a gray tangle of antennas set on the roof of a nondescript building in the south end of the city, known by those who need to know as Canadian Forces Station Leitrim. Twenty-four hours a day, the CSE (Communication Security Establishment) Leitrim facilities intercepted electronic communications to and from embassies in Ottawa. By agreement, decoded digital copies of these recordings were passed on by secured landline to the U.S. Embassy's resident representative of the National Security Agency, America's massive security and intelligence agency. As the Chinese message was still in a new "raw" cipher code that CSE's Cray CX1 computers could not break, he would have no knowledge of its contents when he found it Monday morning at the embassy. He would send it, along with two Russian intercepts, by diplomatic courier express directly to the NSA facilities at Fort George G. Meade in Maryland for decrypting and processing by their more powerful Cray supercomputers.

The agency occupied over eighty-two secluded acres and employed over 1,400 people. Its central building had the longest unobstructed corridor in the US and its complex computers and monitoring technology represented hidden billions of the US citizen's tax money. Over five years ago the facilities – under great strain – had maxed out the Maryland electrical grid that served it, and a new two billion-dollar facility was built in Bluffdale, Utah. Each day, the NSA multiple intelligence collection systems intercepted and stored over 1.7 billion e-mails, phone calls, diplomatic and military messages. Less than thirty percent were decrypted.

It would be two weeks before any attention or time was given to the fourteen minutes of transmission from the Chinese embassy in Ottawa. By then, it wouldn't matter.

Chapter 7

His cell phone rang three times before Vladimir Baryshnikov answered it. Vladimir Baryshnikov was Counselor-Agricultural Attaché at the Russian Embassy in Washington, a large compound of buildings and facilities situated on "Mount Alto" at Wisconsin Avenue Northwest. Baryshnikov, in his late thirties, represented the new breed of smart, young Russian technocrats that have been flooding into the Russian Embassies around the world.

His master degree in agronomy – from Moscow's Timiryazev Agricultural Academy – had established his credentials and reputation as an expert in grain crops and poultry production. In every sense, he was the new Russian international man, polished from consulate and embassy postings in Chile, Cuba and Egypt. He had created a model commercial farm near his home town of Kirovograd in the Sverdlovsk region of Russia, and many of his management reforms and innovations – based on American agribusiness production systems – were now accepted farming techniques throughout the Russian Federation. A regular contributor to *The Russian Journal of Agricultural Science*s, several of his articles on American farming methods had appeared in both *Moskovskaya Pravda* and *Novaya Gazeta*.

Altogether, he was successful, well paid, owned a comfortable flat in central Moscow, and had so far avoided the pitfalls of marriage, in spite of a torrid affair with a dark-eyed daughter of a high Cuban official in Havana. He was tall, slim and boyish, fond his attraction to women – especially American women – had not escaped him. He attributed it to the novelty of his rank and nationality, and his often witty and flawless command of the English language.

He liked his posting in Washington and its easy way of life with parties, receptions and a seemingly genuine friendly attitude from his American contacts, who jokingly called him "Vlad–the Impaler" because of his success with women. His social life was encouraged by Russian intelligence, who debriefed him regularly as a source of inside Washington gossip and social trivia, and his relationship with an important woman in the US Department of Agriculture was encouraged. His code name with the FBI was "The Russian Romeo" or "RR", and they kept a close eye on his amorous adventures about town and when he traveled. He enjoyed his trips across America over the past two years, and constantly marveled at how parts of the rural country were so similar to his motherland.

The cell call had disturbed him. His contact in the Department of Agriculture had always proven to be helpful and accurate, and her latest bit of confidential information was something he could not comprehend. The Department was in a state of controlled panic, trying to cope with apparently disastrous news that was pouring in from field offices and the poultry agribusiness across the country. From all reports, and if his informant was correct, it seemed that of the more than two billion American chickens living at one time, not a single one had laid an egg in the last twenty-four hours. It was impossible.

Baryshnikov ripped his raw notes off the telephone pad and walked around from behind his desk. It was nine-thirty in the morning. At ten, there was the weekly internal meeting with the Embassy's Minister-Counselor and head of the Counselor Division. He decided to say nothing to his small staff. Why appear foolish? Instead he would bring up the matter at the meeting as "rumor intelligence" and see how his superiors reacted. If there was any truth to the story, the facts soon have to be made public. He wondered if it was an unknown avian disease, another bird flu, or some other kind of new and terrible poultry plague.

He left his office and walked down the corridor to the technical library, a large two-room section with its own librarian who stored and catalogued commercial intelligence on discs, tapes, computers and in paper form. Baryshnikov spent the half-hour before the ten o'clock meeting skimming through all the latest poultry intelligence that was on file.

Sergi Shalimov glanced at the wall clock between the aging portraits of Putin and Lenin, and then lowered his Slavic eyes to stare at the face of Boris Yakushev. Shalimov was the Minister-Councilor, he was sixty-seven, big and burly, with a stare that could bore a hole through a wall. Yakushev, the head of the Embassy's domestic staff, was thin and balding and had just turned forty, but looked ten years older.

Since eight o'clock, Shalimov had chaired a long and detailed review of the various department's expenses and listened to the rising costs and outside purchases brought about by "stagflation." The Chancery compound housed a large residential building, school kindergarten and sports ground, and with over 200 Russian adults and children living on site, the cost of feeding them was rising every month.

Right now, Boris Yakushev was putting forward his proposal for importing – under diplomatic privilege – almost all of the Embassy's meat and poultry provisions by Aeroflot Cargo. In great detail; he outlined how these Russian provisions could be stockpiled in new commercial freezers in the residence buildings. Over time, the savings could be substantial. As usual, Yakushev had thoroughly documented his proposal and projected in boring detail both the immediate and long-term benefits from such a scheme.

Baryshnikov had sat silently through Yakushev's presentation, looking at the wall portrait of an older Vladimir Putin. He was sure it was bigger since the last time it was there. Since the Embassy's opening, that wall had hung portraits of Mikhail Gorbachev, Boris Yeltsin, Putin, Dmitry Medvedev, Putin again, and now Dmitry Kozlov, Russia's new president, but the portrait of Lenin never changed because for Russians of Shalimov's generation, Vladimir Lenin was their George Washington.

"How would the bulk importing of the meat and poultry be viewed by the American Department of Agriculture, Comrade Baryshnikov?" asked Shalimov. "Could we do it in such a volume?" Only the military still used the word "Comrade" as a form of address. Shalimov used it to rankle the self-assured young men that Moscow keep sending him.

"Under normal circumstances, it would be frowned upon, but if what I hear is true, it could be something to make us the most popular embassy on the hill, Mr. Shalimov." He knew that his reply would provoke another question from Shalimov and allow him to introduce the American chicken rumor into the meeting.

"Explain," commanded Shalimov.

"They could be lining up to buy chickens from us." Baryshnikov sat back in his chair and looked at his cigarette before continuing. "Early this morning I received a telephone message from my informant in the American Department of Agriculture. She told me that the whole department – at the highest level – was in a crisis panic. There was chaos. Reports had been coming in from around the country that not a single chicken had laid a single egg."

"That sounds impossible," scoffed Shalimov.

"No one knows yet," cautioned Baryshnikov.

"All the more reason for my proposal," said Yakushev.

"Please, Not now." The words were sighed with a smile but coming from Shalimov they were an instant command to Yakushev to shut up.

"What could this mean?" asked Shalimov, turning back to Baryshnikov.

"On the face of it, nothing, but if any of it is true, it could mean a serious poultry plague or group hysteria which can happen to large flocks of chickens. Such things can effect egg production, but not to this extent and not right across the country. After all, we are talking about millions and millions of chickens. I am baffled. I have found nothing in our technical library. Whatever it is, if it's across the country on a large scale, it might cause pockets of economic disaster – even certain food shortages – but I can't see this part of America's agribusiness just falling apart."

"The end of Colonel Saunders," chuckled Yakushev.

Shalimov shot Yakushev a withering glance.

"It may not be that funny," said Baryshnikov, "Last year, we consumed over 380,000 tons of chicken meat, but we produced only 78,000 tons. The difference we imported. The US accounted for about twenty percent of it. If this is true, we could be in big trouble."

Shalimov pondered for a moment on what he had just heard, and then said in a tone that ordered up performance, "Comrade Baryshnikov, I want you to contact your informant. Find out if there is any substance to this rumor. Personally, I don't believe it. America is an excitable country of silly and stupid rumors. Anyway, track it down and phone me your results at my residence tonight."

Shalimov leaned over to requisition a cigarette from Yakushev's package, He took it, lit it and exhaled the smoke before continuing. "Meanwhile, I shall say nothing to the Ambassador for both our sakes. The whole story sounds 'fishy', as the Americans say. I shall be out all afternoon and will expect your call between six and seven this evening." With that, Vladimir Baryshnikov was dismissed from the meeting and the Head of the Counselor Division returned to Yakushev's proposal.

. . .

The man on the screen wore dark-framed glasses. His gray-coiffured hair was backlit to create a halo effect around his head. With a white, carefully-groomed mustache perched over his mouth, to millions of CTN cable viewers he was "The Walter Cronkite of Cable News" – the honest, objective purveyor of the day's events.

It was a tight head-and-shoulders shot that framed him squarely in the screen in front of an electronic wall of slowly moving patriotic ribbons and stars. He leveled his eyes to the lens and began to speak.

"A chicken crisis sends the stock market reeling. Two French university students are killed in Paris during demonstrations. Severe flooding makes thousands homeless in China's Shandong province – and Spain threatens to leave the European Union. I'm Dane Donner – and you're in – *The Hub*!"

This was the nightly cue for the screen to replace Mr. Donner with a montage of graphic world news images that circled toward the center the screen, punctuated by a dramatic musical sting of drum and brass that heralded instant importance.

When the music phrase reached its crescendo, the screen slammed the title *The Hub* in the center of the circle of graphic images.

Mr. Donner then appeared again, now standing in the studio next to a large electronic screen. A mammoth white chicken was projected beside him, creating the momentary illusion that it was about to peck away at his well-groomed gray-haired head.

"In Washington today, the top story concerned America's real silent majority – America's chickens. To tell us more about this chicken conundrum, here's Tuffy Timmons over at the Department of Agriculture. What's happening there Tuffy?"

Dane Donner was replaced by a shot of a large classical revival building held up by Corinthian columns. In front of it stood Tuffy Timmons. She was a young, shapely blonde, new to the job and a glowing testament to the cosmetic miracles of L'Oréal. Tuffy greeted the camera with a brilliant smile. She smiled no matter what the subject or how dire the news. Her reporting was always breathless and excited, and she spoke in a high tinny voice, spitting out up to 150 words a minute.

"Dane, here at the Department of Agriculture there's been a flurry of activity all day. Like chickens with their heads cut off, Department spokesmen have been running around from one meeting to another, while senior officials have been cooped up on the second floor. No one is available for any comment concerning the rumor that American chickens have quit laying eggs. CTN has learned from reliable sources that Secretary of Agriculture, Percy Adams, has cut short his participation in the World Food Conference in Rome, and is flying back to Washington. No official confirmation of Adam's return is available from Department officials." A sudden gust of wind swept Tuffy's golden locks across her face as she continued her rapid-fire delivery eating her hair. "Meanwhile, poultry experts have informed CTN that it's virtually impossible for millions of chickens to stop laying eggs at the same time. Nevertheless, rumors continue to circulate around Washington that America's egg-laying chickens are on a standup strike." Her smile widened and her voice trilled to the silliness of what she had just said. "Something seems to be happening to America's chickens. Just what it is, agricultural officials can't or won't say. In the building behind me feathers are flying, and there's a lot of scratching and pecking here. A statement on just what's going on in America's hen houses is expected sometime tomorrow. Meanwhile, the great American chicken rumor continues to hatch. Tuffy Timmons at the Department of Agriculture. Back to you Dane." Pleased with herself, she tilted her head and smiled.

The picture cut back to Dane's whiskered face. "Excellent reporting Tuffy. CTN has just now learned that Canadian officials in Ottawa have confirmed that egg production in that country has taken a sharp decline. We'll keep you posted on this developing chicken-and-egg story." Behind him, on cue, the large white chicken looming over his head was replaced by the excited faces of French students. They marched arm-in-arm up Boulevard Saint Michel, the girls defiantly baring their breasts in protest.

"In Paris today, left-wing students protesting the French government's decision to close down part of the Sorbonne, staged a series of running battles with the –"

Donner's voice and image quickly died when Shalimov turned off the set to answer his bedroom telephone. It was Baryshnikov calling in as ordered. Baryshnikov confirmed what was just reported on television, adding nothing new except to say that there was now a complete wall of silence ringing the Department of Agriculture.

Shalimov grunted his appreciation and rang off. For a moment he wondered whether he should have brought Baryshnikov's morning intelligence to the Ambassador's attention. He then decided he had been wise to ignore the matter. After all, he had no hard intelligence. Still, he wondered whether Baryshnikov had included the chicken incident into his daily report to Moscow. Then there was the television comment about Canada. He made a mental note to have Baryshnikov check with their Ottawa embassy in the morning. His thoughts were interrupted when his wife, Nelya, entered the room.

"Who was that on the phone? My God, aren't you ready yet? We'll be late again. You'd think by now you'd know how much that annoys the old man."

Shalimov looked at his wife and remained silent. He felt his day's beard, then rose from the comfortable chair and went into the bathroom to shave and change. Nelya sipped at a shot of vodka and fussed with her hair in front of the full-length mirror.

It would be their third official function this week. Tonight it would be dinner at yet another African Embassy – and the main course would probably be chicken.

Chapter 8

A manicured lawn dotted with small cropped shrubs runs for two blocks along the pedestrian pavement of a broad avenue in Beijing. Set well in from the avenue, a low stone building runs the length of this lawn. Only seven stories high, it is gray, monotonous and brutish in design. It is meant to intimidate. It is the headquarters of the Ministry of State Security for The People's Republic of China, and from this building the MSS controls thousands of agents and operatives in over fifty countries around the world.

Major-General Cheung looked out from his sixth-floor office; the city's smog alert level was "orange": the second-highest level possible. The city – now for the fifth day – was shrouded in brownish air pollution that smothered lives, filled the lungs, and burnt the eyes of its citizens. He held a single sheet of paper in his hand. It was as hard to fathom its meaning as it was to see the smog-shrouded buildings at the other end of the avenue.

He lifted it up, looked at it again and returned to his desk. It didn't make sense; the President of the United States holding a secret meeting in the White House with a young Canadian lawyer and a talking chicken, but that's what the agent reported. Chickens don't talk, especially to Presidents. She must be crazy, yet there was nothing in her case officer file that suggested anything but a dependable, dedicated agent during her six years in Ottawa. In the past she had provided human intelligence on the Prime Minister's thinking – not top-grade intelligence – but useful in trade and natural resource negotiations between the two countries. What was this nonsense about a talking chicken?

It was the background information that the Ottawa station intelligence officer had added that caught his interest. The Canadian in the report was a principal in a Toronto Law firm that specialized in international patent and copyright law. One of their clients was Cyber Selection Genetics Inc., a new research facility in farm animal genetic engineering, jointly funded by the US and Canadian Governments.

Cheung Ling knew that there was some sort of poultry crisis happening in America from intelligence reports flowing in from their Washington Embassy and their five Consulates across the country. It was an uneasy unknown that could possibly effect China's long-term poultry plans. He couldn't sit on this Ottawa intelligence, but at the same time he certainly couldn't report a talking chicken. It was too unbelievable. Instead, he would write a short intelligence report from a creditable source reporting that the President would secretly meet with a poultry expert and a chicken specimen, possibly from an advanced genetic research facility. He would cautiously speculate that meeting might be related to the American chicken crisis.

All reports to any member of the ruling State Council were typed on special typewriters with a distinctive font and typewriter ribbons that were numbered and destroyed after typing. The numbered typewriters were manufactured in the municipality of Tianjin in a factory owned by the Ministry of State Security. This was an answer to a growing and troubling concern that the rapidly changing technology of electronic espionage by the Americans was such that neither the Bureau of Security Protection or the Bureau of Info-Communication could guarantee with any certainty that internal government electronic communications were safe from US penetration. Typed reports could be numbered, addressed, tracked and filed or destroyed without fear of their contents being read by anyone outside the State Council. It was a simple and safe precaution.

Cheung Ling spent some time composing a concise intelligence report and had three numbered copies made. The top copy was addressed to Wei Leung, Minister of Agriculture, with a copy to the office of the Executive Vice Premier, and the third copy for his secure files.

Two MSS security officers were dispatched by car to hand deliver the report, both requiring a deliverance receipt that would be time-marked and filed. Meanwhile, Major-General Cheung turned his attention to the problem of an agent who had just defected to South Korea's National Intelligence Service.

Chapter 9

He knew he would have heartburn. The chicken-groundnut stew simmered in the chaffing dish: a steaming concoction of chicken, tomatoes, onions and hot peppers, with a judicious touch of garlic thrown in. Yellow balls surfaced from time to time and then slowly sank back into the bubbling pottage.

Sergi Shalimov watched in diplomatic terror as one of his well-meaning African hosts piled the stew onto his plate beside a dish of three odd yellow balls.

"Chicken-groundnut stew, your Excellency. It is the national dish of our country," said the smiling woman. "And these are 'fufu' – mashed yam balls. Traditionally, you break off part of the fufu ball and dip into the stew–always with your right hand–then pop it into your mouth and just swallow it down. But you can use a knife and fork if it's more comfortable for you. I put some smaller fufu balls in the stew."

Shalimov eyed the fufu balls with suspicion; the pungent odor of the peanut oil started a minor revolution in Shalimov's stomach. Nelya, his wife, feigned rapt attention as a large black African woman – in a lime-green Buba dress topped with a matching head wrap – revealed the secret of the dish's ingredients and careful cooking. Apparently everything depended on the cook's ability to skim off the excess peanut oil that rose from the potion as it simmered.

The room was crowded with black and white diplomats jostling their plates, drinking Zobo, and sampling this new chicken ecstasy. There was also a large contingent of Chinese guests, who smiled at everyone but stayed aloof. This small poor African nation – canopied by a dense green jungle – now enjoyed being competitively courted by both the West and the East for the vast mineral riches that lay buried in its rust-red earth.

. . .

In another part of Washington there was another kind of chicken stew boiling. This chicken brew was bubbling in the U.S. Department of Agriculture. Off the mall at 14th and Independence, lights burned on the fourth floor of the immense bureaucratic building. A haggard Percy Adams, the Secretary of Agriculture, struggling with jet-lag hangover from his hurried Presidential recall from Rome, was trying to grapple with the mounting catastrophe sweeping through America's poultry industry.

Pandemonium reigned in the corridors of the building. Security guards limited elevator access to the fourth floor, while desperate Department spokespersons hassled with the press. The Department had never experienced such a turnout of the Fourth Estate. Besides the editor of *The Poultry Times*, reporters from *Meat and Poultry Magazine*, and *Feedstuffs* – a leading weekly paper on Agribusiness – every major network and cable news channel was represented, as well as two newspaper chains, three Midwest radio stations and even the Washington bureau chief of the august *Financial Times*. Into this melee of scrambling journalists and reporters, an *Al Jazeera* man and a stringer for *The Jerusalem Post* had turned up together in a shared taxi, drawn to the "kill" by the chicken rumors which were now racing around Washington's press corps.

Through another entrance to the central block, a higher echelon of the Capital's inquisitive were gathering in a large walnut-paneled briefing room embellished with a 1930s Federal Art Project mural depicting harvest scenes of fruits and vegetables, and ironically, an angelic. golden-haired American farm maiden feeding a flock of grateful chickens.

Four undersecretaries, aides to the undersecretaries, and aides to the aides, were attempting to calm and answer the questions of this nervous group of senators and congressmen from poultry-producing states, driven to desperation by the thousands of e- mails flooding into their offices.

In an adjacent room, agricultural attachés from concerned embassies were also milling around, trying to pick up any scrap of information which they could piece together in this unfolding poultry puzzle. Into this keyed up crowd came Vladimir Baryshnikov, his intelligent eyes searching for his female friend in the Department. He spotted her speaking to a tall pale man whom he did not recognize. For a brief moment they made eye contact, then quickly looked away. The size and mixture of this anxious group confirmed Baryshnikov's earlier guess that something big and very unpleasant was happening to America's poultry industry.

Like all Federal buildings in Washington, the building was supposedly smoke-free. Percy Adams broke open his second deck and pushed a cigarette into his dry mouth. "For Christ's sake, can't any of you make sense of this? Surely to God you can get a better grasp on the situation than what you're telling me. I've had two calls from the White House and I've got to report to the President first thing tomorrow morning. I'm not going to go into his office looking like a complete bloody fool!" Adams was still smarting over an ad-lib remark he had made in Rome about the Pope and population control. The press had been quick to pick it up and the President had really chewed him out for it. Thank God there was no video.

The smoky boardroom – thanks largely to Percy Adams – contained a large board table that could seat thirty persons in its brown leather chairs. At present the room was in disarray, with agricultural maps papering the walls and additional folding chairs crammed in and around the table. Abandoned coats and ties were flung over the backs of chairs, and reports and confidential documents littered the enormous table top, surrounding islands of empty coffee cups and half-eaten donuts.

Established in 1862, the Department of Agriculture had weathered a good many farm crises in its time, and had usually managed them with the earthy wisdom that seems to emanate from men of the soil. Percy Adams was no man of the soil. His appointment to Secretary of Agriculture had been a last minute shuffle brought about by the untimely death of its intended heir.

Percy Adams had never lived on a farm. He was a landowner, owning a vast number of almond orchard groves in the San Joaquin

County of California's great Central Valley, along with a pretentious thirty-room villa. His great-grandfather, Pirro Adan, brought his almond orchard skills to California in 1912 from the Andalusia region of Spain. In 1929 his grandfather changed the family name to Adams and kept buying up land. Now a fourth generation almond multimillionaire, Percy Adams had served briefly as Under Secretary in California's Department of Food and Agriculture. He had not been a great success then and was even less so now. Still, he was tenth in line of succession to the President. and he liked to comfort himself with the importance of that thought, ignoring the mathematical probabilities of it ever happening.

"Hemming! Give us a rundown on our inventory position." barked Adams. Hemming was a rumpled, lumpish little man from the statistical division of the USDA's Consumer and Marketing Services. He gathered up his computer printouts and fanned them across the table in front of him, his eyes probing the endless lists of poultry and egg statistics. "Eggs or poultry? he timidly inquired.

"Which comes first – the chicken or the egg?" It was a flippant quip uttered by someone at the far end of the table. Percy Adams killed him with a withering look, instantly smothering the few nervous titters.

"Let's start with eggs."

"Right sir," said Hemming, extracting the pertinent printouts. "These are in round figures sir. I'll have them updated by tomorrow morning. Eggs dried," he announced. "On hand as follows: shell eggs broken in total, 790 million, 867 hundred thousand dozen."

"What the hell does that mean to me!" snapped Adams. "Well it's the total number of eggs broken." stammered Hemming. "I'm aware of that!" snarled Adams. "What I want to know is totals: the vital totals of our reserves as they will affect our economy. How long can we hold out? That's the first question the President is going to ask me."

Hemming's eyes extracted the vital figures. "In edible liquid form from shell eggs broken, we have an estimated current production in excess of 915 million, 807 thousand pounds. That's liquid whole, white and yolk. The liquid product produced for immediate food consumption and processing is in excess of 307 million, 365 thousand pounds. That's not storage sir. That's continued on-stream production."

"In other words, these figures would represent volumes flowing through the system if egg production was normal." said Adams.

"Right sir," replied Hemming.

"Well what have we got in the cupboard?' asked Adams.

"In the cupboard sir?" Hemming took the question literally. Percy Adam's face turned red and a small vein across his forehead began to palpitate visibly. His aides knew the signal; he was about to explode. "In storage – under lock and key. What the hell have we got in reserves?"

Hemming cringed. The others sat petrified, listening to the frantic shuffle of Hemming's papers. "Here – here we are." he mumbled. "Right now, including whole plain, whole blends, white, yolk plain, and yolk blends, we have slightly in excess of 380 million under refrigeration in key areas across the country. The same product in dry form comes to over 187 million."

"Million what?" growled Adams.

"Pounds sir – millions of pounds," answered Hemming. "These figures represent product under Federal inspection." Hemming paused before continuing, "Then there's product by production and disposition. I have figures here on mixed emulsions, egg whites, plain yolk, sugared yolk, salted yolk, and of course other yolk."

Hemming continued to rattle off the staggering statistics of egg production and consumption in America. Percy Adams felt himself sinking in a scramble of numbers. It was becoming painfully clear that chickens were no laughing matter. The figures droned on and on – eggs in storage were over seventy-eight million dozen – exports to American territories averaged sixty-two million dozen – the military alone consumed over seventy-three million dozen – civilian consumption topped forty-eight billion dozen last year.

"It averages out to a per capita consumption of 247 eggs per person per year – down from earlier years – but of course that doesn't include eggs consumed in food products and baking.," proclaimed Hemming.

"My God," groaned Adams, "Enough about eggs! Where do we stand on chickens?"

"Now about chickens – based on projected figures, we expect to produce over thirty-seven billion pounds of broiler chickens. Egg flock chickens will, or should be about 371 million at present. The fear is they could all suddenly become spent hens."

"What the hell does that mean?" asked Adams.

"Spent hens. Spent hens are chickens no longer able to lay eggs." Adams gave Hemming a look as if he were personally responsible for every spent hen in America. Hemming's eyes returned to his stat sheets, "Now back to broilers sir. We estimate that Americans will consume well over 1.25 billion Buffalo wings on Super Bowl Sunday. This will average out to more than 500 million chickens representing slightly more than eleven billion pounds of finished poultry meat." Hemming's fingers raced along the lines, seeking more awesome figures. Chicken consumption in America was beyond Adam's comprehension.

"Only 213 million pounds were under storage at this point of the year. The military consumed over 6,805 million pounds. In pure chicken terms, domestic consumption has risen to around eight billion broiler birds that Americans ate last year. Sir, this averages out to almost eighty-four pounds of chicken per person a year."

Percy Adams breathed a long and low whistle. "Eighty-four pounds of chicken per capita. My God!" exclaimed Adams again, dropping his cigarette butt into this half-cup of cold coffee to join the other one floating around in his Starbucks mug.

"Then there's our export market. We are the world's largest producers of chicken and the world's second-largest exporter of chicken meat, measured in metric tons."

"We're not the first? Who is?"

"Brazil Mr. Secretary, but not by much. Last year we exported over eighteen percent of our broiler chickens valued at over three billion dollars. It would be terrible to lose that market."

Adams stared at him, but said nothing. "Then there's Phoenix Talons," said Hemming.

"Who the hell is Felix Tilon?" asked Adams.

"Sorry Mr. Secretary, I mean chicken feet. The Chinese call them 'Phoenix Talons'. Chicken feet are a delicacy over there. They deep fry them, drench them in some kind of spicy-sauce and nibble the meat off the bone. What we do with chicken wings, they do with chicken feet." Percy Adams winced at the thought and a look of disgust came over his face.

"It's a growing market and very profitable for us. Last year we exported over 410 million dollars' worth of chicken feet to China. Before, they were ground up and put into chicken feed."

"Mr. Secretary!" It was Fred Cleaver, the U.S. Food and Drug Administration representative. "We also have to take into account the hot dog consumption."

Percy Adams blinked his eyes. "What the hell have hot dogs got to do with chickens?"

"Well sir, decades before your appointment, the FDA put through a ruling allowing that up to fifteen percent of 'All-Meat' hot dogs could contain chicken meat. The ruling went into force in 1971."

Before Adams could respond to this new unpleasant fact, Hemming continued his statistical disclosure of chicken parts and where they went, speaking as forcefully as he could for a timid man. "And we can't forget other industries."

"What other industries?" Adams feared the answer.

"Well Sir, Mr. Secretary, a large amount of inedible eggs and chicken goes into the pet food industry. Poultry carcasses and parts are made into animal meal. Feathers into feather meal that's recycled into poultry feed. There's also recycling as fertilizer, and pharmaceuticals. And we can't forget egg shells."

"Egg shells?"

"Yes Mr. Secretary. The poultry industry generates about 150,000 tons of shell waste a year. Some is recycled as fertilizer and animal feed. Some is processed as a flavor enhancer, or used in pulp paper, or in ink jet printing, or tooth paste, even as a calcium supplement in orange juice. Again I don't have any breakdown on these figures in front of me, but our department can provide you with them by tomorrow morning."

Percy Adams looked blank. He was past the point where he could relate the bewildering barrage of chicken statistics to any concrete conclusion. Instead he delegated subcommittees to deal with the avalanche of multiplying problems. One undersecretary would work with the Economic Services of FDA to draw up contingency plans for possible rationing on a national level. His most senior undersecretary would form an emergency committee of the Poultry Industry. This group would consist of The Poultry Growers Association of America,

The American Agricultural Marketing Association, The National Farm Bureau Federation, The National Egg Council, The Southeastern Poultry and Egg Association, The National Broiler Council, The American Egg and Poultry Association and The Advisory Committee on Criteria for Poultry Inspection.

Under this committee a task force comprised of FDA's Packers and Stockyards Administration, The Poultry Inspectors Local of the American Federation of Government Employees and FDA's Bureau of Food, Pesticides and Product Safety would tackle the horrendous problem of immediate flock slaughter and refrigeration should the situation deteriorate beyond a point of passive resistance from the millions of striking birds.

There were also the problems of the Agribusiness giants and the turmoil that this unfolding poultry disaster was causing in the corporate boardrooms of Minneapolis, New York and Chicago. These big food conglomerates dominated the poultry industry, supplying the chicks, feed, medicine and transportation to farmers on a contract basis. This corporate-integrated system of agriculture accounted for over ninety-eight per cent of all chickens in America – processed under contract to integrated corporations.

Outside the Department of Agriculture, the chicken crisis was causing rising panic in the world of business. Food futures danced up and down by the minute, driven by reckless rumors on the New York and Chicago stock exchanges in response to the uncertainties of the poultry industry. Shares in fast food service industries dependent on chicken plummeted. The large poultry corporations saw their shares shaved in half by mid-afternoon. Everybody who was in chickens was getting out of them.

The powerful Agribusiness food lobby was now leaning into the Department of Agriculture with all the corporate muscle it could muster. Percy Adams knew that if his department couldn't satisfy their wailing concerns about production and profit, they'd put their weight against the President. Percy didn't want that to happen, especially as next year was an election year.

"Hemming, what are we talking about in dollars – the economics of this disaster." demanded Adams.

Hemming glanced down at the sheets in front of him, pulled one out of the clutter and studied it. He was about to read out the figures, but thought better of it and passed it over to Adams who snatched it from his hand.

The paper had a large pie-shaped graph divided into many colored wedges with arrows and numbers running around the outside of the pie. Adams tried to make sense of the jumble, picking out the salient information. The US poultry market was now a staggering 526-billion-dollar annual business. Mexico was its biggest export market, but China was second and growing at such a rate that we'd soon have to breed chickens with four wings and four legs to keep up with their demands. Georgia, Alabama and Arkansas were again the three largest poultry producing states where the industry was a major employer. The meat and poultry industry's economic ripple effect generates 848.2 billion dollars annually to the U.S. economy, about 6 percent of the nation's entire GNP. This made it a major generator of revenue to Federal, State and local taxes, especially in the South.

Adams bit his lip. These were awesome numbers. "What do you have on employment figures?" Again Hemming dipped into his papers, pulling out a sheet that seemed to have very little printed on it.

"Well Mr. Secretary, there's no hard single figures for poultry right now. But the latest study shows that the meat and poultry industry together directly employs over 1.6 million people, paying out 45.6 billion dollars in wages and benefits. An estimated 524,000 people have jobs in production and packing, sales, packaging and direct distribution of meat and poultry products. Wholesale directly employs an estimated 63,000 individuals in every state in the country, and over 1,225,000 employees' retail jobs depend on the sale of meat and poultry to the public. We 'guestimate' that the poultry industry makes up about sixty-five percent of these figures, but we'll have the exact numbers for you by tomorrow morning."

Hemming proceeded to read from the paper, his voice slightly shaking. "Then there's another 60,000 employed in feed mills and hatcheries. Then there's the family farms. Family poultry farms within this category account for only about two percent of poultry production. We calculate two poultry employees per farm, that's another 60,000. Then there's illegal immigrant poultry farm workers. We have no figures, but estimate that it could be as high as 300,000. "

Adams did some quick mathematical additions while he lit yet another cigarette. "So the poultry people numbers could be almost two million, not counting the illegals."

Hemming gathered his courage, and then introduced a final figure that was to stun Percy Adams. "But the biggest unknown is the total number of people dependent on chickens in the service industries, restaurants, fast food chains and processed food products. If there were no chicken, eggs or poultry products for any great length of time, we estimate that more than three million people would be out of work".

"Jesus Almighty!" exclaimed Adams in a voice wavering in weakness. The present unemployment rate stood officially at seven percent. An added total of five million more would sink any incumbent President seeking a second term.

A new group of men and women now crowded into Adams' improvised command post. The first faction was led by Dr. R.C. Woodman of the University of Ashton, Georgia. He was an advisor to the Department and one of the world's leading authorities on avian animal behavior.

"The Gallus gallus domesticus —"

"The what?" said Percy. "The Gallus gallus domesticus–the scientific name for chicken," said Dr. Woodman. "Listen, save the fancy words for your classroom. In here, call them chickens."

"Yes Mr. Secretary," replied Dr. Woodman, who then proceeded with a lecture. Percy found him a bore and confirmed his opinion after listening to him give a tedious monologue on the American Standards of Perfection for the maintenance and occasional modification of poultry breeds. Dr. Woodman divided the breeds of chickens into classes, breeds, varieties and strains, classifying the breeds by place or origin, such as American, English, Polish, Mediterranean, Dutch, Continental and other classes. He then illustrated how each could be determined by such factors as difference in size, shape, weight and form. He was starting to work his way into the fifty standard breeds of chickens when Percy cut him short with a not-too-diplomatic question concerning the chicken's ability to reason.

Dr. Woodman rose to the question. "Newly hatched chickens are capable of skills that can take human babies months or even years to master," he proclaimed. "New research by a professor of animal welfare at Britain's University of Bristol revealed fields of intelligence ranging from structural engineering to self-control appear to come more naturally to chickens than to toddlers. We should no longer think of chickens as stupid. In fact, they are quite bright.

"They have a sophisticated social behavior – what we call a pecking order. Animal scientists have determined that they can recognize over a hundred other chickens and remember them. We also know that they have more than thirty types of distinct cries and cackles to communicate information to each other. It's quite amazing.

"In England, a research team from the Biophysics Group at Silsoe Research Institute has discovered that chickens don't just live in the present, but that they can anticipate the future. We're still don't know how they do this, but the fact that they have larger brains than humans' relative to body size might be the answer."

Dr. Woodman then warmed to the subject of the emotions of animals and how "unscientific" it was to attribute anthropomorphism to them.

Adams asked what the hell did anthropomorphism mean, and the good professor launched into an explanation of man's constant desire to falsely identify human values, feelings and characteristics to animals, citing Disney's Mickey Mouse and Donald Duck as pop culture examples. Percy Adams coldly thanked Dr. Woodman for his scholarly briefing and turned to the other scientific faction represented by Dr. Philip Roost, Professor of Agricultural Economics at the University of Fornham. He was a tall lanky man with sunburned features and an ill-fitting suit.

"Mr. Secretary, we have our preliminary summary for your attention," drawled Roost, pointing to a sheath of papers tucked under his lean arm.

Percy Adams eyed the papers before speaking. "Professor, let's dispense with formality. We're all tired, and frankly I've got a long night still ahead of me. Can you give me your observations quickly and to the point? I don't mean to be rude, but you understand."

"Certainly Mr. Secretary. I'm afraid it's not good." Roost paused, looking at his colleagues for their confirmation. "Dr. Hardy of the FDA's Bureau of Veterinary Medicine and Dr. Iba of the ACSS –"

"The ACSS?" interrupted Adams.

"The American Chick Sexing Standards." The voice came from a small neat Japanese gentleman who stepped forward. "It's a recent institution founded to maintain the rigid sexing disciplines of the American Chick Sexing Association. We distinguish the sex of day-old chicks – the telltale signs of the chick's anatomy. No modern hatchery is complete without a chicken sexer."

"I see," said a somewhat startled Secretary of Agriculture.

"Frankly, we've looked at this from all angles." Robert Roost talked glowingly, his sentences having the ring of academic assuredness. "We are baffled. In tests conducted overnight in Georgia, California, Alabama and Upper New York State, the chickens are not conforming to their normal habits and conditioning. Young chicks, after hatching, are not imprinting."

"Imprinting?" asked Adams.

"The process by which they identify with a mother-figure at birth: in natural conditions with the hen. In controlled conditions with the brooder and feeder unit – a balloon or any moving object that will lead them to warmth, water or food. Careful examination has revealed no physical abnormalities, and disease ratios and spectrums are well within acceptable margins. On the surface they appear healthy. We've conducted over eight hundred autopsies to a controlled system through the generous auspices of the Bureau of Veterinary Medicine."

Dr. Hardy picked up his cue to continue the verbal report. "We've tested intestines, tumors, windpipes, heads and brains, fecal matter and hearts, probing for a clue. We've done feed samples and comparisons, suspecting that the industry's rapid development in genetics, feed and animal drugs may hold the answer to this astonishing deviation in chicken behavior."

"Nothing so far." intoned Dr. Roost.

Dr. Hardy continued. "We've even been in contact with NASA to consider the possibilities of earth observation to determine the fowl inventories or changes in Russia, Brazil and China through earth observation satellites. In fact, all modes of collecting data: satellites, drone aircraft and existing intelligence surveys. We are even considering multi spectral electronic analysis of film data. It is difficult to measure energy radiation from flocks, particularly when they are enclosed in roofed environments. Also, the military are concerned about losing low flying drone aircraft over a belligerent country for what they term is 'chicken-shit' intelligence."

Percy Adams' face flushed red again. "What you're telling me gentlemen, is that you have no answers – no answers at all! You're stumped, baffled and just as goddamned confused by the behavior of the birds as we are. Is that right or isn't it?" Adams' face was now turning a light shade of purple and his voice was tight and strained from exasperation and too much smoking.

The three scientists mumbled their reluctant agreement. Watching and listening to all this was a dark-skinned man at the back of the room. He wondered if this was an unknown type of bird disease that attacked the chicken's brain? Whatever it was, was it contagious? Could it mutate to infect or even kill humans? All of these thoughts went through the mind of Dr. Abrar Khanzada, from the US Centers of Disease Control and Prevention (CDC), but he kept them to himself.

"Thank you. Thank you anyway gentlemen," there was a sarcastic ring to Adam's voice. "Please keep at it and keep me informed."

Percy Adams was stumped and was now scared. The long flight from Rome had landed him into the greatest disaster and disorder the Department of Agriculture had ever experienced. Why did it have to happen on his watch? Even with the resources of over 114,000 employees, he had not found the answer to give to his anxious and alarmed President. He dreaded tomorrow morning in the President's office.

"I want everything you got in two binders, tabbed, and I want it tomorrow morning by seven o'clock. Is that understood."

He swilled cold coffee inside his musty mouth, oblivious to the cigarette butts floating on its surface, and surveyed the surrounding group of experts, charts and advisors. All of it worthless to him. Regardless of what happens, he made a mental vow to himself: Percy Adams would never, ever eat a goddamn egg or chicken again. From here on in, he was going to be a strictly meat-and-potatoes man.

. . .

About the same time that Percy Adams made his secret vow never to eat chicken again, Sergi Shalimov – having left the African embassy reception early – was lying in his bed, listening to his stomach gurgling and rumbling away as strange expanding gases pushed through his intestinal tract, seeking a way out. Now and then he would belch and the taste of the chicken groundnut stew – or was it the fufu balls –

would surge up his throat to soil his tongue.

Nelya had enjoyed their African evening and was now blissfully asleep beside him with no digestive after-effects. He hated her for it, for he knew it was going to be a long night with many trips to the toilet.

Chapter 10

A summer shower was steaming off the pavements of Washington as the chauffeur maneuvered the State Department Lincoln through the iron fence gates of the most guarded 18 acres in the world.

They had flown into Ronald Reagan Washington National Airport from Ottawa late yesterday evening. Throughout the flight the chicken had remained silent, and so had Trent, neither revealing to the crew that they could communicate with each other.

The drive across the Potomac River into Washington took less than twenty-five minutes before they reached the Canadian Embassy, a sleek contemporary six-floor building on Pennsylvania Avenue. Trent had spent the night cooped up in a small bed-sitting room on the third floor. The chicken had slept in the bathroom, its open traveling basket placed in the bathtub next to a pan of feed and a bowl of water.

Now, driving up to the northwest executive wing of the White House, Trent broke the silence to speak to the ever-silent security officer in the front seat. "Will you take the chicken in? I think that I have to go through some sort of special security check. Isn't that right?"

"Just a standard security measure," answered the State Department official from the front seat. He turned his heavy body to look back at Trent.

"How about the chicken?" said Trent.

"We don't body search animals unless there's something unusual about them." replied the official in his most serious and concerned tone.

They entered into the West Wing lobby, comfortably furnished with leather chairs and couches, turning left and walking down a wide hall past the Roosevelt Room to a solid door guarded by a secret service man. Their credentials were checked against the day's visitors list and the electric lock snapped open to allow them through the door. Once through, the State Department official was asked to wait with the chicken in its basket while Trent was taken by an aide into a small side room for the security ritual. Several minutes later he emerged with one of the President's aides. Another secret service man then appeared and took the basket. As Trent and a uniformed escort went down a second hall, the secret service man with the basket trudged along behind at a discreet distance. They stopped in front of an impressive white door with ornate brass fixtures. From the opposite wall, a large melancholy portrait of Thomas Jefferson gazed back at Trent in sadness.

"This is it," thought Trent.

"Please wait here. I'll inform the President of your arrival." The aide opened the door just wide enough to slide through and disappear.

"Do you want me to carry the – carry her inside?" asked Trent, nodding at the chicken in the basket.

"Whatever the aide says, sir," replied the secret service man. Trent could see two other similar well-groomed protectors at the end of the hall. They waited until the aide appeared again through the door.

"The President will see you now, Mr. Marshall. You should know that the Secretary of State Arthur Brandon and your Ambassador are with the President. At the mention of the Canadian Ambassador, a slight smirk sneaked across his face. He immediately killed it, resumed his official air, and turned to the secret service man, saying, "I'll take the chicken."

Trent was ushered through the door and into the famous Oval Office of the President. His first impression was the size and brightness of the handsome room, a subdued blend of gold, beige and whites. The massive Resolute desk dominated one end of the room. The President was behind the desk, rocking his huge frame back and forth in a green swivel leather chair, while a bust of Mandela – on the credenza behind the desk – peeked over the President's shoulder. In front of it, two ribbed chairs revealed the tailored backs of the Secretary of State and the Canadian Ambassador.

As Trent was led across the lush oval carpet – careful to step around the Presidential seal woven into its center – the President stood up and walked from behind the desk and the other two men turned to look in Trent's direction. The President was a big man; the first American President to have a Spanish surname and Latino blood in his veins. He had been the former governor of California, and later a senator from that state, before putting himself forward as a presidential candidate. He had won hands-down, especially with the woman's vote, ethnic minorities and those under 35 years of age.

"Mr. President, may I present Mr. Trent Marshall." announced the aide who had now assumed a formal stance with the chicken in the basket in front of him like a court offering.

"Ah, Mr. Marshall. Nice of you to come –" he paused, looking at the covered basket, and then continued, "– to offer your services for our feathered friend."

"It's a great honor to meet you sir," replied Trent. The President, now standing in front of Trent, was a solid man with big hands and a large handsome head. He was dressed in a course tweed sports coat, buff colored pants and a brown shirt open at the collar. His hair was coal black and his sharp Latino features had the appearance of being chiseled into his face. In person, he looked even more rugged than his pictures. His manner was friendly and direct, and his great outstretched paw offered itself to Trent. Clasping Trent's hand, he pulled Trent forward and guided him until he faced the other two men who had now risen.

The resonate voice of the President eased itself through his broad grin. "I presume you know your Ambassador, Marc Brunet." The Canadian Ambassador took a small step forward and nodded his head in recognition. He was sixty-two years old; a short, sleek little gentleman and very French Canadian. Brunet was a seasoned diplomat, slightly vain, artfully charming when it suited him, and smart and savvy to the many machinations of international diplomacy. Gregarious by nature, invitations to his monthly Embassy dinner parties were much sought after by Washington's rich and powerful. Trent noticed that today his blue-striped suit had sprouted a pompous boutonniere next to his *Order of Canada* lapel pin.

"We met last night – that is we were his overnight guests. Good morning Mr. Ambassador." The diplomat flashed a complete smile of expensive dentures, his small eyes gleaming with the importance of the occasion.

The President waved a hand in the direction of the Secretary of State. "And of course, our indispensable Secretary of State. Brandon came in from London for this meeting. It was London, wasn't it Brandon?" Secretary Brandon's eyes were riveted in fascination on the basket. On command of the President, he looked up to acknowledge Trent with a blank expression. Only his eyes revealed the shrewd and discerning intelligence that simmered inside his oval head. Trent was amazed at his compact stature and the paleness of his complexion. His skin had a chalky tint to it. His thick-rimmed glasses gave his puffy face an owlish aspect that suited his overall gray appearance.

"Why don't we sit over there, around the coffee table. It's more comfortable." The President waved at two sofas flanking a low colonial table. The group moved toward the other end of the oval office, followed by the aide with the wicker basket.

"Where shall we put it?" inquired the President of Trent. "May I suggest the ottoman sir. We could move the ottoman up to the edge of the coffee table."

"Fine. Fine. Take a seat Gentlemen." The President, with a nod of his head, directed his aide to implement Trent's suggestion. "Just put the basket on the ottoman, would you Jack. I think that's all for now." The aide retired from the room as the four men seated themselves around the table. Trent noticed two silver bowls on it; one filled with corn kernels and the other with ice water.

"Mr. Marshall, let me lead with a question." The President leaned his heavy frame forward and dipped his head in the direction of the basket. "That chicken in there, can she understand us, or am I to understand that she understands only you?"

"Mr. President, I can assure you that her intelligence has comprehended every word and sound since we entered this office. Not only that, but she is probably peering at you through the ribbing of the basket."

A skeptical expression flashed across the President's face to be immediately wiped away by a warm smile. "Forgive me. I wasn't to know?" He turned and spoke directly to the basket. "I think our friend should join us, and hopefully put our bad manners down to ignorance. This is certainly not my style of opening discussions." His eyes returned to Trent and back down to the basket. "Would you, Mr. Marshall?"

Trent placed the basket on the floor, unlocked the lid and flipped it back on its leather hinges. There was silence. Nothing moved or appeared. Slowly, Trent dipped his hands into the basket and gently lifted the white chicken up and out, placing it down on the leather ottoman. The bird stood up to its full height, stretching body, neck and wings in a total gesture of riddance from its confinement. As it did so, several black droppings hit the ottoman and dropped onto the carpet. Then it settled back down, puffing itself up, its head moving in a series of jerky actions to peer at its surroundings and the four humans looking at it. The President studied its every move, prudently deciding to remain silent until Trent initiated introductions.

"Mr. President, may I introduce you to Ceres, a Plymouth Rock hen, and the representative of the World Council of Chickens." said Trent. The President nodded and smiled at the beady-eyed bird, automatically putting out his great paw of a hand, then stopping it in mid-action to place it on his knee. The bird's tiny red eyes burned with danger and defiance as they followed the sudden movement of the President's hand.

Trent then introduced the Secretary of State and the Canadian Ambassador. The bird swiveled its head toward Marc Brunet, glaring back at Trent and uttering a long series of annoyed cackling sounds.

Trent felt an immediate flush of embarrassment. He nervously moistened his lips and wiped his hand across his mouth before translating. "Gentlemen, the bird wishes to know why the Canadian Ambassador is part of this meeting, and further, why your Secretary of Agriculture is not present?"

Marc Brunet bristled at the question, his face reddening at the effrontery and insolence of the chicken. The Secretary of State looked at the bird, his face now relaxed and open in its expression, his voice soothing and sincere as he put forward his diplomatic explanation.

"Please understand that you being here was arranged through the courtesy of the Canadian Government in response to your request to meet with the President. You are, after all, a Canadian chicken. That is, in the eyes of international law, a possession of Canada. Ambassador

Brunet represents your interests and also the interests of your fellow Canadian chickens. It is a normal and diplomatically correct procedure for the Ambassador to be present at this meeting to put forward the views of his country – and to offer you advice and safeguard your interests."

The chicken appeared to be listening intently. It seemed that it understood the Secretary's remarks and was weighing them carefully before it replied. Suddenly it burst forth with a series of high-pitched noses that propelled Trent into rapid translation.

"Let's make one thing perfectly clear – we recognize adherence to no government of humans. How you organize your societies politically or geographically is of no interest to us other than how it effects our species. We are not Canadian chickens, or American chickens, or Chinese chickens, or chickens of any geopolitical map. We are chickens of this earth. I am here meeting with you as a representative of the World Council of Chickens. The Council represents more than twenty-one billion chickens living on this earth at any one time, outnumbering you three to one. I'm here because we've had enough. You humans have made us your largest source of protein meat. You take from us over a trillion eggs every year. In your land alone, we have calculated by your calendar that twenty-one million of us are killed every day for food. By your measurement of time, we have reasoned that comes out to 269 deaths per second. This cannot go on. United, we are a mighty force. And we are not alone: what you humans call turkeys, geese, ducks, pheasants, ostriches, in fact all of the fowl where you take their eggs and eat their bodies, they are with us, ready to join our movement."

The brashness of the bird's sudden outburst took them by surprise and they sat there speechless staring at the chicken. It was Ambassador Brunet that broke the silence.

"What credentials have you got to make such blatant claims?" Marc Brunet' snarled the question, his voice harsh and arrogant. "You speak of some international animal organization – an organization of chickens that was neither known of – much less recognized – by any state three days ago. Why should we believe you?"

The chicken twisted its neck and glared at Brunet, its feathers ruffled in furry. "My feathers, and my beak, and my very presence in this room are my credentials! The fact that we communicate attests to my being. The catastrophe of your poultry industry, brought solely about by the will of my species, gives testimony to the power I represent. We are your food Mr. Brunet. Food is a weapon Mr. Brunet. We are our own weapons against you Mr. Brunet. A weapon that can disrupt and even destroy your society as you know it. Sir, you ask a stupid question. You affront me with your blind defiance of the facts."

"I affront you!" sputtered the Canadian Ambassador.

The President decided to defuse the bombastic exchange. "Let's not hamper a historic, and I might say, incredible dialogue between what you represent and what we represent. Provoking each other gets us nowhere. I acknowledge your organization. I have to, the events speak for themselves. There's no question in my mind that you speak for an international movement of fowl. But you must give us time to understand. This is a startling phenomenon to us."

The President paused and glanced over at Brunet before continuing. "We are all aware of the poultry events in our two countries. Our scientists and agricultural experts can offer no explanation. We have no other course but to believe you. Now as to your other question, the absence of the Secretary of Agriculture is another matter. Let me explain. Percy Adams is under very heavy pressures because of the events triggered by your actions. His department is attempting to grapple – to even understand a serious – no not serious – a calamitous problem that is affecting the agricultural balance of this nation. The ramifications of this will have serious consequences on our obligation to provide foodstuffs to our citizens and the hungry of this world. We have to reappraise our obligations. The obligations we made to the World Food Conference in Rome. These are Percy Adams' immediate priorities."

This was not true. The President had met with Adams earlier in the morning and found him wanting, befuddled and incoherent. He had not measured up in a time of crisis. He was coming apart under the strain and would have been of no use at this meeting. He would have to be replaced.

"I tell you this because I don't want you to take any offense in the fact that Percy Adams is not here, that he is not present at this meeting." The President then ran his hand through his thick hair and lowered it to point his finger at the face of the bird. "I met with him very early this morning. He gave me a detailed briefing. I am fully aware of the situation. As President, I have the ultimate authority in this nation and the ultimate responsibility for the health and security of its people –" The President hesitated before adding, "and the animals of this nation." There was an authoritative echo to the President's voice, as if its full force was coming from deep inside his massive chest.

The chicken sat motionless, then bent down to peck at the silver bowl of corn in front of it. The four men watched its action, listening in silence to the bird's beak rap out a metallic note on the inside of the bowl. The bird raised its head to slide the corn down its gullet before replying. Again, through Trent, the chicken spoke. Now Trent's translation was slow and even, as if the chicken was measuring every word carefully for its total effect.

"Mr. President, I fully understand both your position and your authority. You have, as you would say, established the pecking order." The bird's head turned to look at Marc Brunet. "I will recognize the Canadian Ambassador as an observer to this meeting since our actions have affected his country as drastically as they have affected yours." The bird then dismissed the Ambassador by turning away from him. "The Secretary of State is your representative and spokesman to other human societies on this earth and I welcome his full participation. Mr. Marshall is my voice. Now, let us come to the crux of this situation. Allow me to state our position."

The President nodded his agreement. "Perhaps we should have coffee while you put forth your position." The Ambassador pulled the trolley to the edge of the coffee table and the four men poured themselves coffee as the chicken continued.

"You live in a world populated by over twenty-one billion chickens at any one time, over five and-a-half billion living in China. This figure does not include the millions of other fowl such as turkeys, geese. ducks and pheasants. Our natural life cycle is much shorter than yours. Left to our own in natural conditions, we can live five or six human years, some of us as long as ten years. Like yours, our population has multiplied. However, unlike you, we have not been responsible for our incredible increase in numbers. You have! You have applied your science of genetics to our breeding, helped by the various pharmaceutical cocktails that you force down our throat or put into our feed.

"But you should know that we are not a bit thankful for this. For as you have deliberately multiplied our population, you have decreased – with callous calculation – our life span. Did you know that it is quite normal for what you call a broiler chicken to hatch from an egg, be force-fattened, and end up as a chicken nugget on your plate in just forty-two days?"

"One of your most popular fast food chicken chains boasts that since it opened its first Kentucky outlet in 1930, it now has more than 18,000 outlets in 117 countries, and boasts that it has served enough chickens to circle our earth more than seven times.

"Thanks to humans, there's millions more of us living less. Our shorter lives serve your glutinous food habits. If you could fatten us up from cage to carcass in a week, you would."

The President looked over the rim of his raised coffee cup. "I don't quite understand your point."

There was a heavy sigh from the bird as it cocked its head quizzically to one side and studied the President. "Let's approach it from a historical perspective. For centuries, through all your social changes, through all your cultures, we have played a role in your retinue of domesticated animals. We were even one of the first. You have fed and looked after us, protecting us from many predators. In return we furnished you with the richness of our embryos – our eggs.

"Under your protection we were once free to run around, free to scratch and root in the soil, and after a decent time, giving up our plump bodies to your tables. Once we lived on farms with other animals. Less than sixty years ago you ate us only on special occasions, like you eat our turkey brothers today."

Now Trent sensed a caustic and bitter tone to the chicken's thoughts forming themselves in his mind for translation.

"But you have changed all of that. Somewhere you determined that we chickens surpass all other domestic animals as a productive meat factory. For every ten animals you slaughter for food, nine of them are chickens. You married our bodies to the systems of your industrial technology. You discovered that three pounds of grain could equal one pound of poultry, and you set to work with ruthless efficiency to mechanize our life, our growth and our death. And you have changed our bodies. We're now more than twice the fat and about a third less protein than forty years ago.

"Today we are condemned to an ever-shortening life, crowded and confined in buildings which can hold up to 600,000 of us and process up to 200,000 in a single day. Male chicks are not profitable; they take too long to fatten. In one of your 'poultry processing farms', over 150,000 male chicks are hatched every twenty-four hours. They live and die the same day, thrown into chutes that take them to be ground-up alive. One plant grinds up thirty million little lives every year, yet your egg cartons, Easter cards and children's books present idyllic images of little red hens, strutting roosters and cute cuddly chicks."

Trent was becoming more uncomfortable as he translated the chicken's scathing remarks directed at the President.

"You have replaced the broody hen with mechanical incubation: shelves holding tens of thousands of eggs at one time, automatically rotating them three times a day. Some of your hatcheries can hatch as many as a million at one time. Think of it – a million brought into this world, often never to touch the ground from the moment their hatched until the day they are slaughtered for their meat. Our days consist of sixteen hours of artificial light in a totally programmed environment. We are unnaturally rushed into growth, fed enriched feed that makes many of us so obese that our legs can't hold us up; that we die of sudden heart attacks or from lung failure living in cramped conditions with the air fouled by ammonia, dust, bacterial and fungal spores."

The chicken stopped, then leveled his eyes to meet those of the President. "Obesity, heart attacks, air pollution! Now that's something you humans can relate to: urban air pollution, heart attacks and obscene obesity from the junk food you eat."

"Now wait a minute –" protested the President, anger simmering in his voice.

The bird lifted a wing. "Please, hear me out!" It hunched its great feathered body forward to shout out its cackling indictment. "Your crowding of our species causes disease. This cooped-up imprisonment creates stress and the spread of harmful bacteria such as coccidiosis.

We suffer from other diseases, in fact twenty-six diseases that are common to humans and fowl."

The chicken turned to look at Marc Brunet. There was almost a smirk running along the side of its beak. "Oh don't worry Mr. Ambassador. I can assure you that I am free of all of them – and I have no fears of catching anything from you."

Trent watched as the bird's eyes turned back to the President. "Most serious of these diseases are salmonella. psittacosis and New Castle disease, but it doesn't stop there. Your methods of raising us in rigid confinement from egg to dinner table causes stress. Have you ever seen the results of mass stress Mr. President? It does frightening things to social groups. In our case it causes cannibalism. But don't worry, you debeak us with lasers to keep us from destroying each other. In some cases, you give us tranquilizers, but that's natural in your society."

The Secretary of State had now opened a small leather notebook and was doodling in it with a slim golden pen. He was doodling eggs. He thought of his grandchildren and for some silly sentimental reason, the annual Easter Egg Roll – a White House lawn tradition – came into his mind. Every year he brought them to this event. It was a tradition that had survived nearly one hundred years. Children hunting, rolling and racing with eggs; military bands near the White House fountain; crowds in the thousands; and a costumed cast of lovable cartoon characters. Young Sebastian loved Bugs Bunny and Oscar loved Donald Duck. A lover of historical trivia, he knew that it was Roosevelt who had stopped it in wartime; Eisenhower resumed it in 1953. Now it would probably be stopped forever. There were so few good and decent traditions in Washington. Did it matter? The Secretary snapped the notebook closed but his sketching had not gone unnoticed by the chicken.

"Please draw eggs Mr. Secretary. Let me continue. Would you like to know of another problem in your poultry-processing farms? Cancer! That's right. The one disease that strikes fear into the hearts of you humans. We have to thank you for that. Stress and overcrowding cause it with us, but there's also the little matter of arsenic."

"Arsenic?" what are you talking about?" asked the President.

"Arsenic is put into our chicken feed. It makes us grow faster and adds color to our skin. Bigger and more attractive thanks to arsenic. For years your FDA and the poultry industry said to your people that there was no reason to worry. Finally, your FDA admitted arsenic can be cancer-causing in large doses. The arsenic in our flesh ends up in yours. Who's to say that over time by eating us, you ingest enough arsenic to trigger some form of cancer in your own body. Don't believe me? Check with your Department of Agriculture. Check with your egghead scientists."

The President squirmed in his chair and suddenly longed for additional knowledge, certainly not from Percy Adams – but from a career undersecretary – to blunt or refute these aggressive accusations. He decided to tough it out, his face set in a grim mask of repugnance.

The chicken, now passionately aroused, drove on with its vengeful oratory. Even through dampened by the monotone translation from Trent, the bird's words stung and pushed the horrible truths into the minds of its listeners.

"Do you believe that over thirty-seven million chickens in your nation were destroyed because of cancer. Thirty-seven million slaughtered because of a disease that you caused."

The President's stiff composure was dissolving under the arguments of the chicken, He was becoming aware that he was helpless to refute this terrifying testament, and even more, unable to defend the human actions with any moral justification. Throughout the translation, Trent's voice disarmed the passion from the bird's arguments, turning it into a calm and objective situation briefing. The effect was chilling to the listeners.

"Did you know Mr. President that ninety percent of what you call 'poultry' is raised – actually fed – on a diet of pesticides, antibiotics and other drugs from birth until slaughter. Did you know that almost eighty percent of your nation's antibiotic production – and that's over sixty companies – goes to livestock and chickens. Antibiotics make us grow faster and put on weight. But antibiotics are responsible for drug-resistant bacteria on your farms: drug- resistant bacteria that reaches your people through the food that they eat. Yes, we certainly share your drug culture, don't we?"

The Secretary of State peered through his owlish glasses. "But these drugs are medication to improve and maintain animal health. I must question the inference you place on the antibiotics." It was the first time that the Secretary of State had voiced any strong opinion. The bird cocked its head toward his voice.

"Medication! More like medical experimentation!" the bird shrilled.

"You have us at a disadvantage," interjected the President. "We are not aware of these drugs or their uses,"

"But I thought you were briefed by your Percy Adams," retorted the chicken. The sarcasm filtering through Trent's translation.

"Not from this perspective," replied the President defensively. The President's toleration of the bird's tirade had reached its limit. He resolved to bring the meeting back to the basics of the issue. Being both a political and a practical man, he knew his first priority was stemming the immediate agricultural calamity. He lifted his palm to silence the bird. "Let's return to the reason for this meeting. You requested this meeting through the offices of the Canadian Government after – and I emphasize after – your kind had thoroughly disrupted our poultry industry, threatening our food chain. You are speaking to us from a position of ... of ... of insurrection! Not from a position of power. Just what the hell is the ultimate point of your actions?"

The chicken worked its heavy body over to the edge of the ottoman, its yellow claws gripping into the soft leather. "Our actions are not directed toward Americans – or Canadians. Our actions are directed toward humans and their inhuman exploitation of us. Our rebellion only began in Canada and continued into your country. Why? Because you are the most powerful nation in the world. You are the richest nation in the most essential commodity of life: food! If our actions can influence you, then the whole world will listen. You are the world's largest larder of grains, meats and poultry. All three are linked together. Because of this fact, we give you an ultimatum to present to the world."

"Nobody gives the President of the United States an ultimatum!" shot back the President, his voice quivering with suppressed rage. Around the room, paintings and busts of Washington, Franklin and Lincoln looked on in silent support.

"We do!" snapped back the chicken. "We give an ultimatum that may mean the end of our life – the sacrifice of our species – but it will also mean a sudden crippling change to yours!" The bird's feathers had now ruffled to give it a scruffy and furious appearance. "It is this! Use your commanding position of power to call an urgent session of the General Assembly of your United Nations. Arrange for me to address this universal gathering of human societies.

"We have something to say to all humankind. If you don't do this, we shall commit mass self-genocide – call it *henocide* – leaving only a handful as 'endangered species'. We will die by the hundreds of millions across your nation and around the world faster than you can eat, freeze or bury us. Our sudden mass deaths would rip your agriculture apart, crippling the combines of your agribusiness empires, pharmaceutical industries, and grinding your process food industries to a halt, throwing millions out of work."

The President thought of the sudden unemployment numbers that would be added to the nation's current unemployed; a nation in deep national debt, burdened by ever-continuing natural disasters, climate change, droughts, drug addiction and inner-city poverty. America's wavering confidence in itself might not stand the blow.

"Without eggs and chickens, the marketing of your food industry collapses. Collapses! Your energy problems will be nothing compared to this. You can't eat oil or electricity Mr. President. Food is a weapon. We could cripple you economically if we were to allow ourselves to continue multiplying in certain other countries like Russia, China or Brazil, but commit mass suicide in your land. I'm sure your adversaries would welcome our death in your nation and our life in theirs."

Trent twinged in discomfort as he spoke Ceres's harsh words to the President whose eyes were coldly fixed on the chicken.

"If you think I am bluffing, pick a state Mr. President. Any state you wish. Every chicken and rooster in that state could will itself to death upon the command of our World Council. In less than twenty-four hours there wouldn't be a single hen alive in that state."

The implications of the bird's threat were not lost on the Secretary of State. He flashed a troubled glance at the President, He knew that look: it was enough for the President to concede to the bird. There was madness to this entire meeting. The insanity of this freakish animal's ultimatum could not be ignored. The economy was sinking back into recession. This could plunge it into a deep depression.

"Suppose I yield and arrange for this special session, what would you say and what would you do? Today the big powers are the minority. The Assembly represents the views of the numerical majority of the day, often adopting one-sided unrealistic resolutions that cannot be implemented. I mean, there must be responsibility to proposals put forward on such a platform."

"Why?" taunted the chicken, now sure of itself. "Murderers, terrorists, thieves, liars and nut heads have all been welcomed as heads of state by the UN. They've been cloaked in the dignity of the UN and allowed to spurt out their venom and hate of other peoples. So why not a chicken?"

Always juggling policies and priorities in his agile and cunning head, the Secretary of State interjected with his smooth voice. "Please understand our position at the UN. We are, quite frankly, losing our confidence and faith in its ability to provide answers to the problems of the world."

"You mean you're frustrated at your loss of leadership and power," retorted the chicken.

The Secretary's mouth tightened. He hesitated and then asked, "What is the nature of your proposal to the UN? It would help us to know in facilitating any appearance you might make."

The chicken tossed its comb back in a gesture of defiance. "It's an ultimatum to humankind – to all human societies on this earth. It is not for your nation to know it unilaterally. I'm sorry, but I cannot tell you."

A look of exasperation swept over the President's handsome features. "This is blackmail you know."

"Call it what you will," replied the chicken, "Either I speak for my species to the United Nations, or your poultry industry ceases to exist. You have no alternative. But I must emphasize that the sooner you cause this to happen, the sooner the possibilities of your poultry industry being restored under our conditions. Otherwise, eggs will become as expensive as caviar, and chicken as expensive as truffles. I have my instructions."

There was silence in the room. The President rose and strode over to the large windows that faced out into the garden. He stood there with his back to them for several minutes. It seemed like an eternity. The only movement or sound in the room came from Marc Brunet's cup as he poured himself another coffee.

Suddenly the President wheeled around and approached the chicken. He stood in front of the ottoman, his big frame towering over the white bird, "We will request a special UN session," his voice now gruff and hard. "But we can't guarantee it. It won't happen overnight and there must be conditions. We must have time to brief our UN ambassador and explain this fantastic situation to the Secretary-General." He turned to look at his Secretary of State.

"Brandon, where is Ambassador Skillet? Is he at the UN or here in Washington?"

"He's here at the State Department Mr. President, getting briefed on our position for the UN vote on the Arctic resolution."

"Good. Get him over here. Eight o'clock. A casual dinner upstairs. Just the three of us."

Secretary Brandon knew that meant big bowls of hot chili con carne, stacks of toast and Mexican beer late into the night.

Then the President leaned forward to stare down into the eyes of the chicken. "I must also inform the leaders of the Congress and the Senate. And I must address the nation – and you must keep your promise or I will order every damn chicken's neck wrung in America."

"Fair enough," said the chicken through Trent. "I understand and will accept your conditions, providing you act at once."

"We will act at once," snapped the President, then he turned to look at Marc Brunet. "If the Canadian Ambassador concurs, I would like the chicken to stay here with Mr. Marshall."

"I have no objection," said the Ambassador.

"I will stay here," replied the chicken. You have a lovely garden and I'm sure your staff can provide me with natural grains and pure water."

"They will," said the President. "And the secret service will make sure you don't wander down Pennsylvania Avenue."

"But –" continued the chicken, "I shall have no further need of Mr. Marshall's services until the UN. He has translated fairly and well and I thank him."

Trent found it uncomfortable to translate the bird's praise of him in the third person, but it was made easier by the fact that all eyes were on the chicken. "Now that our meeting is finished, I am going to revert back to my natural state and normal habits."

Brunet' turned to look at Trent and asked, "What does the bird mean?"

The chicken wiggled its body around to face Brunet. It tilted its head, shaking its comb and wattles. "It means that I shall sit and peck and root and strut and cackle and brood and not communicate with any human again until the UN session, and then only through Mr. Marshall."

"I would like Mr. Marshall present or at least nearby," said the President.

The light glistened off the thick lenses of the Secretary of State's glasses as he turned his head to look at Trent. "I agree. It would be best. We shall arrange for you to be put up at the Hay-Adams Hotel with a secure cell phone to my office. It's a very comfortable hotel and we'll make sure they look after you."

The President smiled. "It's close by, Mr. Marshall, just at Lafayette Square." It was the first time the President had spoken directly to him since he introduced the chicken and this incredible meeting began.

*Jerusalem, Jerusalem, you who kill the prophets
and those sent to you, how often I have longed to
gather your children together, as a hen gathers her
chicks under her wings, but you were not willing.*
Jesus Christ, Matthew 23:37

Chapter 11

As the secret and surreal meeting between the President of the United States and a Plymouth Rock hen was taking place behind the closed doors of the Oval Office, Reddit and Instagram – two news and social networking web sites – were posting early chicken news items from Canadian Press, the Lancaster Intelligence Journal, CNN, Fox News, CTN and now Associated Press. Brief news reports from odd poultry behavior were coming in from California, Iowa and Arkansas; frightened farmers were tweeting, posting photos and videos, adding to a growing stream of rumors, opinions and speculations. Federal and State agricultural officials stayed tight-lipped, which only ramped up the intensity of internet "chicken" traffic.

The chicken is deeply embedded in American mainstream culture. It holds a peerless place in the hearts and stomachs of Americans, pecking its way through great American literature, children's books, art, film, television, and every manner of objects and collectibles. It is the stuff of farm folklore and urban legends: cultural side effects of its mass consumption. In the deep Dixie South, it is the cultural comfort soul of their identity, where Southern fried chicken is appreciated as both symbol and sustenance. North or South, no matter how it's cut or cooked, the chicken is as American as apple pie.

In an urban America – still unaware and untouched by the growing poultry crisis unfolding in faraway factory farms – over the next two days, the chicken became a hot topic in a cool medium. A great chicken tsunami began making waves in that untamed public sea that pundits called "The Social Media". It was a tidal wave that flooded YouTube, Facebook, Twitter and Yahoo, and surged into more than 230 million mobile devices that Americans now used. Bloggers went crazy with more than 190 million "chicken" blogs of text and images suddenly inundating and straining web hosting services.

Two "Chicken Dance" videos appeared in short order on YouTube; the first presented four white-haired geriatric citizens reliving their youth when the Chicken Dance first became popular in the early 1960s. To happy grins and unsure footing, they moved their hands, flapped their arms and shook their bottoms to a scratchy oom-pah pah polka recording of the Chicken Dance song. The second was a video clip of a flock of over 70,000 people clucking and dancing like a chicken at the Canfield Fair in Ohio in 1996. The staggering silly steps of the smiling seniors won out and went viral worldwide within the hour.

From out of attics and cellars, eBay was flooded with chicken posters, paintings and prints for sale, as well as all kinds of chicken crockery and ceramic figures. Old chicken comic strips and comic books appeared, some going back as far as 1924, but it was the number of chicken songs that emerged: tunes from the late 40s and 50s like *Chicken Feed*, played by Guy Lombardo's orchestra or the Boston Pops. Over twenty-two songs were posted in six hours, including *The Chicken in Black*, sung by Johnny Cash, *Hen Party Blues*, *Do the Funky Chicken*, and Country and Western tunes like *Chicken Fried* by Zac Brown's Band.

For those over seventy, one song kindled youthful memories with its lyrics. Popularly known as *Chicken Fat*, its official title was The Youthful Fitness Song that was part of President Kennedy's 1961 Physical Fitness Program, a recording that had been sent to school districts throughout the United States.

In Ithaca, New York, Olivia Marsh, a retired spinster school teacher had momentary fame on YouTube with a tour of her small "chicken house" bungalow home, leading the camera room-to-room with all the aplomb of a First Lady hosting a tour of the White House. Each room was walled with chicken pictures, chicken posters, and chicken paintings, while silent flocks of ceramic, plastic, wooden and stuffed chickens perched on tables, roosted in cabinets or stood silently on carpets and floors. The joyous result of thirty-eight years of collecting over 2,112 chicken memorabilia, her crowning object was a carousel "two-seater" chicken, rescued from an old merry-go-round and lovingly restored. Miss Marsh stated that she did not collect roosters or eat chicken.

Across America, costume stores were overwhelmed by customers wanting to buy or rent chicken costumes. On the internet, chicken costume manufacturers – some as far away as Hong Kong – were running out of inventory as Americans suddenly wanted to wear a chicken costume to parties, birthdays and even wedding events.

There was numerous YouTube proud posting by members of poultry clubs who owned selected breeds of chickens only for their striking plumage and ornamental beauty. Most of these birds were *Cochin* or *Silkie* chickens that could trace their heritage back to the Imperial Courts of ancient China. These pampered docile birds, with their silky, fluffy, plumage, lived a life of luxury and were affectionately groomed by their owners, many of whom were Asian-Americans.

From nowhere and everywhere, pirated film clips of chickens in movies began being posted on YouTube. Woody Allen's big chicken sequence in his 1973 film *Sleeper* was the first, followed by a skeletal chicken sequence in *The Bride of Frankenstein*. Someone posted the revolt of the hen's sequence in the 1954 British animation film of George Orwell's *Animal Farm*, completely unaware that it had been secretly financed by the C.I.A. as part of a Cold War propaganda campaign to create anti-Communist art.

They just kept coming: a film clip of Charlie Chaplin transformed into a succulent chicken by his hallucinating starving partner in *The Gold Rush*; the farm scenes from *The Egg and I*; jerky silent black and white chicken films; the sexual banquet scene in *Tom Jones* where Albert Finney sinks his teeth into white soft meat as Joyce Redman slides her tongue across a fleshy drumstick. It seemed there wasn't a Hollywood film that didn't have a chicken in it – or a mention of a chicken in it.

Waves of videos and photos were being posted in a torrent of chicken images in an unending collage of Chicken Americana: children in chicken Halloween costumes, chicken puppets, chicken poetry, chicken pet owners gushing over their feathered family members, brutal video footage of industrialized chicken slaughter, cartoon chicken jokes, chicken dishes, and from somebody's archives, *Foghorn Leghorn*, Warner Brother's large leghorn cartoon rooster, speaking in his stuttering Southern accent in a series of Kentucky Fried Chicken commercials made in the 1990s. Someone with a quick pen posted a cartoon of a headless Percy Adams running amuck through a flock of startled chickens.

Some chicken postings took a distinct American literary turn as English students, teachers and avid bookworms posted chicken excerpts from the novels, writings and essays of Mark Twain, O. Henry, John Steinbeck, F. Scott Fitzgerald and Gertrude Stein.

Ralph Waldo Emerson's 19th century quote, "I dream of a better tomorrow where chickens can cross the road and not be questioned about their motives" was posted more than 300 times, mostly by advocacy groups, whistleblowers and individuals flailing against government' intrusion and surveillance.

Talking heads popped up on every talk show to shed an opaque light on the situation. Scientists, agricultural experts, poultry professors and economists were put before the cameras, but their ponderous utterances did little to clarify an unbelievable reality, as they knew little of why or what was happening.

At one food channel, a thirteen-week series entitled *Chicken Delights*, scheduled to premiere on the following weekend, was put on the shelf for later programming. Management believed it would be in poor taste to promote chicken dishes during the evolving poultry crisis. An expensive production filmed in eight countries, it featured local celebrity chefs cooking the classic chicken cuisine of their native land.

In Petaluma, California, a city that once proudly boasted it was "The Egg Capital of the World" and the place where the egg incubator was invented, they were silently counting their blessings that the community had long ago got out of eggs. Concerned about the chicken crisis, city fathers were debating whether they should go forward with the annual heritage "Butter & Eggs Day Parade" that celebrated their golden ovum days.

Extreme religious groups posted that this poultry apocalypse was God's forewarning of more bad things to come, while the more orthodox religions posted pictures and prayers of Saint Francis of

Assisi, Patron Saint of Animals, and called upon a litany of minor Patron Saints for birds, geese, and doves to add their heavenly blessings. Over 30,000 mentions of Matthew 23:27 where quoted where Jesus makes mention of the mother hen and her baby chicks. In a more down-to-earth moralistic tone, environmentalists and animal rights organizations like PETA – People for the Ethical Treatment of Animals – with more than 3 million members and supporters – joined in with their voices and videos. The Agricultural Department's web site and several poultry industry web sites crashed as the number of hits flooded in faster than the servers could handle.

Anxious to quell chicken humor, the White House placed calls to the presidents of all the television and cable comedy networks "requesting" that, because of the mounting poultry crisis, the Government didn't think it was in the national interest for Late Night hosts and comedians to do chicken monologues or tell chicken jokes. This "request" was passed down as a stern directive to the producers, and comedy writers in Hollywood and New York were soon ripping up pages of henpecked and cocksure jokes, many of which in showbiz lingo would have "laid an egg" anyway.

In Washington the CERT (Computer Emergency Readiness Team) of Homeland Security was successfully blocking sophisticated waves of hacking attacks on the Department of Agriculture's computer system that, even if rerouted, they knew were coming from Russia and China. The bells went off when one got through a security hole, and while it was downloading, they traced it to a computer in North London. They passed it over to the U.K.'s Home Office's e-crime unit, and two hours later the Metropolitan Police raided a four-story building of flats on Foley Street. In the basement flat they found the hacker. He turned out to be a skinny ashen-faced teenager in his underwear. They took him to the e-crime unit at Scotland Yard to teach him a lesson – and perhaps, under duress, for him to teach them one or two. His computer and hard drive were turned over to the American Embassy (but not before they had made a copy).

The stock market continued to reel, with shares in anything connected to the poultry industry getting hammered on an hourly basis. Packers, processors and chicken foodservice companies took the biggest hit. At the Chicago Mercantile Exchange, broiler chicken futures were collapsing as speculators stampeded into feeder cattle futures.

In Asia, the stock markets in Singapore, Hong Kong and Japan were taking a beating on food futures, and ugly predications were voiced on what would happen when the European stock markets opened.

Reports by the media that the chicken crisis was now a matter of national concern in the White House prompted postings on YouTube of past presidents and chickens. An archive photo of President William Howard Taft eating chicken supported the revelation that he had raised chickens on the White House garden grounds for eventual serving on White House dinner plates, and that perhaps the present President should give it a try if the chicken crunch reaches a point of no return.

This started a flurry of presidential chicken trivia, the two most popular being Teddy Roosevelt's ability to wolf down a whole chicken at one White House sitting, and Richard Nixon's inaugural ball in the Smithsonian Institute in 1973 where a live chicken escaped from the American Farm Exhibit and fled under a VIP table, assaulting the legs of a terrified female guest as the Nixon revelers danced the night away.

In the "Broiler Belt" – a great swath of the American Southeast from eastern Texas, north to Maryland and Delaware – there were also waves of anger from frightened poultry farmers scared stiff by the disastrous economic predications of Fox News. This was the heartland of America's poultry industry where, in some places, short-lived chickens outnumbered long-living humans four hundred to one.

Some wit in San Francisco dug up an unflattering photo of the President taken during his campaign two years ago. This unfortunate photo conveyed a sly expression that could be taken as an evil gluttonous grin. The San Francisco satirist photo shopped a hand holding a juicy chicken drum stick up to the President's mouth. Below it was the wording, "Wing-Ding-Daddy-O."

Chapter 12

Pedro Alberto José Silveria was an early riser. He was up at 6 am, showered, shaved and now dressed for the day, sitting in their fourth floor family room going through his personal correspondence. His wife and two teenage daughters were still asleep in their rooms just down the hall.

He treasured the family room. Unlike the rest of the town house that was so dignified and formal, this room was casual and wonderfully messy, with the walls cluttered with happy family photos of their home on Lake Paranoá. Two large couches, smothered in pillows, flanked a gigantic coffee table displaying glossy copies of the Brazilian teen magazine *Capricho* beside the dishes from last night's family snacks.

Near the only window in the room was a white table with a twenty-one-inch desktop computer and two bright red swivel chairs. His daughters spent endless hours on Skype, sitting there chattering to their friends back home in Brasilia or streaming in Globo network's endless glut of television programming: crazy reality shows, telenovelas and their "adora" singer of the moment. A salmon-colored landline phone sat on a side table beside one couch. All of the family had their own cell phones but his wife Gabriela had installed landline phones in the family room, their bedroom, and the dining room downstairs. They had an unlisted number and the girls were not allowed to use them or pick them up when they rang.

In the early morning light, Pedro Silveria was sitting upright on the couch nearest the window, reading a letter from his ninety-year old mother and marveling at her flowery penmanship. Gabriela and the two girls would be up by seven. The Silverias were a close-knit family with strong Catholic values, and breakfast was a special time to be together before he left to tackle the day's worldly problems.

Pedro Silveria was the tenth Secretary-General of the United Nations and they lived in a five-story townhouse in Sutton Place, Manhattan. Silveria had been recommended by the Security Council and elected by the General Assembly with an overwhelming majority. Tall and slim with movie-star looks, after obtaining a degree from the Law School at the University of Sao Paulo, he chose to become a career diplomat, graduating from Brasilia's Rio Branco Institute, the nation's diplomatic academy.

A gifted linguist, he spoke Portuguese, Spanish, French and English, and had served abroad in five countries before serving one term as Brazil's Ambassador to the UN. Only one Secretary-General before him had come from South America and lived in this official UN residence, and that was back in 1982. Latin Americans saw Silveria's election as confirmation of South America's growing importance in the world.

The phone on the side table rang and he picked it up on its second ring. "This is the White House," said a woman's voice. "Am I speaking to his Excellency, Pedro Alberto José Silveria, Secretary-General of the United Nations?"

"You are."

"One moment please." There was a second of silence before the deep resonate voice of the President of the United State came on the line. He spoke in Spanish and what he said shocked Silveria. A global poultry food disaster was coming within two weeks at the latest – and an urgent emergency session of the General Assembly must be called. The United States must immediately address the entire Assembly. As Secretary-General, he needed to be briefed and shown the evidence by Ambassador Skillet. The Ambassador was now on his way back to New York and could the Secretary-General meet with him today in the US Mission Building at the United Nations Plaza. What he had to reveal was incredible and could only be safely said outside of the UN building.

The conversation had lasted no more than eight minutes, but for the President to call Silveria so early, and on his personal unlisted telephone line, was so exceptional that it gave weight to his words and he had no option but to meet with Ambassador Skillet.

Pedro Silveria sat thinking of the global ramifications if there were suddenly no more chickens. In his own country it could be disastrous. He knew that Brazil's poultry industry now employed almost four million people, and Brazil was the world's largest exporter of chicken meat. It would be a staggering blow to the southern state of Santa Catarina where the poultry industry was a major contributor to the economy. Chickens were a part of its culture and cuisine, and the state's seaport city of Itajai boasted that it was "the chicken export capital of the world."

Food was becoming the next big problem for the world. It was something that he feared most for his own country. He took a minute to compose himself before leaving the family room to join Gabriela and the two girls for breakfast.

. . .

The UN Security and Safety Service is responsible for preventing hacking or cyber espionage in all UN buildings. It is a never-ending vigilant battle, except when it comes to the Secretary-General's townhouse residence. Twice a year they do a cursory sweep, but there is nothing of vital intelligence to steal on any of its five floors. There are no UN secrets hidden in the house. There is a large wall safe in their bedroom, but it holds only personal documents and Gabriela's most treasured jewelry. The house is girded with burglary prevention devices and the NYPD keep a sharp eye on the building and on the famous and the fortunate few who live on the same street.

Any UN activities in the townhouse are strictly social, limited to cocktail parties, small lunches or dinners, and confined to the dining or reception room. Pedro Silveria makes it his business to never talk UN business at home except in the most general way, and only about human or humorous incidents that have happened on his global travels.

There are five TV sets and the girl's desktop computer in the townhouse. Two months after the family moved in, the Chinese invaded the girl's computer during one daughter's Skype chatter with a boy in Brasilia. This cyber penetration was done from Shanghai with "Dragon's Ear", a dormant cyber device that audio activates their iMac computer's built-in microphone whenever anyone entered the family room. It operates only when the computer is not turned on.

In Shanghai, a rotating unit of twelve Chinese Portuguese-speaking monitors listened and record every word uttered in the family room. There are many monotonous hours of listening to silence or to muffled conversations that were unintelligible, plus the kittenish chitter-chatter of the teenage girls. Over time, the slim file on the personal life of Silveria and his family bulked up, providing an intimate insight into the man beyond his UN persona.

The telephone ring and voice of Silveria activated the microphones in the computer and the tape recording in Shanghai. Although the Chinese could only hear one half of the telephone conversation, it was more than enough to cause alarm. Silveria was speaking with the President of the United States about chickens and the need for an emergency General Assembly meeting and someone named Trent Marshall.

Their end of the eight-minute conversion was translated verbatim from Spanish into Mandarin and sent by secure telephone line to Beijing. In Beijing, a typewritten copy was delivered by courier – marked urgent time-sensitive intelligence – to the office of Major General Cheung Ling at Ministry of State Security. When he read it, he quickly realized its implications and the possible impact it could have on "The Great Move Forward", China's new grand plan yet to be unveiled. He telephoned Leung Yang, Minister of Agriculture, and then raced over by car to the Agricultural Minister's office.

Chapter 13

After showering and shaving, Trent put on a white hotel bathrobe and walked across the room and gazed out of the tall windows onto Lafayette Square. He could see the straight symmetrical lines of the White House through the trees, and the towering granite obelisk of the Washington Monument. He glanced with amusement at the folded page of *The Washington Post* on the bed, then at the black security cell phone that connected him to the White House. It had remained silent. The only call he'd had – rung through on the hotel telephone an hour ago – was from Ambassador Brunet inviting him to lunch. He cursed himself for not bringing more than two shirts. He would soon run out of clean underwear and his blue shirt would only take one more wearing. The shirt decided it. He would select his dark blue suit, preferring it over his gray-striped Hugo Boss,

Quickly dressing, he left his room and decided to walk down to the lobby. A somewhat foppish desk clerk gave him broad instructions to the restaurant, and he was lucky to grab a taxi that was discharging a three-star Marine general at the hotel entrance.

Café du Parc was one of Washington's top French restaurants nestled in the Willard InterContinental Hotel on Pennsylvania Avenue. Trent had a feeling that the cabby had gotten him there by way of Boston, but the fare was reasonable and he arrived on time. It was a modern, sleek Parisian-style bistro restaurant in soothing tones of blue and creams, with stylish tables and chairs in white and chrome that seemed to float over the floor. The time was just past noon, but already the place was crowded with sophisticated patrons, and several political personalities that Trent recognized as former *Time Magazine* covers.

The restaurant hummed with mannered sociability, punctuated occasionally by the tinkling of cutlery and glasses. He found the maître d', who greeted him like a French cousin, eyed but ignored his tired shirt, and led him to the Ambassador's table which was outside on the terrace.

Marc Brunet faked a rise from the table and offered his small hand to Trent. "Good to see you again," he said as he gestured for Trent to sit down.

"Did you have difficulty in finding this place?"

"No, not at all," replied Trent. "The hotel directed me and the cab ride over was quite a pleasant tour of the capital."

"Washington is so attractive at this time of year. I thought we should eat outside" cooed Brunet. They were softly interrupted by the waiter who took Brunet's order for a Dubonnet on ice and Trent's Vodka Gibson straight up. "Well, the hotel is nice. No?" inquired Brunet.

"Very comfortable."

"But I imagine you are wondering what's happening. You have had no calls from –" Brunet paused and whispered, "– the President, and you are wondering. Am I right?" Brunet's habit of conversing in questions began to irritate Trent.

"Mr. Ambassador, obviously you are more privileged than I am to what's going on. As instructed, I've toughed it out at a palatial suite at Hay-Adams, watched TV and read the papers." Trent paused and a humorous twinkle danced in his eyes. "By the way, *The Washington Post* had a small item about a white chicken being spotted in the White House grounds. I think they mentioned the South Lawn. I'm assuming that's the feathered house guest of the President."

Trent returned to his main theme. "I'm running out of underwear and I'm down to my last shirt, which incidentally, I'm now wearing. Could you tell me what's going to happen, and when?" There, thought Trent, I hit him with a question for a change.

"Certainly," soothed Brunet, "Would you care for another drink before lunch?"

"No thank you."

"Well then, let us order. This restaurant is, in my opinion, a corner of France just down the street from the Whitehouse, offering interpretations *magnifique* of French classics. Normally I would recommend the *Poulet Bio Roti*, but considering the circumstances –" Brunet's eyes twinkled and he gave his shoulders a slight shrug. "What would you like?"

"What would you recommend?" countered Trent.

"Let's do Bistro. *Un steak frites!* – with sauce Béarnaise, though sometimes I find that their kitchen sauces tend to be a little overly thickened. How's that?"

"Sounds good. I'll have the same."

"Fine."

"With a salad?"

"Fine."

"Now, let us choose our wine?"

"Fine."

"How about a boutique wine?" asked Brunet, looking lovingly over the wine list. "Fine," said Trent, wondering what the hell a boutique wine was. "Ah – a red *Reine et Pape* from the Languedoc region of Southern France. They only bottle 240 cases a year."

"I didn't know that," said Trent, who really didn't care. The Canadian Ambassador's head pivoted around in search of the waiter. Trent watched Brunet's hand creep up his lapel to fondle his fresh boutonniere. Trent noticed that his *Order of Canada* lapel pin had been replaced with a deep red stripe running from the edge of his lapel to disappear into its buttonhole. Suddenly his hand shot up with one finger pointed heavenward, spearing the waiter's attention. He rushed over and they both broke out into an effusion of French. Brunet's fingers pinched the air and his hands made invisible measurements which Trent interpreted as portion size, or cooking instructions, or both. It was obvious that Brunet was in his element: a completely changed man from the one at the meeting with the President. Brunet turned back to Trent, "There," he said in a satisfied tone, "I have arranged our lunch. You will be pleasantly surprised."

"I couldn't help noting the red ribbon in your lapel. What is that?"

"I was once our Ambassador to France. During my posting I researched and wrote a three-volume history of the first French settlers

– *the Pure Laine* – who colonized Quebec. It took me three years. It was acclaimed by scholars and became a best seller in France and in Canada. Two years later they awarded me the *Légion d'honneur* for my contributions to Canadian-French relations." Brunet smiled and fingered the ribbon in his lapel. "This comes in handy in a French restaurant, especially if the waiter is from Paris"

"Now you're our Ambassador to Washington. That's quite a step-up I should think."

"Yes indeed, I love the Americans, but part of my heart remains in Paris. Washington is not Paris," sighed Brunet, and then quickly added, "But I serve where they send me. Now you had a question?"

"I had a question?" parried Trent.

"You had a question!" insisted Brunet.

"Oh yes, I was wondering, could you tell me just what the hell is going on?" Brunet leaned across the table. A look of profound seriousness descended upon his face. His tiny eyes scanned the nearest table before he spoke. His voice was low and conspiratorial.

"The White House called me – the President's aide. Ambassador Skillet is briefing the new Secretary-General – possibly at this very moment – and is arranging for a special session at the UN."

"Ambassador who?"

"Skillet, Franklin Skillet, the American Ambassador to the United Nations." Trent had never heard of him, but then, like most North Americans, he didn't follow the workings of the UN.

"The new Secretary-General is quite concerned. He's Brazilian, you know. The crisis could affect his country"

"How so?" asked Trent.

"I'm told that after China and America, Brazil is the third largest breeder of chickens. Anyway, he's called the Assembly for a Thursday morning session. The White House is arranging for the President to address the nation on television Wednesday night."

"What about the chicken?" Trent asked.

"He will not be speaking – oh I see what you mean." Brunet gave an embarrassed snicker.

"We will have to tell Ceres," said Trent

"Ceres?"

"Ceres! The chicken!"

"Oh yes, yes. We mustn't ruffle her feathers," observed Brunet.

"Very funny. When I get back to the hotel, I'll call Secretary Brandon and arrange to see Ceres and bring her up to speed on how things are progressing."

Brunet nodded approvingly and replied, "Until Thursday, the chicken will stay on the White House grounds and will be transported down to New York shortly before the session. You will have to be in New York to meet her. We have arranged for you to stay at the Plaza. You will fly down on a U.S. government plane early tomorrow afternoon."

Brunet looked at his Dubonnet drink and added almost as an afterthought, "And while you're in New York, they want to look at your brain."

"They want to do what!" blurted out Trent.

"Take photos of it, from the outside of course," added Brunet, trying to lighten Trent's angry alarm.

"It will only take an hour. Then you can go shopping for underwear and shirts."

"What the hell do they think I am?" snapped Trent.

"Mr. Marshall, you are a man with a rare – no, a not rare – a miraculous gift. You owe it to humanity for us to understand what is inside your brain. What gives you this gift? You may have a special gland inside your brain or ear. Who knows? Wouldn't you like to know?"

"I don't think there's any special glands in my brain, and the only thing inside my ear is wax," said Trent sarcastically, cooling down as he digested the thought.

Brunet pulled a piece of paper from his pocket. "It's a private hospital on 1st Avenue – the New York University Medical Center, not far from the Plaza. A brilliant professor is flying in from the Mayo Clinic in Minnesota. His name is Dr. Helmet Hirnstien, and he's one of the world's leading neuropsychologist." Brunet glanced again at his notes, and smiled back at Trent. "He's one of the leading scientists in a brain-research program. They're spending millions on innovative neuro – neurotechnologies – brain-to-brain communication. They've already got a lab mouse to wave its tail when a human thinks him to do it." Trent threw Brunet a look of skepticism that turned into a shallow smile.

Brunet rushed on. "You don't have to do any tests. You just go in. They scan your brain – and you go out. Simple as that. You can even leave your tie on."

"Well that's encouraging, I hate tying two knots in one day," scoffed Trent. Inwardly he longed to know why he alone possessed this sixth sense: this bizarre telepathic ability to communicate with chickens without the use of any of his basic five senses. It was both a wondrous gift and a confusing curse.

"Okay, I'll do it, but only for an hour." Trent stared sternly at Brunet before continuing, "Look, I've been away from Toronto for almost three days. I've got a law practice, a living to earn, and frankly I miss my girl." Trent waited for Brunet's reaction.

The Ambassador's face spread into a knowing grin that just missed being a suggestive leer.

"I understand."

"You don't understand," retorted Trent. "I'm asking if Janice can come down to New York.

She's never been there. " Out of the question!" snapped Brunet harshly. "The Canadian government can't pay for girlfriends and trips to New York City."

"I could charge you for my hourly legal fees instead, if you like," countered Trent.

Brunet's voice took on a fatherly tone. "My boy, I understand, but think of the possible publicity you'd be subjecting your lady to. You and the chicken will be the focus of world attention, hunted down by the media. This will take all of your concentration and all of your energy, believe me. Leave your lady out of this. She will be there to warm and comfort you after this is all over. It would be best."

Ted popped the Gibson onion into his mouth and crunched the small white bulb. "I've been on this chicken-treadmill alone. I'd like Janice to be with me. She'd like to be with me. We both would like to be with me. Besides, if I remember correctly, wasn't it one of our Prime Ministers who said that Government has no business in the bedroom of the nation.

"I'm sure that also includes hotel bedrooms in New York City. Also, I found that my translation ability with chickens was much improved when Janice was nearby. I wouldn't want to make a mistake at the UN, if you get my meaning."

The Ambassador sighed and finished his Dubonnet in one final gulp. "You've made your point," he conceded. "I'll have an aide bring the money to you at the hotel."

"For two," interrupted Trent. Brunet continued, "With a UN translator's identity pass and detailed instructions."

"For two," asked Trent again. "For two," nodded Brunet.

"Thanks," smiled Trent. The waiter danced into the conversation with their lunch. There was a flurry of French as he flourished the salads and steak-frites onto the table. Three tables away, two secret service men gnawed into their Salade Niçoise. They were old hands at the job, and would time it so that they could enjoy a liqueur with their coffee before Trent got up to leave.

The Ambassador swirled, sniffed and sipped the wine and then tasted the sauce Béarnaise: He still sometimes thought that the kitchen sauces did tend to be a little overly thickened, but then again, maybe not. He couldn't make up his mind.

. . .

Late that afternoon, Trent was admitted to the South Lawn of the White House where he found Ceres pecking away in the vegetable garden planted by a former First Lady. The chicken was rooting around in a row of cabbages as two secret service men, standing in a row of carrots, watched her every move. He knelt down to stroke her so that he could be closer to her and whispered in her ear. Ceres's head tilted in response, nodding as he talked. When he was finished, he stood up, smiled at her two puzzled guardians, and walked away toward the gate, passing a large sycamore tree planted in 1831 by President Andrew Jackson. Trent didn't notice the flock of starlings hidden in its dense green foliage.

Chapter 14

China's growing middle class now was greater than the middle class of North America and Europe combined. Its growth was unstoppable, as were its citizen's expectations for a better, richer life. China's new leaders could foresee that its expanding middle class would demand higher incomes, greater social equality and more services from its government. It was inevitable that China's present workforce would become increasingly no longer competitive as a global source of cheap labor.

By 2015, over 500 million Chinese – more than forty-five percent of the population – had entered the global middle class, making them the greatest consumer market in the world, even though it would be years before individual wealth would equal that of America's shrinking middle class. It was now the right time to accelerate the transformation of China from an export economy into a state controlled consumer-driven economy.

Behind this decision was China's increasing concern about the economic long-term health of America and the hollowing out of its middle class consumer base. The driver of economic growth, America's middle class was now less than forty-two percent of the population. America's staggering national debt, unemployment, political polarization, and its relentless printing of more and more dollars was slowly weakening its status as the world's Reserve Currency.

China now had trillions of dollars in official reserves, held mostly in U.S. treasury bills, notes and bonds. China – worried about its holdings in U.S. debt – would soon set out on a fiscal strategy of selling off this massive debt position and embarking on a global buying spree. China began buying international corporations and assets, minerals, oil and food resources, wineries, biochemical research and quantum computing companies, as well as pharmaceutical and high-tech industries, including major interests in two international aeronautic and transportation companies. It also began to dramatically increase its investments in Africa and South America. Allied with this, the People's Bank of China quietly began accumulating gold bullion by the ton.

At the same time, China began promoting the international use of its own currency: the Yuan. It began lobbying for a new international currency system consisting of the Dollar, the Euro and the Yuan. All of this was designed to weaken the power base of the U.S. dollar with the long-term objective of eventually establishing the Yuan as the world's new Reserve Currency.

This could only happen if it became a stable "guided" capitalistic society that eclipsed America as the richest nation in the world. This would require a tremendous drive by the Chinese government to dramatically accelerate the urbanization rate. The share of its population now living in cities was now over fifty-five percent. The central government's goal was to relocate another staggering 350 million people from rural areas to new inland cities within the next ten years. This would get them up to eighty percent urbanization.

In three weeks' time, the Chinese government would announce the national launching of "The Great Move Forward", a bold audacious plan that would change the face of China and astonish the world with its size, scope and global repercussions.

Twenty-eight new pollution-free super cities would be built inland. They and the rest of the country would receive electric power from a combination of seven million wind turbines, hundreds of solar farms and millions of roof-top solar panels, as well as eighty-three nuclear power plants and expanded hydroelectric operations, phasing out the use or need for fossil fuels, coal, or long-term dependency on Russian oil and natural gas. This was designed to employ twenty-three million people, and reverse and eventually eliminate China's massive urban air pollution problem that was now threatening civil unrest, effecting world climate change, and drifting across the Pacific, fouling America's West Coast atmosphere.

Chinese hydrologists had calculated that China's water needs would double every twenty years and that climate changes, global warming and its current supply of potable water in its lakes, rivers and water tables could never supply its human, agricultural, and industry needs.

"The Great Move Forward" would build thirty-two gigantic sea water Desalination Plants along China's coastline. These plants would extract the salt from the sea water through high-tech polymer distillation techniques – drawing sea water out of the South and East China Seas – to create freshwater and irrigation-grade water flowing through huge water pipelines inland to fill new lakes and mammoth underground reservoirs.

Shanghai would be transformed into an international Silicon Valley: a great center of technology, tolerance, and talent, where creative people from all over the world would be welcomed, nourished and rewarded.

Under a proud nationalistic banner, a second wave of "The Great Move Forward" would be announced in the following weeks outlining the building of new hospitals, health care facilities for senior citizens, schools, universities, a transportation infrastructure of highways, railways, rivers and mass public transportation, plus a ten-year domestic automotive industry transformation to electric cars, and great changes and advances in agriculture.

China's agricultural production would need to be substantially increased – by sixty percent – in the next four decades to meet the demand for food to feed a projected population of more than 1.75 billion.

To feed this expanding population, The State Council had secretly decided that the potato – "the earth nut" – would replace rice and noodles as the main source of carbohydrates. Unlike rice, the hardy potato could be grown anywhere in China, required far less water, and was labor-intensive. The State Council also decreed that the chicken would become the main source of meat protein, followed by pork, and beef as a distant third. It was a question of simple mathematics; chickens produced one pound of meat for every three pounds of feed, while one pound of pork took five pounds of feed, and one pound of beef ate up seven pounds of feed. A pound of beef would cost in feed more than twice as much as two pounds of chicken. Beef consumption must be discouraged, and the best way to do that to would be to price it so expensive that only the very rich could afford beef on any regular basis.

Like many indigenous processed food products, the Chinese people had very little faith in the quality and food safety of their domestic poultry industry. The Ling Jirou Poultry Co. Ltd. in Shenzhen, was negotiating a five-billion-dollar deal to buy Sunnyhen Foods Inc., America's largest broiler and egg producer with 48,000 employees in twenty-three states and four countries. This would give them a quality international brand name and access to America's factory farm technology, in addition to a guaranteed source of poultry products for the Chinese home market.

The proposed deal was before the US Treasury Department and an interagency panel that reviews foreign investment for national security threats, food security and the protection of American agricultural technology and intellectual property. Fifteen senators on the Agricultural Committee and the leaders of the Senate Finance Committee were against the deal, arguing that it would weaken America's food independence. There was only a fifty-fifty chance that the sale would be approved.

Wei Leung, the Chinese Minister of Agriculture – responsible for feeding one fifth of all the humans on earth – knew that even if China purchased Sunnyhen Poultry, it couldn't begin to fulfill China's poultry needs, but could provide the reassuring brand name and farm factory poultry technology that China needed. If the Sunnyhen purchase was blocked, China would attempt to buy a privately owned Swedish poultry farm, since Sweden, as a trusted national brand, rated above all other nations in Chinese public opinion polls.

Under a foreign name branding, China would build ninety-two poultry factory farms inland. Each one would be immense in size: an industrialized management system combining egg- laying factory, broiler hen factory and incubation hatcheries under one roof. The size of these factory farms would dwarf even the largest American factory farm in comparison. Electric power would be generated by the incineration of the millions of tons of fecal droppings produced by the birds. The estimated six to eight-billion pounds of feathers collected annually would be shipped to nearby processing factories to produce diapers, filters, insulation, feather meal – a high protein product, – and thermo-plastics that could be used to manufacture plastic furniture or be molded into automotive dashboards and door panels.

The Chinese poultry industry was constantly plagued with various strains of avian influenza, some of them deadly to humans. Recently in Hong Kong, an outbreak of H7N9 – a highly infectious respiratory disease – had infected thousands of its citizens, causing 132 deaths, forcing the closing of all outdoor chicken markets, and the putting down of over twenty-eight thousand chickens. The increasing number of such avian flu outbreaks throughout China was becoming an international embarrassment and a constant concern to the UN's World Health Organization. If chicken was to become top of China's protein food chain, Minister Wei knew that draconian measures had to be taken. Over sixty percent of China's poultry output comes from small individual backyard farms, with the birds in close proximity to humans and domestic animals. This private breeding of chickens and their sale in traditional markets would be curtailed and eventually outlawed.

The government would control all chicken and egg production under stringent sanitary conditions. Backing this up was the classified development by Chinese scientists of an avian liquid vaccine to be introduced into the chickens' drinking water that would build up their immunity over a ten-day period. Eventually, all chicken would be sold only through supermarkets, and the urban Chinese consumer would never see a live chicken again.

Chickens must be fed, and all of this would require millions of tons of protein-rich soybean meal as the main ingredient in processed chicken feed. China was the earliest producer of soybeans and by the 1930s was the world's largest producer. But no more. Through incompetence, war and heavy industrialization, it had long since lost that lofty position. America was now the world's largest producer, with China importing twenty-five percent of its soybean crop: over sixty-nine million tons annually. In the grand scheme of "The Great Move Forward", this dependence on American soybeans could not continue, and another and larger sustainable source must be found. Minister Wei had turned to Africa for the answer.

Tumpawie is a small republic of thirteen million people in southeast Africa with a coastline along the Indian Ocean. A fertile land about the size of Texas, for over four-hundred years it had been a colony of Portugal. In its War of Liberation, it won its independence in 1970 – supported by China.

Today, China's influence can be seen and felt everywhere in this African republic. China built its National Parliament Building, its National Stadium, its Conference Center and its International Airport. Generous loans to Tumpawie's government have also been given and forgiven.

Minister Wei had twice visited the capital Jomewa to negotiate a secret 50-year agreement between China and Tumpawie. His Ministry of Agriculture would create vast soybean "plantations" that would employ thousands. Railways and highways would be built to carry the soybeans to plants at the seaports of Januwa and Kalwanzi for processing into soybean meal.

In China, a fleet of eight bulk cargo ships would be built at the Jiangnan shipyards in Shanghai. They would carry the soybean meal across the Indian Ocean to four large port factories along China's coast for final processing into chicken feed and delivery by rail to the inland poultry factory farms.

During his last visit, Minister Wei – waxing poetic – had stated that in only five years, his Ministry would turn Tumpawie into a "Soybean Saudi Arabia" making everyone rich beyond their dreams. The Tumpawians eagerly embraced his vision.

. . .

In central Beijing, the conference room in the Ministry of Agriculture was large and square with no windows. Two opposite doors offered entry and exit. The walls were painted a dull grey-green, and the only thing on each wall was an impressive red and gold circular emblem of The People's Republic of China: a graphic reminder of who ruled the room.

Under an ugly fluorescent lamp, a large circular table was surrounded by twelve upright wooden chairs. Five of them were occupied by middle-aged men wearing starched white shirts and black suits and ties. The sixth man wore the uniform of a Ministry of State Security general. On the table was the debris of their two-hour meeting: plastic bottles of Perrier water, glass cups, overflowing ashtrays and red and gold packages of Zhonghua cigarettes, the status smoke of these powerful men. Recently, the government had banned Party cadres and government officials from lighting up in public places. Here, they could smoke their lungs out.

Unfolding events in America were causing concerns in these men's minds about ongoing negotiations to buy Sunnyhen Foods. China couldn't commit on the Sunnyhen deal – or go forward with the Tumpawie government venture – until the President's speech and the UN session revealed the source and size of this evolving chicken calamity.

In addition, the government's planned proposal to the world's largest multinational fast- food company to triple its more than 5,400 fast food chicken outlets in China to 17,000 would have to be put on hold. It would be an enticing offer of generous tax benefits and prime locations in the new cities to be built.

"We now have some hard decisions to make," said Minister Wei. Wei was tall and fat. He was sixty-two years old, but in an effort to appear ten years younger, he dyed his hair and wore a hair piece and contact lenses. His power in the party far exceeded his powerful position as Minister of Agriculture. He was a committed nationalist and the leader of the inner party's ultra conservative wing. His power could be felt by the men around the table.

"General Cheung has provided us with hard intelligence. We know that this man Trent Marshall will speak at the UN for the chicken." Minister Wei stopped to light up another cigarette. "We know from the intercepted e-mails that they will hide his appearance in some way, possibly a mask or a hood. But we know what he looks like – and that he will be staying at the Plaza Hotel in New York City with his woman."

He paused, closing his eyes in thought as the other five men sat motionless waiting for his next words. When he opened them, he stared hard at each man around the table before speaking.

"No one knows that we know all this. And no one is to know. Is that understood."

Minister Wei tapped the red and gold state folder in front of him on the table. "The Great Move Forward is the future destiny of our nation, our people and our party. This chicken crisis threatens our grand poultry plans here and in Tumpawie. We would have to undertake an agonizing reappraisal of everything we've planned. We would have to find a new sustainable food source. At this stage, we can't permit that to happen." He fixed his gaze on the state emblem on the wall opposite him before continuing.

"This man Marshall, he has the answer. If the Americans have a new scientific way to control animal behavior, we must know. If so, maybe they have lost control."

One of the men, a Ministerial vice-president, ventured a thought, interrupting Minister Wei. "Didn't your animal scientists say that controlling the minds of animals is not possible?"

Minister Wei stared at him before answering. "If you are too close to the feathers, you do not see the whole bird." There was silence in the room as they pondered that thought and waited for the Minister to continue. Minister Wei looked over at General Cheung, "We must get our hands on this man and squeeze the truth out of him. With what you know, could your people get him? You've done this sort of thing before."

"Anything is possible, but there is little time to mount such an operation. And there would be great risk," replied the general.

"But it could be done. Your people could do it," urged the Minister.

"As I said, anything is possible. It would be dangerous and very risky, but we have people who know how to do these things."

"Exactly what things?" asked a vice-president of the Agricultural Ministry.

"Making people disappear," replied the general matter-of-factly, "We have a major in Department 2 in Shanghai. He has people very skilled in these matters."

"But how would they get him out of America?" asked the nervous vice-minister of Foreign Affairs.

"They have their ways," answered General Cheung, a sly smile slipped across his face.

"Do it!" commanded Minister Wei, fixing his eyes on the general with a fiery look. The meeting was over.

Chapter 15

The chauffeured Red Star luxury sedan purred its way down Lianhua Road. Behind the car's tinted windows, Major Feng Yong studied the tall, modern condo building that flanked both sides of the road. He was 61years of age and was reflecting over how much things have changed in this part of Shanghai in just the last fifteen years. What was once open farm country, was now an upscale residential district. The car turned the corner, passing more condo towers and a gray building set back from a walled forecourt. To those passing by, the gateway signs into the forecourt identified it as the "Shanghai Municipal Auditing Bureau." The building was eighteen stories high and the first fourteen floors housed 837 calculating accountants dedicated to keeping the city's books in order and to ferreting out corrupt citizens and city officials.

The top four floors had fewer windows. They were bulletproof, soundproof and double glazed to trap six inches of air between the glass panes. This trapped air was constantly filled by a small speaker booming irritating radio static that slightly vibrated both panes. In addition, the outer pane contained a thin electrified metal mesh. This made the windows virtually impenetrable to parabolic directional microphones, invisible infrared laser listening devices and camera lenses. The interior walls and ceilings were painted with two undercoats of a metallic paint that blocked invisible infrared laser beams from any inquisitive thermographic cameras. Cell phones were inoperable in this sealed environment, and all communication was by courier, or telephone or cable, delivered over secured landlines.

Major Feng's sedan drove twenty yards past the building before turning into the driveway of the adjacent condo building's entrance to its underground parking garage. The sedan slowly spiraled down to the third level which was reserved for government parking. On command, a garage door opened and the sedan drove through a tunnel to stop at the same level underneath the Shanghai Municipal Auditing Bureau building. Feng got out of the sedan and took one of two private elevators up the top floor of the building. This top floor housed a specialized section of Department 2 in the MSS (Ministry of State Security) that reported to the Ministry of Public Security in Beijing.

Department 2 was responsible for "special reconnaissance abroad", their polite phrase for aggressive overseas espionage. Major Feng's special section of Department 2 controlled ten "white" agents in Western Europe and North America. These were long-term agents known as "fish at the bottom of the ocean" who were Chinese in everything but their physical appearance. The three floors below Feng housed a section of Department 11, responsible for computer, electronic and cipher espionage. Though in the same building, both sections were kept separate and seldom interacted with one another.

In one hour's time, Feng would meet with Ping Huo and Ping Tong, two of his most prized "white" agents. They had been hastily recalled from Berlin and had flown in overnight on one of Lufthansa's daily flights to Shanghai's Pudong International Airport. He would take the time to review again their dossiers and active files before they arrived. Feng had a proud and private interest in them. These two young men were his personal and brilliant creation.

Years ago, Feng had directed an operation to penetrate the French Embassy with a beautiful French-speaking Eurasian woman who would seduce a senior member of the embassy. The Deputy Head of the Mission was the target. He was handsome, filled with vanity and a philanderer. Six months into the affair, she presented him with the news that she was two months pregnant. He went to the embassy's DST security officer, confessed the affair, and the next day was bundled onto an Air France flight back to Paris. The Eurasian woman was Ping Mei-Hua, the mother of the two agents.

When she gave birth to the twins, her Eurasian beauty and the father's strong Bourbonnais genes, delivered two fair-skinned babies without a trace of Chinese features. Feng realized that these two babies – the sons of a Department 2 agent – could be reared from birth to become elite MSS agents – Western on the outside; Chinese on the inside.

Now both twenty-six years of age, Huo and Tong, both blue-eyed and blond, had been raised and indoctrinated by their mother to love and serve the Motherland. They had been schooled at MSS's Intelligence College, taught the dark arts of espionage, spoke flawless English and French, and as their first immersion into the Western world, sent to Australia. They lived there for three years in a spacious flat, supposedly as sons of a rich English businessman in Hong Kong, attending the University of Sydney under the supervision of their mother, who posed as their cook and maid.

Feng closed the files and slid them over to a corner of his desk, then got up, lit a cigarette and went over to look out the window. They should be here in a few minutes. It would be good to see them again. How they have grown up and how professional and loyal they had become to a China that changes every day. Now you could no longer say "comrade", a street word used by today's new generation to mean homosexual. He would call them by their first names so as not to embarrass them.

There was a knock at his door and Chin Wu, his secretary, opened it to usher in the two young men. There were sparkling smiles, warm words and fatherly embraces as Feng blinked back tears of happiness. He was so proud of them. Feng then suggested that they all sit around a low table near the window, and ordered Chin Wu to bring them a large pot of Longjing tea and a plate of powdered fruit buns.

"I know you never question your orders, but you must have wondered why you were so suddenly recalled overnight to Shanghai six months before your planned return." The two young men said nothing in response.

"There is an urgent need for your special talents on a time-sensitive dilemma of the greatest national importance," said Feng. Huo and Tong's special talents were assassination, abduction and "desired disappearance" of enemies of the State, and they were good at it: a two-man killer team not known to exist by any foreign intelligence agency.

Chin Wu returned with a tray of tea, cups and a plate of fruit buns, placing them on the table in front of Feng. Feng nodded his approval and gave a slight nod which was Chin Wu's cue to leave the room. Feng poured the tea for the three of them.

"I have never sent you on any mission without telling you why it was important to China and its people. So listen carefully. Our leaders have decreed that the next ten years will be a great and grand leap into the future that will stun the world." Feng paused to drink his tea, placing the empty cup on the table and leaning forward to stare into the two pair of blue eyes looking back at him.

"In ten years every citizen will have health care, corruption will be stamped out, there will be no more pollution, and healthy food and clean water will be plentiful for all our people. We will lead the world in technology, medicine and science. This will all be accomplished within our lifetime."

He hesitated before continuing, his voice now almost like a whisper. "America is almost bankrupt, its people deep in debt, divided and morally diseased. Every day they're shooting each other. In ten short years America will no longer be an economic superpower. America is now in a slow descent, but we will make it faster for them. It is now a "democracy" only for the rich who know America's time is up, but dare not tell their people. And as for Europe – Europe is poor, fractured and spent." Feng broke into a smile before continuing, "Now in the twenty-first century, it is China's time again to be the center of the world."

The two young agents focused their attention on every word and gesture of Feng. Huo sat motionless with an unlighted cigarette clamped in his mouth, reluctant to light it and break the mood of Feng's oratory. Tong absently stroked his left leg, his eyes suddenly misty with emotion.

Feng leaned back in his chair, opened a red file, studied two pages and paused before continuing, "Food is the fuel of the people. Bellies must be filled. Without food we cannot reach these noble goals. Anything that threatens our food supply – and anything that threatens our chickens – threatens our future." Feng paused to let what he had said sink in to their two young minds before continuing.

"I cannot stress the importance of your mission. Over twenty-one million of our countrymen are in our poultry industry: an industry worth billion and billions of Yuan. We produce and consume more eggs than any other country in the world. My figures here say forty percent of the world's eggs."

He could tell them all this, for he was confident that they could never be taken alive, and knew ways to kill themselves if ever caught, but he did not read them the summary page on the social and political consequences of a sudden Chinese poultry and egg collapse, ominously predicting millions of Chinese farmers descending on the cities, inflaming unrest, rebellion and deadly confrontations with the government.

His voice now took on a chilling tone. "Something is happening to America's poultry industry. The American and international press are reporting that their chickens are refusing to lay eggs or breed with the roosters. Stupid rumors are flying about that the Americans have somehow managed to master a new technology that can totally control animals by some kind of direct communication: to actually communicate with animal societies on an intellectual level that can manipulate their minds."

Feng hesitated, and then added, "The American President is going on TV to address the chicken crisis. We don't know what he will say." The two young men stared at Feng with identical looks of disbelief as the potential power of his revelation turned in their minds. Huo wrinkled his brow and pursed his lips as if he had just bit into a lemon as his eyes followed Feng's hand placing the red file back on the table.

"Believe me, this is true," said Feng, before a small skeptical smirk crossed his face. "But is it? Our own scientists say that it is impossible to communicate with the brain and intelligence of chickens. The real probability is that there is possibly a new and unknown avian plague that is destroying the American poultry industry. They don't know what it is, but they will not admit it.

"And so they concoct this absurd story of a new scientific discovery that gives them the power to control the animals of the world. It is just not believable. But our scientists say that if – and only if – it was true, then they believe that the Americans have lost control and are grappling with an experimental disaster. Their Department of Agriculture is silent and so is the White House. So what do we do? We cannot take chances. We suspect that it is a new avian brain disease, and so we are stopping all imports of American poultry products into China. Today we ordered two American cargo ships with frozen chickens to turn back – that they could not enter Chinese territorial waters."

Feng picked up a pale green file from the table and studied its contents as the two agents sat in silence, waiting for him to continue. His eyes moved quickly over the paper before raising them to speak. "This American fairy tale becomes even more questionable. Our agents report that a chicken – with a Canadian translator – has met secretly with the American President and his advisors in Washington. There is even intelligence that the chicken will then go on to New York to appear before the General Assembly. If this UN appearance happens, this chicken translator would be the most important man in the world."

Huo and Tong sat upright and expressionless, absorbing every word while Feng studied the green file in his hand. "So what do we do? We kidnap him. We bring him to China and find out if there is any truth to this ridiculous story. If there is, then we have the human key to that knowledge. If not, we find ways to make America look foolish to the world.

"This will be the greatest and most daring challenge of your careers. He will be guarded day and night. We believe he and the chicken are in the White House. New York is your only chance. We have a mole in the FBI and a 'deep-water' agent in the office of the President, so we will know when and where this chicken translator is at all times. He may be disguised for his appearance at the UN, but we have many photos of him and we know what hotel he will be staying in. I have activated a supporting network of agents in New York to provide you with everything you need, or to assist you. As usual, they won't meet you and you won't meet them."

Feng leaned back, placed the green folder back on the table before continuing. "If an egg is broken from the inside, life begins. If an egg is broken from the outside, life ends. America' is breaking its eggs from the outside."

Huo and Tong smiled at Feng's sage statement. Feng enjoyed the moment, then again affirmed their mission by speaking in an official and assertive manner. "Your mission is to go to America and bring back this chicken translator. To the world he must simply disappear. I have told you much. You now understand the supreme importance of your mission. Failure is not permitted." Feng stared at them and gave them a cold smile and added, "But then, you have never failed me, have you."

He then got up from his chair and went over to his desk, picked up a thick brown folder and went to the door, opening it and asking Chin Wu to join them.

For the next hour the four men huddled over the small table as Feng went carefully through the details of dead-drop locations, photos of Trent Marshall, cell phone codes, bridge-agents, contact methods and their false identity package of passports and credit cards. Only Chin Wu made notes that would later be turned into the official briefing document for Huo and Tong's active file.

When they were finished, Tong respectfully ask Feng if they could see their mother before they left Shanghai. Feng studied their earnest faces before answering that it would not be possible, given the urgency of their mission.

. . .

That night, Air China Flight 1590 took off from Shanghai's Pudong International Airport for the direct flight to New York's JF Kennedy Airport. The flight was long, uneventful and boring.

Nineteen hours from takeoff, two young men, traveling on Australian passports as tourists, checked into the Americana Inn, five minutes from Times Square.

Fair would I kiss my Julia's dainty leg,
which is white and hairless as an egg.
Robert Herrick,
English poet 1591-1674

Chapter 16

An elongated sliver of pink flesh danced in the mirror. It was soft, warm and curved diagonally against a thin rectangle of white bathroom tiles. Occasionally it disappeared, only to slither back into sight, repeating the pink and white erotic pattern. Sitting on the edge of the hotel bed, Trent studied this living abstract, savoring its movements and the promise of pleasure it offered.

He had downed his Dom Pérignon and was holding the empty champagne flute glass up to his right eye, looking at this slinky sensuous shape through the curve of the glass This improvised lens spread the pink pattern into a graceful crescent of flesh which he could undulate by rotating the stem of the glass between his fingers. He played with this newfound image, then placed the glass on the floor and inhaled deeply. He was getting aroused.

"Honey, are you ready for champagne?"

"In a sec," replied Janice. "I can see you." Trent informed her. The bathroom door slammed shut. He sat there on the bed and shifted his eyes along the wall to study the rest of the room. It was long, high and elegantly furnished in the style of the Plaza: a beautifully balanced study of browns, creams and golds disturbed only by the television set throwing out blatant incandescent colors.

Trent could hear the clinking of bottles against tile and he could imagine Janice in the bathroom neatly setting up house, arranging her cosmetics and creams in orderly rows along the counter. She was so orderly, and he loved her for that. He lived out of his suitcase, never using drawers or closets; she moved in, unpacking two small cases, and like a magician, conjuring forth a seemingly endless collection of costumes, shoes and frilly undergarments. If he had his way, she wouldn't be finding much time to wear them tonight. It was her first trip to New York and if he knew Janice, he knew he wouldn't have his way.

She came out of the bathroom dressed in a kaftan. Her hair was loose and shiny and her feet were bare. She tossed him a little kiss and moved lightly over to the window. He watched the loose robe wrestle to contain the curves of her body, the slit sides now and then parting to reveal tantalizing glimpses of her naked legs.

"Very sexy," he murmured, with an exaggerated huskiness in his voice.

"I'll have my bubbly now if you please," she announced. Picking up his glass, he got up and crossed the room to the writing desk where a silver ice bucket held the champagne bottle. He poured Jennifer her flute of bubbly and refilled his own flute.

Janice had swept back the curtains and was surveying a green and grassy Central Park from a height distant enough to smudge away dirty details. From this same window and in the same pose, the American socialite Mrs. Oliver Harriman had looked down on a quieter and calmer New York. It was Tuesday, October 1st.,1907, when the hotel first opened and the room was then part of her choice corner apartment. On that memorable evening, she not only looked, but also listened to the distant roaring of the lions in the zoo park several blocks away.

A palatial hotel of social opulence, the Plaza had started life as a residence for only the very rich. The room that now hosted Janice and Trent had a long history of lodging fruitful and failed wedding nights, carnal couplings of opposite and same sex lovers, political plots, business ploys and once, even the unexpected birth of a baby.

"I wonder who else has stayed in this room? What famous person? Janice mused. She scanned the view with inquisitive eyes. "New York is beautiful from here. Distance does lend enchantment. It's not like everyone said it would be. Everyone's so polite. I've been here five hours and no one's tried to pick my purse or fondle me." Trent took her glass over to the window and stood behind her.

"How about me?"

She turned to face him, her body brushing against his in the pivot of her movement. With a tender whisper she replied, "You don't count." She arched up to kiss him gently on the cheek, lifting her drink from his hand in the gesture, and then stepping past him to curl up in a chair. Her unexpected retreat was a sudden, comely action, designed to break their physical intimacy and calm her rising impulses.

"You're a tease," said Trent softly, downing his flute of champagne.

"That's why you love me."

He hesitated, lowering his gaze to the inviting and revealing neckline of her robe. "I think I'll have another drink." He returned to the desk.

. . .

In Washington, the President of the United States sat upright as the makeup woman reverently removed the Kleenex tissues from around his light blue shirt collar. The brilliant and intense television lights were beginning to bring out tiny beads of perspiration across the top of the President's forehead and upper lip. He closed his eyes as the makeup woman deftly dabbed away with a small sponge. One of the technicians stepped behind the President and removed an original Frederic Remington bronze from the credenza The bucking bronco bronze was then replaced by another Remington bronze, this one of a pioneer Conestoga wagon pulled by a straining team of oxen: a more suitable pioneer symbol of American tenacity and courage. The technician looked hopefully into the lenses of the cameras, waiting for confirmation of his action from some unseen voice. The new Remington was approved and he stepped out of the shot, ignoring the still and stately presence of the national father figure. Earlier, the Nelson Mandela bronze had been struck off the credenza and replaced with several framed photos of the President's family, large enough to "read" on camera. They presented a tableau of a smiling, outdoor and folksy family.

. . .

Now on her second glass of champagne, Janice's voice brightened with excitement. "This is all so sinful and delicious. You and me in a classy New York hotel room. I feel like a jaded woman having an afternoon affair with a rich Wall Street broker, seduced by champagne. A Plaza Affair! Like a play or a film." She made the statement sound theatrical.

"Well it's a government-sponsored affair," quipped Trent. "Planned and paid for by the Ottawa boys from the tax revenue of its citizens. That sort of takes the edge off this romantic encounter. Mister and Mrs. Smith – not very imaginative – booked, reserved and paid by the Canadian Embassy."

Janice smiled and her voice bubbled with happiness. "It's a government plot so you can keep me in this room. You've enticed me to New York only to do with me what you will. You're an evil man." Her eyes now sparkled and she ended her protest with a saucy sticking out of her tongue.

"Christ! What time is it?" Trent's mind was suddenly pulled back to reality. Janice glanced at the clock on the bedside table, rolling her head back to squint at Trent. "It's eight – it's eight o'clock. Why?"

"The President's chicken speech!" exclaimed Trent. He turned to the television set in time to see the colored outline of the White House facade fade away to reveal the Great Presidential Seal. It dominated the screen, singing out its colors like the national anthem. He turned up the volume.

At the same moment, and unknown to Trent and Janice, two Diplomatic Security men in the room next to them, sat in front of their television set, confident that the two lovers they were guarding were tucked away safely in their room for the night.

"In a few moments an address of national importance from the President of the United States." intoned the voice of the network announcer. It was a deep, amber voice, and like rare cognac, reserved by the network for state occasions, national disasters and momentous news events. This could be all three.

"I've got to listen to this," said Trent, returning to the bed and plunking himself solidly down on the edge. Janice looked over at him, aware of his abrupt interest in the set and suddenly curious herself. The Great Presidential Seal continued its glow on the screen with the religious imagery of a stained-glass window,

"How long will it be?' she asked, sipping her champagne.

"Before he talks?"

"No, how long will he speak?"

"I don't know. Probably a half hour."

"Will he mention your name?"

"I doubt it,"

"Why wouldn't he?" The smooth network voice silenced her questions with his national pronouncement, "And now, from the White House Oval Office –" There was a dramatic pause, "The President of the United States of America." Silence reigned.

The Great Seal was replaced by the stately head and shoulders of the President. He was sitting at the polished Resolute desk, his notes before him, behind him the credenza top held the carefully placed Conestoga bronze and family pictures.

The President looked out to the cameras with unblinking brown eyes. As one camera gently moved towards him, his features slowly shuffled to present the proper arrangement of authority. It was a subtle expression of confidence and sincerity.

The President was a master communicator. He had honed his teleprompter skills so that he could read the scrolling words with a sense of understanding, getting all the inflections right. He insisted on large type fonts, not because of his eyesight, but because with large lettering, viewers couldn't see his eye movements reading the prompter. He always ran through the teleprompter text twice so that he had a sound grasp of its content and meaning, and he usually preferred to deliver his televised talks to one camera only. He believed in keeping his addresses and sentences short and simple, and it was rare that he addressed the nation from the Oval Office, reserving it only for occasions with a sense of supreme grave consequence or of great national importance.

Trent was amazed to see how the television lighting and lens flattered his features and shaved ten years off the face of the man he had sat next to in the White House that week.

"My fellow Americans – tonight I wish to speak to you about a situation that affects us all, rich or poor."

"Tall or short. Fat or thin," added Janice aloud.

"Before I go further, I want to stress that this is not a situation for either alarm or panic. Rather, it is one of courage and challenge for all of us. It will test us, and that is good. We have, in the course of over 230 years as a nation, been exceptionally blessed with an abundance of Nature's wealth. Our land rolls rich in resources. Our country, unlike many others in this world, has provided us with a cornucopia of the good earth's offerings."

By now the camera had continued its slow crawl toward him until his massive head dominated the screen. The Conestoga bronze had disappeared. He looked intensely into the lens which could now focus on minute beads of sweat on his forehead, visible only to those with High Definition. The television lights made them glisten like tiny sequins.

"Since the Pilgrim Fathers, we have tilled our fertile land, turning it into a provider of plenty." Out of sight, the President carefully turned his backup script in case the teleprompter seized up. "Through our own hard work, our skills and our imagination –" The turning of the page had severed the flow of the thought – "We shall continue to do so. America's true strength was born by its pioneer farmers. It is rooted in our land. Our love of the farm and the good earth fills our heart, even though many millions of us have never turned the soil, planted a seed, or milked a cow. This inherent strength is our heritage. From it we have put the blessings of Nature on our tables – and in a spirit of generosity and goodness that is so much a part of our national character – we have provided our food to the hungry of the world."

"Hurray!" cheered Janice, holding her third glass of champagne up high in a salute of approval. Trent ignored her patriotic outburst.

The President had worked his way to page three on the teleprompter, and with a look of satisfaction, glanced down at the pages and then returned his eyes to the intimacy of the lens. "We have become the world's larder, feeding its millions with our meats, our grains and our cereals. We have always shared our abundance with others, for that is our way." Another pause. "We can be proud of that." He let that thought simmer before continuing, "In the past ten years we have born our share of weather extremes: wildfires, floods, droughts and terrible storms in much of our country. Nature has not always been kind to us – but perhaps we have not always been kind to Nature."

He lowered his voice to grasp sincerity. "Now as I speak to you, we are confronted with another challenge – a challenge to our continued food wealth and prosperity." Slowly he read his question. "What is that challenge? First let me state that it was unpredictable. In the past few days you have read, seen or heard that there is a threat to our poultry industry. What does that mean? How does it affect every American?" The President took a dramatic pause. "What does it mean? It means that through an unaccountable change in animal behavior, thousands of chicken flocks across our nation have stopped propagation and the laying of eggs."

Janice, now a little giddy from the champagne, couldn't let that pass. "You mean they're not getting it on?"

There was no response from Trent. "Maybe it's mass flock menopause?" declared Janice, delighted by her own humor.

"Quiet!" snapped Trent.

"This is a vital continuing cycle process that is necessary to our standard of living and our food habits. Let me give you just two statistics that illustrate this. Every week Americans consume over 169 million pounds of processed poultry on a ready-to-eat basis. Every year, on a per capita basis, every American consumes approximately 265 eggs, many in the form of baked goods and many other processed foods. You can see that Nature's gift of the chicken is important to every one of us."

"And finger-licking good?" quipped Janice. The camera had now loosened the shot to put the Remington bronze back in the picture "How does this matter of national concern effect every American? Well it affects the ability of every poultry farmer and every segment of the food industry that uses poultry products to put food on your table." The President again paused to give his next statement weight.

"Your government, through the Department of Agriculture and its Secretary, Percy Adams, is moving quickly and efficiently to assist these two prime producers to finding the solutions to get our nation's poultry and egg production moving again."

The President was now speaking with vigor and determination, turning pages without really looking as he gained confidence in the scrolling text of the teleprompter. "With the joint resources of the poultry industry, the food industry and your government, we can harness the best agricultural minds and animal scientists in the world to find a sustainable solution. As your President, I have instructed that the full capabilities of every government body and agency concerned be applied full-time to this solution. I am confident of the results."

The President was now boring Janice, and the third champagne that Trent had given her was having its effect. She had given up on witty barbs which weren't being appreciated. She uncurled her body from the chair and crossed to the bed, pulling Trent back from its edge to lie down beside her on the crumpled spread. He made the move back into the middle of the soft mattress with three shifts of his rump, adroitly balancing his glass while still keeping his eyes on the screen.

The President continued. "How will it affect you and your family? If it's over a prolonged time – which we must consider – there will be a decline of poultry meat and eggs available in the stores and supermarkets where you shop." Here he paused again for emphasis. "I ask every American family to limit their consumption of eggs and poultry meat for now. I ask you to temporarily seek alternatives to your food needs."

A frisky Janice leaned over and nipped Trent's ear with her teeth. He winced in silence, determined not to let her divert him from the screen. He would take his revenge later.

"I ask you to conserve. I ask you to refrain from hoarding. As your President, and acting in the best interests of the nation, I have instituted the following Presidential Executive Orders to the responsible government departments. These will take effect tomorrow morning at 6 a.m., Eastern Standard Time, and simultaneously in each of our time zones."

A second camera cut to a close-up of the President. He missed the change of cameras by a full two seconds before turning his head and eyes to the proper lens. This angle was not flattering and was further hampered by the fact that any movement of the camera created the optical effect of a slightly out-of-focus oxen and a Conestoga wagon rolling into his ear.

"He's got very sexy eyes and he's on page six," announced Janice.

"One – that a price freeze be immediately placed on eggs by the dozen and on a pro rata basis per individual egg. These price freezes to be announced tomorrow morning by the Secretary of Commerce.

"Two – that a price freeze be immediately placed on all poultry meats, poultry products and food stuffs containing more than fifteen percent poultry meat to prevent unwarranted price hikes. In addition, price caps may also be imposed on a variety of other animal meats. These price freezes and price caps to be announced tomorrow morning by the Secretary of Commerce.

"Three – I have instructed that a national system of poultry and egg rationing for both the consumer and the food industry be drafted up for consideration by the Congress and the Senate. This action is a precaution only, should the ultimate unthinkable happen.

"Four – I have instructed the Department of Agriculture, working with the Department of State, to temporarily rescind all existing contracts for the sale of poultry products, meats and grain sales to overseas markets. Further, I have asked them to critically appraise our food commitments to the World Food Organization and the World Food Bank. This is a step I deeply regret having to take, even if only temporary.

"Five – finally I have asked the Department of Agriculture to draw up a concise inventory of poultry meats and eggs currently under government and commercial storage."

Trent watched a tiny rivulet of perspiration start its descent down the President's forehead. It was stopped and eliminated by the President's broad hand sweeping across his brow. The director now cut back to camera one and the President reacted with a quick shift of his eyes. This new scene presented a wider shot of the President, including the full credenza and the glimmering Remington bronze. The President took a deep breath, grasping the last page with both hands.

It's his last page," whispered Janice. "I know it's his last page cause he's holding it with both hands."

The President paused to rub his lower lip with his finger. It was an odd gesture. "In addition, I have asked our Ambassador to the United Nations to request an emergency session of the General Assembly of the United Nations."

"Here it comes," said Trent.

"The United States," continued the President, "has requested this session to be called tomorrow morning, or at the soonest possible convenience to the UN General Assembly. The purpose of this session will be to bring this vital food problem to the forum of world attention and participation." He tilted his head forward and down to give a penetrating look into the lens. It was extremely effective.

"Hunger knows no nationality. It is the common concern of all humankind. It is a world challenge for us today–and for our children tomorrow. And we must rise to that challenge."

"That's it!" declared Trent, a feeling of disappointment fell over him. "The bastard didn't mention the chicken. Didn't tell them the real problem. Are they in for a surprise at the UN!"

The camera now started to move toward the President, favoring the American flag to the left of the credenza at the expense of the Remington bronze.

"I began my talk this evening by stating that this is not the time for Americans to lose faith or lose courage. I would like to end with this thought." He paused, placing the final page down on the desk. He crossed his hands and a new surge of sincerity filled his voice and steadied his gaze.

"The farms of America and the kitchens of Americans can, and will, through their collective skills, continue to feed America and maintain our nation as a land of milk and money."

He immediately realized his Freudian slip of the tongue and without hesitation instantly repeated the phrase, "As a land of milk and honey."

The camera held its unblinking position. The President made his final pause before saying, "God bless our farm animals. God bless America."

The image of the President faded from the screen to be replaced by the Presidential Seal, again heralding its authority and power in the rigid formal stance of the eagle.

"El Presidente really gave us the bird tonight. Jesus – a land of milk and money." Janice broke into spasms of laughter, falling back on the bed.

"He's even got a bird on his Boy Scout badge. She continued to laugh as Trent rolled over on top of her to take his revenge.

CTN's Dane Donner came onto the screen. He intelligently and concisely summed up the key points of the President's address to the two tangling bodies on the bed.

Chapter 17

The effect of the President's speech and the harsh and unexpected controls announced by him were felt the next day on every major stock market in the world. The New York and American Stock exchanges reflected immediate uncertainty with one of the lowest Dow Jones averages ever recorded. Anything remotely connected to the poultry industry suffered severe losses, especially the Processed Food industries dependent on eggs or poultry meat as an ingredient. In Chicago, Food Futures tumbled in the morning with a quick and aggressive afternoon rally in lima beans, grains, cereals and soybeans, a major export to China as a chicken meal feed in China's rapidly growing poultry industry. Soybean futures reached record high, but by mid-afternoon wavered, and then plunged.

Overseas stock exchanges quivered with the shock that America was closing her larder stores to the export market. China, which had the world's third highest poultry industry, and always concerned about its food security, remained strangely silent and secretive. While the government exerted significant control over the nation's more than 600 million internet users, it could not stem the sudden surge of chicken-posted messages and bloggings on popular websites like Sina Weibo and Renren.

In Brazil, where some poultry factory farms kill over four million chickens each month, and others produce more than more than five million eggs a day, the large Brazilian poultry industry took a beating on the San Paulo Stock Exchange. Overnight, there was a sudden realization – sweeping through the financial institutions of the world – of the economic importance of the chicken to the world's food needs.

The chicken – coming on the heels of yet another money crisis in the Euro zone and America – was kicking the hell out of Western lifestyle, confidence and stability. Every major American newspaper carried the full text of the President's short speech, along with gloomy editorials and grim predications. All three television networks and their cable competitors scrambled to line up chicken experts, poultry economists, and CEO's of fast-food chicken chains as they hurriedly assembled news documentaries for peak nighttime viewing. The poultry factory farms of America were invaded by battalions of network camera crews and national broadcast commentators. The chickens viewed this broadcast invasion in sullen silence, refusing to participate in any natural demonstration or actions that could be recorded on camera. Twitter, Facebook and YouTube exploded with worldwide responses, only this time the content of the posting were serious and concerned.

Russian and American relations were at their lowest point since the Ukrainian crisis of Putin's era, due to contesting ship passage through Arctic waters, differing interpretations of the UN's Laws of the Seas Treaty, and conflicting national claims to the rich mineral wealth and natural gas deposits under the Arctic's frigid waters.

Moscow propaganda experts held hurried meetings to consider what, if any, political opportunities presented themselves from the President's speech and America's fowl dilemma. The SVR – Russia's equivalent of America's CIA – quickly put together a plan of active measures to capitalize on America's misfortune. Working through the diplomatic cover of their embassies and consulates, SVR's Disinformation Department was soon sowing suspicion abroad by circulating false rumors and fake news e-mails that indicated America's secret prior knowledge of the chicken crisis, while grossly exaggerating its political and economic ramifications on various countries.

From its Moscow studios, RT Television, Russia's slick, smooth English-language channel – available to more than 700 million viewers worldwide – was broadcasting interviews and video footage that magnified the chicken crisis in America. In France, the more radical anti-American French dailies published every rumor, and even the stately *Manchester Guardian* guardedly alluded to the rumors, attributing them to the French press.

In the US, PBS, America's public service broadcast network, dug into its archives and resurrected a 2011 *Frontline* investigative documentary on corporate factory farming, recording new voice-over narration and scheduling the program for broadcasting later in the week.

In spite of the Department of Agriculture and the Food and Drug Administration's joint assurances that the chicken crisis was one of animal behavior, having no effect on the safe consumption of poultry meat and products in supermarkets, nervous consumers struck chicken off their grocery list, resulting in a sudden jump in pork and beef sales.

In the UK, Animal Rights activists attempted to demonstrate outside the American Embassy and clashed with British poultry farmers, who were demanding immediate action to insure that America's "contaminated" poultry products did not reach Britain's shores.

The UK's Department for Environment, Food and Rural Affairs, The British Poultry Council and The British Egg Council were swamped by e-mails and cell phone calls from their members and the public. The UK was Europe's second highest producer of poultry meat, and domestically chicken now accounted for half of the UK's entire meat consumption.

The BBC's acclaimed current affairs television program, *Panorama*, hastily put together a one-hour special program on the state of the poultry and egg industry in the United Kingdom. For a country that prides itself on its animal welfare standards, it came as a shock. *Panorama's* hidden cameras recorded "beak trimming", the painful debeaking of chickens, and presented graphic scenes supporting the staggering statistic of thirty to forty million chicks killed every year in the UK. Part of the program originated from Arkansas, with a segment from Brussels reporting on the Council of European Union's decree in1999, setting out more humane conditions for chicken flocks, their sizes and the banning of battery cages, to be implemented by 2012. It reported that only Switzerland, Austria, Finland, Norway and Sweden had completely complied.

In the Berlaymont building in Brussels, the European Union's bureaucrats sat behind their polished desks in shock. The EU had spent decades harmonizing the poultry and egg industries of its twenty-eight member countries. France, the UK, Germany and Poland produced half of the EU's poultry meat, and Europe was now self-sufficient in poultry meat and eggs, importing only high-value poultry products, mainly from Brazil.

The President's words also created alarm in the that rare world of elevated cuisine. Seven Paris chefs of three Michelin Star restaurants, sensing a coming chicken scarcity, bought every chicken that Gerard Prunier had on his farm.

Monsieur Prunier raised only Bresse chickens in the Rhône-Alpes region of France. They were free-ranging, pasture-raised on an all-natural diet of farm insects before being fattened on a diet of grain soaked in buttermilk. Classed as *Label Rouge* – the official sign of superior quality – Prunier's chickens were deemed to be the best tasting poultry in the world.

America's chicken exports had been brought to a halt. Around the world, refrigerated cargo ships carrying American poultry meat or products where suddenly told to stand off and not enter the territorial waters of nervous nations, unsure of what was happening to the American poultry industry. Exporting to more than 120 countries, the broiler chicken market in the previous year had topped 610,000 tons. Chicken paws were over 370 tons and table eggs and processed egg products reached the equivalent of a startling 281 million dozen. All of this was worth more than six billion in export sales.

Mexico was one of America's top six world markets, and some California food chains and restaurants were quietly buying back American-exported chickens so that they could market them at exorbitance prices as "Natural Chickens from Mexico" in their supermarkets and on their menus.

In Toccoa, Georgia, a contract poultry framer, Edwin Novac, with a wife and four children to support, and deeply in debt, went into his hen house and hanged himself. There were unsubstantiated reports that five other poultry farmers in the Southern states had committed suicide.

Altogether, between the stock exchanges, the media, suicides and SVR's efficient rumors factory, America's poultry peril was firmly embedded in the minds of national governments around the globe.

Chapter 18

Harold Dempsy looked down through the window on Broad Street below. From twenty stories up, the people looked like ants: dark dots moving in all directions on the wide pavement, momentarily disappearing under the leafy foliage of the treetops below only to appear again.

"Are you thinking of throwing yourself out that window?" said Frank Costello.

"No. The window doesn't open." sighed Dempsy, as he turned around and gave Frank a thin smile.

"Pour us a bourbon." It was a soft-spoken familiar command. Harold Dempsy was the President and CEO of Sunnyhen Foods Inc., America's largest poultry factory farm company. Headquartered in Augusta, Georgia, every week its ninety-two poultry plants slaughtered and packaged seventeen million chickens, while its 120 million laying hens lived longer, producing twenty-five billion eggs annually.

Dempsy studied Jack's broad back and balding head as his Chief Financial Officer stepped over to the bar. He's putting on weight, Dempsy thought as he sat himself into the soft leather of a Milano chair. Dempsy and Costello were Augusta boys who grew up together, and together they ran the Sunnyhen Empire.

"So give me an update. Where do we stand now?" asked Dempsy.

"The Army sent an e-mail. Their pulling rank. The Quartermaster General, reminding us of the clause in our contract."

"What clause?" asked Dempsy as Costello handed him his

glass of straight bourbon, no ice.

"It's buried on one of the supplementary pages – says that in times of national disaster or state of war, delivery to the army takes precedent over all civilian clients."

Dempsy swirled the amber fluid in his glass before taking a gulp, squinted and shook his head. "Christ Jack, it's not Pearl Harbor. it's chickens!"

"Maybe they know something we don't know?" said Costello.

"I don't think so. It's just Army lawyers covering their ass. What about our prison contracts and hospitals? They're not civilian clients."

"Good point, I'll get our legal department to check into that."

In addition to the army, Sunnyhen Foods Inc. had contracts to provide chicken products to state prisons in the twenty-three states in which it had factory farms, as well as thirty-one hospitals in those same states. This was a highly profitable part of its business that went back to its beginnings during America's Civil War.

. . .

In 1845, Boleslaw Dempski, an adventurous young man, migrated from Poland to America with his new bride. A polarized Poland was then a tormented country of partitions and uprisings, while America promised freedom and golden opportunities to anyone willing to work. They settled near Augusta, and by 1859 Dempski was raising chickens and selling eggs. The Civil War brought four years of horrible hardship for a family that now had two young sons, but through it all, somehow Dempski continued to raise his chickens, freely offering them to help feed the hungering 1st. Regiment of the Georgia Infantry in the Confederate Army.

In the years following, grateful returning veterans repaid the young Pole for his sympathy and sacrifice by becoming his loyal customers. His chicken business prospered and in 1905 he changed his name from Dempski Poultry to The Dempsy Poultry Company.

Before his death in 1908, as his business continued to expand beyond Georgia, Dempsy again changed his company name to Sunnyhen Farms. This name-change introduced the American public to the Sunnyhen chicken: a cheerful white cartoon chicken with a large yellow circular sun behind her, drawn by Roy W. Taylor, a famous cartoonist of the time.

This chicken logo was graphically refined and updated over the years by succeeding generations of Dempsys. In 1955 it first danced into life in a 60-sec black-and-white commercial on the Ed Sullivan Show, a TV variety show watched weekly by millions. It blossomed into full color with a network appearance in 1965 in the Pasadena Rose Parade as a flower float and two 30-second commercials. Now a brand logo firmly imbedded in American popular culture, it appears on twenty-one Sunnyhen poultry products around the world. When the company went public in 1992, it modernized the chicken again and changed the corporate name to Sunnyhen Foods Inc.

. . .

Costello had seated himself opposite Dempsy with his drink and a folder stuffed with papers.

"I've got some more good news."

Dempsy took another swallow of bourbon and waited. "The Chinese have gone silent. Berch & Kohen think that after the President's TV speech, Beijing will suspend talks until the American Ambassador's speech to the UN," said Costello.

"What do you mean our lawyers think! Don't those crackers know. God knows we pay them enough," growled Dempsy. Costello smiled, for he knew how much Dempsy hated lawyers.

"And two other Washington bulletins. I talked to Bentwill. Their advice right now is to keep the press out of any of our farm factories, particularly the television media. No interviews or comments, except to say that your concerned for your employees and, as an American, for the nation's food supply."

"That's stupid. What would the Chinese think if I made a public statement like that? What's the other bulletin?" asked Dempsy skeptically.

"Three of the senators that we thought were in our pocket have gone off the air. The President's speech has spooked them. They're telling The Eastberry Group that they can't push for any action on the bill until this whole chicken crisis resolves itself, and that could take months."

Dempsy groaned in disgust and then grunted, "They all want

to get reelected, love our money and are chummy-chummy, wink-wink, until they have to step up to the plate." One of the senators was on the Senate Agricultural Committee and the other two had strong connections in the Department of Agriculture.

"That Senator Frattini thinks the sun comes up just to hear him crow. Get Eastberry to tell all of them no action on the bill equals no funds to get reelected. It's that simple."

There are over 12,000 registered lobbyists in Washington, but only about a dozen that that have a real clout to make things happen. They mostly represent America's large corporations involved in government relations. The Eastberry Group was one of them and Sunnyhen Foods was one of their largest clients. On their staff, working on the Sunnyhen account, were two former undersecretaries of Agriculture and a former Kentucky Senator.

Bentwill Communications was one of Washington's biggest public relations company, cynically referred inside the capital belt as "bent communications" for their ability to "bend and spin" a client bad news item or "put it to sleep" in the media.

Bentwill earned most of their fees keeping Sunnyhen Foods out of the media spotlight and with good reason. With ninety-two poultry plants, at any one time Berch & Kohen lawyers were always somewhere in America defending Sunnyhen lawsuits related to air and water pollution from processing plants, or undocumented workers on some production line, or false labeling on the overuse of antibiotics, or the dumping of untreated chicken droppings.

Arguing the case on chicken droppings was a losing battle with the Federal Environmental Protection Agency. Each year, America's factory farms' chicken droppings were more than three times the human waste produced by the entire US population, and Sunnyhen Foods was responsible for the lion's share. Sunnyhen's corporate fines and penalties usually averaged about twenty-one million dollars a year. Dempsy did not put all his PR eggs in one basket. The sunny side of Sunnyhen Foods was handled by EventsBuzz, a hotshot Hollywood public relations and events marketing organization. They managed Sunnyhen's program of generous donations to nonprofit organizations, mainly athletic equipment and player's uniforms to over 350 colleges and high school teams, plus immediate response donations of Sunnyhen Foods to any national disaster area. Good corporate citizenship was also fostered by local fund-raising Sunnyhen barbecues in the twenty-four states in which they had plants, and their annual non-profit "Master Barbecue" during the Augusta Masters Golf Tournament was a favorite city event.

In Hollywood, EventsBuzz were masters at getting product placement in feature films and TV series, or paying producers and writers to set scenes with Sunnyhen billboards in the shot. Implied testimonials were another of their specialties, paying current movie stars and celebrities to be cooking or eating Sunnyhen products when "informally" photographed domestically in a homey family setting.

Under their management, the Sunnyhen Foundation funds arts programming on PBS, supports the Augusta Museum of History, contributes to the Morris Museum in acquisitions of Southern artists, and gives generously to the Augusta Ballet and Augusta Symphony. The Foundation, also liberally endows Georgia Regents University, Dempsy's Alma Mater. Both Dempsy and Costello firmly and rightly believed that their corporate citizenship endeavors benefited and enriched the communities they reached, and were committed to it.

When Dempsy built the Dempsy Building on Broad Street in 1998 as Sunnyhen Foods' new headquarters, he insisted that it be two stories higher than the eighteen story River Place Condominiums, then the tallest building in Augusta. Adding to the height, two tall halyard flagpoles flutter the Stars and Stripes and the State of Georgia's official flag thirty feet higher, and can be seen for miles, especially when floodlit at night.

The top floor is Dempsy's office and apartment with swimming pool and private elevator. The five floors below him are the divisional head offices and corporate home of marketing and advertising, finance, and employee and investor relations. The twelve floors below those are a combination of luxury condominiums and professional offices.

It is the first and second floor of the Dempsy Building that is known and loved by the public, for these two floors house "Sunnyhen World", a poultry pavilion that draws thousands of visitors every year and is one of Augusta's major tourist attractions.

Designed by former Disney theme park "imagineers", it features a small 3-D theater, an eclectic collection of folkloric chicken items, and a wall of signed photos of famous personalities with "Emma", the Sunnyhen chicken. Emma was the marketing creation of EventsBuzz. Emma is a popular girl's name in Georgia, and a series of "The Adventures of Emma" coloring books, as well as statues, trinkets, T-shirts and silly hats could be purchased in Sunnyhen World. In addition to a corporate and product web site, EventsBuzz produced an interactive web site of Emma's adventures targeted toward children and driven by the producer's creative mantra that "if you teach the little bastards to love Emma, they'll grow up to eat her."

Collected over the years, "Pysanky" – beautifully colored Ukrainian Easter eggs – and a collection of egg art from the International Egg Art Guild, surrounded a Faberge Czarist egg valued at over nine million dollars. The first floor was home to *The Red Barn Diner*, a rustic farm theme restaurant featuring traditional Southern and Georgia egg and chicken dishes. Locals claimed that the restaurant's hominy grits and redeye gravy was the best in the state. The restaurant's chickens and eggs came from special flocks raised at Sunnyhen's research farm.

In a partnership with a local dairy company, the restaurant's signature dessert is an "Emma Sundae", a large vanilla ice cream egg with an orange sherbet yolk, served in a nest of yellow "straw" candy. It was so popular with children that Sunnyhen licensed the concept and character to the local dairy, and packaged "Emma Sundae Eggs" were soon appearing in the freezers of Southern supermarkets.

Outside, on Broad Street's wide sidewalk in front of the entrance, a life-sized bronze statue of Boleslaw Dempski – Polish pioneer, Civil War Patriot and founder of Sunnyhen Foods – stands on a polished marble pedestal. In his left hand, he holds out a golden egg in his palm. On the marble base, a bronze plaque commemorates how the young immigrant had given his chickens to Augusta's Confederate Army.

. . .

Dempsy had taken off his sports coat and was sitting in his shirt, nursing his bourbon and gazing at *Le Coq* – one of Picasso's 1938 cubist paintings of roosters – that dominated the wall behind Costello's back. Purchased in 1992 – outside of his stationery – it was the only thing in Dempsy's office or apartment that hinted on how he made his fortune. He was wondering what it was now worth, when Costello's voice snapped him back to reality.

"We've got enough chickens for two, maybe three weeks, and then that's it. Labeled chicken products maybe four. As for eggs, four weeks also." Costello paused, and then continued, "Nothing. There's nothing coming down the line. We're going to have to start laying people off. And that's in the thousands."

Dempsy's strong Slavic features winced before replying in a tone tinged with sadness. "When the Chinese hear this – and they will – there goes a five billion deal."

Costello let the moment hang in silence before quietly continuing. "Shares are continuing to fall. Our Investor and Shareholder Relations people are swamped and drowning in e-mails, cell phone calls, faxes and even people turning up on the fourteenth floor, including reporters. Everyone wants out."

For the past five years neither Dempsy or Costello ever visited any one of their ninety-two farm factories. Each factory had its own independent general manager who ran the factory in his way, answering to home office only in matters of facility improvements, operating costs and profit objectives. If general managers met or exceeded their objectives they were rewarded with handsome bonuses. If they got in trouble with Municipal, State or Federal authorities, they were on their own, paying fines out of their own revenue. Three managers had been convicted by the EPA, fined and sent to prison for two years each.

Long ago, Sunnyhen Foods had erected a legal firewall between the plant's actions and the corporation. This tactic kept the problem local and absolved them from national condemnation. It also kept any fines or penalties lower, appropriate to the laws of the municipality or state.

Sunnyhen Foods had its own breeder operations. In warehouse-sized sheds, living most of their lives in darkness, millions of breeder chickens were kept in cramped "nesting" confinement, their sensitive beaks cut so that they won't peck each other out of frustration and stress. Cruelly induced to produce fertile eggs for hatching in a hatchery, they lasted about eighteen months, before becoming "spent hens". Now too worn out to sell, many suffering from lameness and heart conditions, they are usually shipped off to become chicken soup or canned cat or dog food.

Their chicks don't last that long, the males living only minutes. After birth, hatched chicks were grabbed by workers called "sexers" who could study the infant and in seconds determine if it were male or female. Male chicks have little value to Sunnyhen Foods. Each year their farm factories slaughtered over fifty-two million male chicks by grinding them up live and fully conscious in a "macerator". They could have gassed them or killed them on "electric kill plates", but the macerators were the fastest and most economical methods.

Sunnyhen Foods was one of twelve factory farm companies that together now produced ninety-eight percent of the nine billion chickens that Americans consumed every year. Provided with the birds, feed and technical advice, over 6,480 contract farmers raised chickens for Sunnyhen Foods. Crammed into massive windowless sheds in groups of thousands, these normally social birds, beaks sheared, peck away at each other in fervid frustration. Dosed with drugs to make them grow faster, after thirty-five to forty-nine days on these farms, the hens have reached an often obese weight and are trucked back to Sunnyhen's process plants.

Sunnyhen's processing plants were like a modern assembly line in reverse. Whereas parts were brought together in a progressive system to produce a finished car to roll off an assembly line, Sunnyhen did it backwards with killing efficiency. First the live birds were leg shackled upside down and hung on a rail that moved them through a bath of electrified water that "humanely" stunned them before they moved on to a mechanical blade that cut their throats. After being bled, the dead birds were then stripped of their feathers by immersion in scalding hot water. The chicken carcasses traveled down a disassembly line, taking the bodies apart in an orderly manner for further product processing. It was a cost-effective operation that kept their products competitive.

Sunnyhen Foods operated thirty-four egg-laying farms. On these farms fifty-six million hens laid approximately fifteen billion eggs, about one fifth of the seventy-seven billion eggs laid by America's 250 million hens each year. Sunnyhen's egg-laying hens are not contentedly cooing and clucking in soft straw nests as their advertising seems to suggest, but are imprisoned by the tens of thousands, crammed in wire "battery" cages, as many as ten birds in an 11 x 18-inch space. Unable to freely move and constantly standing with their beaks cut to prevent frantic pecking, they are egged on to maximize their egg production by constantly manipulating the light to trick them into laying more eggs than nature intended.

After two years and no longer able to lay sufficient eggs – their bodies now withered and exhausted – they are carted away to the slaughterhouse. Too emaciated to ever be labeled a plump Sunnyhen chicken in any supermarket cooler, their flesh ends up as animal food and canned boneless dice meat, much of which goes to the National School Lunch program.

. . .

Dempsy had returned to gazing at his Picasso rooster. Costello, scanning the e-mails spread across the glass coffee table, had been reading out the dismal details from company reports coming in. Looking up, he noticed Dempsy was somewhere else, his eyes focused on something behind Costello.

"We're going to have to call a director's meeting. Harold, are you listening to me? Where the hell are you? I said we're going to have to call a director's meeting."

Dempsy's blue eyes lowered to focus on Costello. "I never did like that damn rooster?"

"What the hell are you talking about?"

"The rooster behind you. I never did like the damn thing."

Costello shifted his body, and turned to look at the painting behind him. "The Picasso?"

"Alice bought it on our first trip to Paris. I'm going to get rid of it."

"What about Alice?"

"She never comes in here."

"You could donate it to the art gallery."

"I week ago I would have. Now I'm going to sell it."

Costello stared at Dempsy. In all the years he'd known him, he'd never before seen him on the verge of tears. Slowly Dempsy raised his right hand and pointed at Costello's reports spread across the coffee table

"Frank, it's a catastrophe. Let's have another drink."

Chapter 19

Two State Department diplomatic security agents and a third older man left little room in the sleek black limousine for Trent and the chicken in its large wicker basket. The limo had picked him up at the West 58th Street entrance of the Plaza. The chicken's basket was in the rear seat next to an agent and it made a low soft cackle as Trent slid in beside it.

"That's the first sound that chicken's made since we left Washington this morning," said the security driver.

"Really?" replied Trent. There was silence in the limo for several blocks until the security driver looked up into the rear view mirror at Trent and spoke, nodding to the older man in the front seat beside him. "This is Arthur. He's going to fix you up."

"Fix me up? queried Trent, not knowing what he meant.

"You can't appear before the General Assembly looking like you do. Everybody in the world will be after you. We're going to disguise you. It's for your own safety and protection. We've borrowed Arthur here from the CIA. He's a disguise master. When he's through with you, your own mother wouldn't know you." Arthur turned around to look at Trent and gave him a warm smile.

"What if I say no?" said Trent.

"I wouldn't if I were you. I don't know what you're going to do with that chicken at the UN, but when you're finished, you'll have a thousand paparazzi up your nose and some crazy chicken farmer out to shoot you. Think about it." It was said matter-of-fact manner, but it scared the hell out of him.

Ceres, who had heard everything, let forth an approving cackling and cooing sound.

"When you put it that way, I guess It's better to be safe than sorry, so okay, but don't make me look like a fool."

"I see you as a professor in his late forties, possibly with shaded glasses," said the CIA disguise wizard.

The limo was now rolling into the underground garage of the UN building. Trent had caught a fleeting glimpse of the curious crowds penned behind police barriers along First Avenue. Some of them had signs, but the limo was moving too fast for him to read them.

They pulled up in front of an underground elevator flanked by two UN security guards. The party climbed out of the limo to meet a waiting UN official, and the grim little group, after polite courtesies, was ushered into the elevator. It rose in silence, holding five humans and one chicken in a basket. Trent noticed that the CIA man was carrying what looked like a large black legal briefcase.

When the elevator stopped, the group moved down an empty carpeted corridor to an equally empty small VIP lounge. Both had been sealed off from prying eyes. Throughout this whole transportation exercise, no words had been exchanged between Trent and the chicken.

"Sit down, let's take a good look at you," said the CIA man. "Yes, we'll give you an academic image. Could you take off your tie, put it in your pocket and then button your collar." Trent did as he was told.

In fifteen minutes the disguise expert "aged" the natural wrinkles in Trent's face with skillful applications of flesh latex, emphasized the hollows under his cheek bones with a subtle shadowing, and then applied a natty mustache and spade-shaped goatee to his chin with spirit gum. From his magic briefcase he produced several wigs, selecting one that was curly and flecked with gray. He popped it on Trent's head, securing the front hairline with more spirit gum.

"I think I'll add a small mole on your left cheek. We don't want you to look too perfect. I haven't got time to do anything with your eyes. Their too young for the rest of your face. So what we'll do is wear these tinted glasses, They'll hide your nice baby-blues. Finally, this clip-on bow tie completes the picture." He held up a mirror to Trent's face. He couldn't believe it; he'd been transformed into another person and the feeling was eerie yet exciting. The chicken had watched this makeup magic with keen interest. Trent stood there and wondered what would happen if this incredible chicken in front of him decided to suddenly stay mute, or worse still, if he were to just as suddenly lose his gift to translate its cackling, clucking sounds.

They passed through a tall redwood veneered door and found themselves behind a small curtained wing of what appeared to be the stage of an enormous theater. It took several minutes for Trent to realize that they were backstage in the newly refurbished General Assembly Hall, behind the massive wall slab that held the lofty symbol of the United Nations above the Secretary-General's green marble desk and the matching speaker's lectern below it. On either side of the UN symbol, a giant LED flat panel TV screen presented a large image of the speaker lectern. He could hear the coughing and shuffling of the delegates and could see a portion of the curved Assembly Hall that fanned out from the raised speaker's platform.

Glass walled booths overlooking the Hall held interpreters and UNTV broadcasters, cameras and photographers. The interpreters would simultaneously translate proceeding into the six official UN languages: Arabic, Chinese, English, French, Russian and Spanish, while via satellite, UNTV would feed the world's television networks.

From its beginning in 1945 with fifty-one nations, the UN had grown to now have 193 member states and this morning every one of its more than 1,896 seats was occupied. The public gallery at the back had been limited to just 172 seats. These were occupied by representatives of The World Health Organization, The UN Food & Agricultural Organization, The Word Bank, The International Monetary Fund, The Center of Disease Control and the US Department of Agriculture.

The lisping Brazilian voice of UN Secretary-General Pedro Silveria had called the extraordinary meeting into session and was now calling upon the American UN Ambassador, John Skillet, to address the session. Trent, cradling the chicken in his arms, could hear polite murmurs as the popular Ambassador made his way to the speaker's rostrum, but his partial view was now blocked by two UN security guards who had moved in front of him. The security guards wondered what the hell a chicken was doing in the Assembly Hall, but they had their orders and said nothing. Trent could sense that the American

Ambassador had reached the podium when the murmuring subsided and the Hall gradually settled into silence.

The Ambassador stood rigidly behind the lectern, then turned to glance up and back at the Secretary-General seated above him. "Mr. Secretary-General, I would first like to convey the earnest and sincere appreciation of my President and my government for your immediate response to our request for this urgent and unusual General Assembly session. Your confidence and trust in the incredible reason behind our request will be justified – in spite of the many – and may I add – false rumors circulating as to our reasons, that is, the real and true reasons of the United States to call this Assembly."

The rustle of the Ambassador's notes sputtered and crackled over the Assembly sound system. He paused a minute to look out into the global gathering before him, and then continued. "Throughout the history of the United Nations, this Assembly has witnessed many momentous world events within this great hall that have tapped our collective abilities to the limit – events which have often taken us to the brink of confrontation – events which have both challenged and ennobled our common cause, proving that the brotherhood of humankind, through the United Nations, can resolve and control our different destinies with mutual respect – if we meet and work together in this great world forum."

The assembly was packed with its full representation of all member countries. The Ambassador paused to sip a glass of water and clear his throat before continuing. "Today we are faced with perhaps our greatest universal and international challenge. It is a challenge that transcends all political, social, racial and economic factions represented here. It is a challenge that can affect all of us in terms of life itself – greater than economic and energy resources – it is the challenge of Food!

"I need not tell you of the catastrophe that has befallen the poultry industry of the United States and Canada. It is monumental. It is not, as some have suggested, a political ploy, a Machiavellian plot, or a terrible misadventure by our scientist. It is a confrontation – an unexpected confrontation – an unexpected confrontation between humans and chickens. And, if not resolved, it will be global." There was a buzz of surprise and disbelief from the Assembly members in response to the Ambassador's statement. He waited for his astonishing warning to sink in before continuing.

"And now I must tell you something that will startle you. That you will find unbelievable, absurd, that contradicts any and all human reasoning." He paused for dramatic effect. "My President has had a long and arduous discussion with – a chicken!"

There were gasps of surprise mixed with giggles, laughter and outrage at such a tasteless joke; that such an outrageous and fatuous statement would be uttered from the podium of the United Nations by the respected American Ambassador.

The American delegation sat there in shock, for in the entire General Assembly Hall, only the Secretary-General knew in advance what Ambassador Skillet would announce to the delegates. The Ambassador put up his hand to quiet the Assembly and waited before he continued, every word carefully measured and spoken in a slow deliberate tone.

"It is the chickens that have caused this poultry crisis through their collective will." There was another rumble of disbelief from the delegates. "While discussion with the chicken was open and frank, the outcome has not been satisfactory for either side and the implications, my President realized, were of a universal nature. We immediately recognized our responsibility to the United Nations to terminate unilateral discussions with the chicken and to bring this most crucial matter to the attention of this Assembly.

"In doing so, we must emphasize that this is a potential global crisis that we share. The universal importance of chickens to our food system has also been recognized by the World Council of Chickens, an international body new to all of us, but nevertheless existing. They have sent their delegate representative to put forward their position to the Assembly. The position which they will put forward is not privileged foreknowledge to the United States government, and we look forward to its presentation with the same openness that we believe the rest of this Assembly also shares."

Ambassador Skillet turned back once again to address the podium above him. "Mr. Secretary-General, I do not think that there is any more that my government wishes to comment on at this time, except to state that we shall listen in good faith and act, as we believe we always have, for the interests and the betterment of all peoples – and all things on this finite planet that all living things share. Thank you Mr. Secretary-General."

The American Ambassador then collected his brief notes and slipped them into a green file as he turned again to acknowledge the Secretary-General behind him. He moved quickly from the rostrum to return to his delegation. The Secretary-General waited until the American was seated, then leaned forward, grasping the desk microphone in front of him with both hands. He spoke slowly and deliberately, his Brazilian accent ornamenting his excellent English.

"This is a momentous moment in the history of the United Nations. Never before has an animal addressed this Assembly. I ask all members to observe the dignity and protocol offered to all speakers to this Assembly."

The Secretary-General then cupped his hand over the microphone as he leaned over to engage in a few whispered words with the President of the General Assembly. He straightened back up, removing his hand from the microphone and announced, "The Secretary-General now calls upon the Delegate Representative of the World Council of Chickens to address this Assembly. It is understood that the chicken representative will address its remarks through a human translator at the podium."

Almost immediately Ceres pushed its talons into the stomach of Trent, propelling itself out of his arms onto the floor. Before either Trent or the security guards could react, it had reached the edge of the stage, hopped up the three carpeted steps and was now strutting out into the view of the General Assembly. The chicken moved slowly, conscious that every human eye in the Assembly was watching it – or its gigantic image on the two TV screens. Its white feathered body moved regally across the dais toward the speaker's lectern. There was a growing buzz of excitement throughout the Hall as delegates started to rise from their seats, straining for a better view of the small white Plymouth Rock hen strutting across a field of blue carpeting

When it reached the lectern, the chicken spread its wings and fluttered up in one gentle graceful movement to perch beside a battery of three slim microphones. The hidden lectern lamp acted like a stage light to reflect itself on the whiteness of the chicken's breast feathers. Slowly the chicken settled itself, ruffling its great tail feathers and tucking in its wings. It stared down at the delegates and waited as they, in a bewilderment of nervous giggles and remarks, slowly sat back down.

Trent was immediately pushed onto the dais by the security guards. He moved quickly, self-conscious and uncomfortable in the makeup, his eyes avoiding the sea of faces before him, as he crossed the dais to join the chicken. He stood there, waiting for some sign. The chicken turned to look at him, nodded, then craned its neck forward and began to utter cooing and cackling sounds which were seized by the microphones and amplified in screeching intensity throughout the Hall. Trent began to translate, moving closer to the nearest microphone so that his voice rode over the chicken's cackling through the sound system.

"Mr. Secretary-General and humankind delegates, I have the honor to address you as the chosen delegate of the World Council of Chickens. The World Council of Chickens represents all of the chickens now – and in the future – on this planet. As such, we do not recognize your geopolitical divisions of the earth's land and oceans. We recognize only Nature."

The chicken paused, and then continued, "I am an individual chicken with no lasting importance to this Assembly, speaking solely for the twenty-one billion chickens who populate this world all too briefly. I shall be here this one time only."

. . .

In their Plaza suite, Janice was watching the television intensely, waiting for Trent's appearance. Instead a gray-haired goateed man was translating the chicken's speech. Who was this man and where was Trent? Then it hit her. His voice gave him away. It was Trent in disguise! What a brilliant idea to keep his true identity secret. Now she watched with even greater interest, smiling to herself and looking forward to teasing him on his premier performance before the whole world.

Less than ten minutes away from Janice, another woman in a room in the Helmsley Park Lane Hotel was also watching the UN session on television. Aurolyn Turner – though not registered by that name in the hotel – couldn't believe what she was seeing and hearing.

. . .

By now the chicken had reduced the volume of its voice and backed away from the microphones, directing its sounds toward Trent for translation. Trent's voice, in turn, was being instantly translated around the world into several dozen languages. The chicken was spurting out its speech in short staccato sentences, allowing Trent time to accurately translate each thought.

"For centuries you humans have lived in balance with each other and with the living things of the earth and of the oceans. In that balance, we, a fowl of the earth, have played our part. Like you, we evolved, multiplied and endured the sometimes cruel but honest balance of Nature.

"We accepted our fate and took our place in the chain of predators. We ate and allowed ourselves to be eaten. We marched down the road of evolution with other species – including you – knowing and accepting our part in the endless cycle of life and death. But then we faltered. We allowed ourselves to be domesticated by you. In that act of domestication – which is an act of animal slavery – we doomed our species to a life of eternal breeding solely for you to kill and eat us. We became the only 'domesticated' animal you eat before they're born and after they've died."

The chicken halted in its remarks, dipping its beak several times into the water glass left by the American Ambassador. It raised its head to look down upon the silent Assembly and continued.

"You have imprisoned us with your technologies of death. Your greed we tolerated when it was directed toward your own species, be they white, black or brown. We accepted it as a brute part of your animal culture; the fact that of all the animals on this earth, only humans are their own predator. But your greed has spread beyond itself. It has distorted and unbalanced all other forms of life: forms which have an equal right to this planet, and which are necessary for you to survive upon it.

"You have wiped out whole species of animal and marine life, and we can see no end to it. You have consumed the resources of this world and polluted it in your selfish consumption of more and more.

"Those that you have not decimated, you have domesticated, breeding them in unnatural forms to suit your purpose. You have done this through massive and modern industrialization in the frantic need to feed your exploding and undisciplined populations.

"You are breeding yourself at such a speed that it can only destroy this world, and you must recognize the limit. Your vast factories of death systematically birth and butcher us by the millions every day. As 'animal slaves', you experiment with us, searching for ways to fatten our bodies and enlarge our eggs, scientifically hatching us into shorter lives through your metal incubators, then castrating and debeaking us to be crowded into your concentration camps ready for your frying pans."

Trent looked out into the Hall. The delegates sat there in dead silence, stone-faced and grim. The bird paused, shaking its head before staring down into its audience.

"To you we are not equal living things with our places on this earth. We are 'animal agriculture' – a consumer commodity – with our proper places in your stomachs, to be programmed down your throats without a murmur. We are sub-animals: food to be fried, boiled, broiled, boned, barbecued, steamed, stewed, pressed, diced and packaged. Our embryos are shirred, scrambled. fried, poached, eaten raw and mixed hundreds of ways into thousands of your food recipes. To feed you we must out-populate you on an ever- shortening terminal calendar."

Trent's eyes moved from the silent Assembly to the chicken. Its whole body was quivering with tension and its outstretched neck projected a tiny head bobbling with anger.

"You persist in this madness, knowing that your own world food authorities have almost completely written off 'animal agriculture' as a sustainable food source for many of your developing countries and as a long-term food source for your world in general. Your petroleum shortages cause you fertilizer shortages, which in turn, cause you grain and cereal shortages. It is a diminishing cycle. Soon, you will no longer be able to afford the luxury of converting field crops to feed animas for human consumption.

"You worship your technology. You believe it will solve everything: that through it, you can manipulate Nature. Well you have, but in the wrong direction. Your reckless use of it to relentlessly consume more and more in an ever-increasing world population has caused droughts, floods, raging wildfires, torrential rains, atmospheric pollution and the mutation of new and deadly diseases. I believe you call it Global Warming. You have abused and injured weather to a point where there may be no return, forgetting that in the long run weather is the true farmer of food. Without it there is none.

"Your scientists know that animal production is a very inefficient way to feed populations compared with consuming plant products, yet you ignore this fact. Your ever-increasing world population is quickly reversing a once favorable food balance. You are doomed upon this path you choose. You in this General Assembly represent over seven billion people on this earth. According to your own UN Food and Agricultural Organization, we chickens are almost twenty-one billion at any one time, or almost three per human. Your own UN says that you could be almost ten billion by 2050, over seventy percent living in cities. Think about it, you'd need to raise and slaughter almost fifty percent more chickens just to stay at your present rate of consuming us.

"Well, we won't let you. And you cannot continue to force-breed ruminants to consume plant food unfit for you, and then convert it into meat protein. At the rate you're going, your own UN Food and Agricultural Organization claims that global meat production will more than double before 2050. You cannot continue to waste grain and cereals on animals to fatten them for food."

The chicken paused, breathing heavily for a moment before looking over at Trent and then continuing, "There are just too many of you. Humankind has put the natural world out of balance with its ever-increasing numbers, driven to consume more and more, to have more and more, preferring wealth to wellness in life. This finite earth will not be able to sustain your breeding, and you will eventually become an endangered species. You need a world revolution in values – and it must start here. You cannot continue to measure your progress in annual incremental growth. It is unsustainable. We won't allow it. We have the power to destroy ourselves and in so doing, bring many of you to the brink of starvation, turning many large parts of your world into famine areas, disrupting your food patterns and economies, as we have in North America. We – and others – can bring you down through starvation until you turn against each other for the diminishing animal food resources on this earth. All of this we can begin overnight, anywhere we are on this earth. We can do this by refusing to breed, refusing to lay another egg, and you cannot stop us!"

Trent noticed a chilling edge to the chicken's cackling, and could sense the rising emotions and conviction of the fowl's pronouncement by the quivering of its head and the flame in its eyes.

"If you wish to eliminate hunger from the face of the earth, you must live in concert with its elements You must use its resources wisely and share them equitably. Most important, and I say again, you must control your own breeding. You must, through the Food and Agricultural Organization in this United Nations of yours, concentrate all of your sciences and all of your energies on fruits, vegetables, beans, grains and cereals. Hear me! Fruits, vegetables, beans, grains and cereals! They are your only long-term food source. There is no other. You cannot do it overnight, but you must start tomorrow. We will work with you to this transition, but to do this you must change your thinking and your attitudes. We must become a part of this organization of yours."

There was a great sound of surprise and some actual yells of protest. The rumbling continued for several seconds before quieting down sufficiently for the chicken to continue with its stunning proclamation. "You have the mechanisms. You need only vote for changes to your Charter: A two-thirds vote by members of the General Assembly, ratified by two-thirds of the members of the United Nations Security Council. You need only add two words to your Charter to read as follows: "Chapter 2 of the Charter membership, Article 4, Point 1: 'Membership in the United Nations is open to all other peace-loving states and species which accept the obligations contained in the present Charter and, in the judgment of the organization, are able and willing to carry out these obligations.' You need only add the words 'and species'. Let me continue.

"Point Two: 'The admission of any such state and species to be membership in the United Nations will be affected by a decision of the General Assembly upon the recommendation of the Security Council. Surely this is not difficult. If we look at your Charter and the chapter on purposes and principles, these can be easily amended by the addition of the words 'and species', Chapter 1, Article 1,

"Point 3: 'To achieve international cooperation in solving problems of economic, social, cultural or humanitarian character, and promoting and encouraging respect for human 'and other species rights' and for the fundamental freedom for all without distinction to race, sex, language or religion – 'or species.'

"To make this function within your council, you need only change Chapter 4, Article 9, Point 2, dealing with member composition to read: 'Each member shall not have more than five representatives 'of their species' in the General Assembly.'

"In addition to these Charter changes which will allow us to be constitutionally represented, we demand representation on the Third Committee dealing with social, humanitarian and racial discrimination and to the World Food Program and the Food and Agricultural Organization. We also demand that a core animal rights treaty be drafted by this Assembly. You have dithered too long on a so-called, non-binding 'UN Universal Declaration of Animal Rights', or 'Animal Welfare'. We will wait no longer.

"We demand a rights treaty guaranteeing inherent rights to all living animals and that an Office of the United Nations High Commissioner for Animal Rights be established alongside the Office of the United Nations High Commissioner for Hunan Rights in Geneva, Switzerland."

The Assembly sat in silence, stunned at the turn of events and the demands of the chicken. Trent looked up to the Secretary-General who sat hunched in his chair with his head buried in his hands.

"Now listen, and listen carefully. We will give you one month from today to organize and reply to our demands. For one month from today – across North America – we will lay no eggs, nor reproduce." Ceres stopped to let her words sink in, and then added, "And on other continents and in other countries of our choosing, we will lay no eggs or reproduce. In one of America's states, we shall sacrifice ourselves by willing ourselves to death. We do this as a warning to the world.

"Depending on your answers one month from now, we will give you six months from that date to phase out your fowl factories of death. Six months only. During that six-month period, we have resigned ourselves to the continuing sacrifice. We will allow you to consume our carcasses, but there must be more 'humane methods of killing us. We will continue to lay eggs for you, subject to how you comply with the phasing out of your death factories. We will do this for six months, but if you breed us to simply eat us, we shall immediately destroy ourselves. We have the power and we have the will. There is no alternative to our decision. We leave this with your General Assembly to consider. We expect your reply within one month from today on your human calendar. Until that time, there will be no eggs or chicks in North America." The chicken paused, studying its audience. It knew that millions were watching the live telecast of its appearance, and that among those millions, the President of the United States would be watching his television screen in his Oval Office. The chicken then twisted its feathered body to stare at Trent as it continued to speak.

"This helpful human being who has translated my words will no longer be our messenger to this forum. Shortly he will lose his translation ability. In two months we shall speak to this gathering through the lips of another human being from another part of the world to give our message global impact. Some fowl, perhaps some bird of another breed, will next address you from this platform."

The chicken ruffled its feathers, stepping back and stared over the Assembly audience. "My part is now played and my worth is now nothing. I am useless to you. I am grateful for your attention and ask that you consider with grave concern what the World Council of Chickens has, through my interpreter and myself, said to you today. Let me end with one statement which is not a threat but an inevitable certainty."

The entire Assembly seemed to strain forward in anticipation of the bird's final pronouncement, eager and yet nervous to hear what it would say. The chicken, realizing the charged atmosphere of the Assembly, and aware of the television cameras focused on it, reared up to its full height and glared down into the Assembly.

"Humankind, change your ways – or one month from today you will eat your last chicken dinner." The white Plymouth Rock then turned and hopped from the lectern onto the dais carpet.

Turning its rear to the Assembly, it marched past the Secretary-General seated above and proceeded toward the wing from where it had entered. It glanced neither right nor left and moved with the same dignified strut that had heralded its entrance on this platform a half hour earlier.

The Assembly remained silent, awed by this incredible moment of history that had unfolded before them and aware of the implications of the chicken's speech. Some of them rose from their seats to stare in numbed silence as the chicken strutted out of their sight.

Vladimir Baryshnikov stayed seated in the Russian delegation, his mind swimming with the agricultural tremors that an ultimate chicken revolution could have on his nation's food economy.

As the last feathers of the Plymouth Rock hen disappeared from the dais, the Assembly rumbled into an uproar of questions, accusations and concerns. Some were shouting at each other and the Secretary-General began to call for order on the floor. Trent watched the commotion for a moment and then moved from the podium to follow the chicken. He was suddenly mentally exhausted, his mouth was dry, and the excitement of this incredible surreal experience had caused his heart to race and his legs to feel slightly wobbly. He arrived behind the wing and was ushered into the secured lounge just in time to see the chicken voluntarily entering a large wicker basket now held by two security men.

The White House had arranged that following the chicken's speech, it would be secretly taken to a little free-range poultry farm in upstate New York and released into a very small flock of egg-laying Plymouth Rocks to disappear back into its own natural world. The poultry farmer – loyal to the President – had been sworn to secrecy, and had been assured that the introduction of this exceptional and now famous chicken would in no way cause harm to her flock. In any case, it didn't much matter, as her flock, along with all the others throughout the nation, was refusing to produce eggs.

When the chicken turned and settled in the wicker container, its eyes met those of Trent. They looked at each other, and Trent could feel the burning intelligence of the bird emanating from its penetrating stare. He turned his eyes away from it. As the lid came down to safely secure it inside, it cackled in a long low sound that ended in a series of muffled cooing noises.

For the first time since his involvement with this incredible bird, Trent heard only the natural uttering of this chicken. There were no words – no thoughts – no meanings to this bird's sounds in his inner mind. He realized, that true to the bird's predictions, he had lost his ability to understand or translate the clucking of this chicken. It was like the sudden release from a long throbbing migraine headache.

The two security men carefully lifted the wicker basket by its leather handles. Gently, as if carrying a live bomb, they left the little group in the lounge and proceeded down the hall to the elevator that would take them to the waiting car in the garage below.

Trent watched the wicker container until it disappeared through the tall door at the end of the corridor. Ceres had left his life.

It took only ten minutes for the smiling CIA disguise master to remove the makeup from Trent's face. It felt good to be facially free again as he unclipped the bow tie, replacing it with his own, tying in his usual half-Windsor knot. He was free to go, escorted by a UN security guard who led him through the building to the north exit. As he went through the large and handsome nickel and bronze doors, he neither noticed or cared about the four base-relief panels arranged vertically to present "Peace, Justice, Truth and Fraternity."

Trent hailed a taxi to take him back to the Plaza. It had been a day like no other in the history of the United Nations.

Chapter 20

The taxi pulled up in front of the Plaza and Vladimir Baryshnikov slid his lean body across the seat to unfold himself out of the opening rear door. It was as if he and the doorman had rehearsed their movements. A quick physical motion jackknifed him to attention beside the cab. He paid the cabby and tipped the doorman. Baryshnikov hated New York but loved the Plaza. It was an island of old world elegance in a sea of glass boxes and pushy people. Baryshnikov was convinced that all of America's arrogant "indispensable" people lived in New York.

He stood there for a moment looking out to Fifth Avenue admiring the graceful *Fountain of Abundance* sparkle in the afternoon sunlight. Fifth Avenue vibrated with traffic and people hurrying past the delicate lines of the fountain. For some reason, it always reminded him of a similar and smaller fountain in the center of the dining room in Moscow's Metropole Hotel.

He turned away from the fountain, not knowing it was erected to the memory of the great Journalist, Joseph Pulitzer. He also didn't notice the silver-gray Cadillac with diplomatic license plates parked in front of it as he picked his way through the privileged people and their expensive luggage that littered the entrance steps of the Plaza.

Baryshnikov was early. He knew that. He had relieved himself from his duties at the UN's Russian delegation to meet his date at the Plaza. He headed through the lobby to the Gentlemen's room and spent five minutes adjusting the half-Windsor knot in his tie and combing his thinning hair until satisfied that his balding spot had been artfully covered. Coming out of the washroom, his eye caught the slim figure of a beautiful black woman standing in the hall. She appeared to be idling away time waiting for somebody. Her left leg took the full weight of her body, thrusting out her hip in a provocative pose that curved her lean figure and caused her cream summer dress to cling to the contours of her body.

She glanced at her watch and turned away from his gaze, then sauntered across the lobby and out the hotel's main entrance doors. In Moscow, beautiful black women were as scarce as Faberge eggs – and almost as expensive. Baryshnikov sucked in his breath and then turned and walked into the Palm Court. He would have loved to have followed her but he didn't quite have enough time and besides, duty comes first.

He had made a late lunch reservation for two. The maître d' guided him through the tables to seat him next to a tall green palm plant that stretched and fanned up towards the luminous domed yellow-and-green skylight high above it. Baryshnikov informed the maître d' that he was expecting a lady to join him. The maître d' glided away to be immediately replaced by a waiter. It amused Baryshnikov to order a double Black Russian, warning the waiter that it must be made with genuine Moskovskaya vodka, his silent support to Russian export.

The heart and soul of the Plaza was The Palm Court. It blended the subdued chatter of exquisitely dressed people with the soft notes of a piano, bathing the court in a dulcet hum of sophisticated richness. Baryshnikov knocked back his Black Russian, caught the waiter's eye, and indicated a refill with a swirl of his finger. The warmth of the drink in his body caused a pleasant glow to his senses, and he sat there assessing and appreciating his surroundings.

This court always made him feel good and somehow stirred his emotions with its fleur-de- peche marble columns, its marble caryatid figures, and its walls accented with a giant order of polished pilasters, topped off with gilded bronze capitals. All of this was reflected in the tall mirrored arches around the court, creating a kaleidoscopic vision that seemed to go on into infinity. Baryshnikov sipped at his second double Black Russian as he drank in the classical ornamentation.

His mind conjured up the elegance of the Czarist regimes, comparing the atmosphere of The Palm Court with the opulence of a smaller room in The Grand Kremlin Palace that had a similar color palette of French blue, marigold yellow and ivory. He then thought of the Imperial eggs. He could see the white enameled egg presented by Czar Alexander III to his Czarina. He could remember this display in the Kremlin Armory. It leapt vividly to his mind: a large white enameled egg created by the genius of Karl Faberge. It opened to disclose a golden hen with brilliant ruby eyes, a replica of the Imperial crown on its head. He decided that some forms of decadence had style, and for no real reason, he hurried through his second drink.

Five minutes later he glanced up to see the maître d' approaching with Aurolyn Turner. He stopped half way and she proceeded on her own, passing between the white linen tables with a delicate and disciplined movement that grazed every man and avoided every woman. Baryshnikov rose to meet her and they exchanged smiles of greeting. Aurolyn Turner was 29 years old. She was attractive but not beautiful. Her most notable feature was her bright green eyes and peaches-and-cream complexion. She had a slim torso held up by slender well-shaped legs and a carriage that set off her small breasts. He had met her at an official function when he first came to Washington. Later he discovered that she held an important post as a Deputy Assistant Secretary in the Department of Agriculture with access to sensitive information.

Motivated by his need for agricultural intelligence and his physical attraction to her, he had cultivated their friendship. She had responded and it had grown into an affair. The Embassy gave its blessing and with typical efficiency, now had an extensive dossier on her, in addition to some interesting photos taken in a small woodland cabin in Maryland. As a result of these cabin photos, her Embassy code name in Security and Intelligence was "Raunchy Raccoon".

"You look beautiful," said Baryshnikov, kissing her lightly on her soft pink cheek. He could smell her freshness; something he admired in American women.

"I feel beautiful, specially here," she replied, surveying the court with a quick turn of her head. As she sat down, the waiter took his cue and Baryshnikov ordered another double Black Russian while she settled for a Bloody Mary.

"Wasn't this morning unbelievable? It was quite a shock. None of us knew what Skillet was going to say. What did your people think?"

Baryshnikov gave her his best smile. "Diplomatic secret. What did your people think?"

"I honestly don't know. I watched it in my hotel room. I wasn't part of the American UN delegation, though I thought I would be."

"Let's just say it has been quite a day for the chickens of this world." He broke into a wide grin and she returned his expression with a cheeky popping of her eyes.

"To hell with the chickens darling, or should I say Mr. Shapiro?"

[SEP]"You can't be too careful," he parried, referring to the name he'd used to reserve their table.[SEP] She leaned forward, plucked a cashew out of the small silver bowl and nibbled on it suggestively. "Let's have a wonderful time. I don't have to be back in Washington until tomorrow night."

"Good"." He moistened his lips with a quick touch of his tongue as she reached across to touch his hand. The thought of the evening ahead shone in her eyes and she took off in a cheerful babble of happiness, telling him of her adventures on the flight down, and the red negligee she had spotted in Bergdorf Goodman.

The waiter interrupted with their drinks. She took a greedy little gulp and continued. She had registered in the nearby Helmsley Park Lane Hotel as Mr. and Mrs. Shapiro, double bed, with husband expected later. They could take in some galleries along Lexington Avenue, window shop, have a long French dinner and return to the Helmsley for a nightcap.

He nodded his approval and looked at the soft slender lines of her shoulders and arms. Another night of boundless lovemaking for Mother Russia. Aurolyn's eyes continued to dance.

Just outside the entrance to the Palm Court, a well-dressed couple were discreetly observing Aurolyn Turner's luncheon rendezvous. They were an FBI surveillance team and had followed her in the short walk from the Helmsley Hotel to the Plaza. Aurolyn Turner's affair with Baryshnikov had been under surveillance for the past three months by the FBI, including her e-mails and cell phone.

· · ·

Janice had great fun teasing Trent about his appearance on television, declaring that the gray-haired interpreter was much-more handsome and distinguished than him. He was also much-more sexier with his cute butterfly bow tie. She told him she was leaving him for her newfound lover. Trent took it all good naturedly as he used the house phone to confirm a table for two in The Palm Court.

"Did you know that no one ever succeeded in obtaining the Plaza's secret of their famous chicken soup?" Janice tossed the question off with a smugness in her voice that Trent had long ago come to recognize. She always posed such questions when she wanted to reveal new knowledge. Trent was thankful that they were alone in the elevator.

"What famous chicken soup?" he asked, deciding to play her game.

"The Plaza's Cream of Chicken Soup! Everybody's talking about chickens! I learned all about it from the room service waiter this morning. He's been here for years. The Plaza was famous for its cream-of-chicken soup. It was a guarded secret. But they don't serve it anymore. I thought you'd like to know. I mean, with us here in New York because of that chicken, and staying at the Plaza. Well – well maybe it's an omen or something."

He looked at her upturned face and maneuvered her into the corner of the descending elevator and gave her nose a gentle kiss, and then her mouth "You're the only chicken in this hotel that interests me." He was still tasting her kiss when the elevator came to a buoyant stop at the lobby.

As Trent and Janice stepped out of the elevator, a slim healthy-looking young man observed them. He had been sitting in the lobby reading *The New York Times*, waiting for them. Now as they headed for The Palm Court, he uncrossed his legs, tossed the paper aside and stood up, one hand smoothing the back his of blond hair as the other hand brushed off the paper dandruff from his tailored French suit.

Ping Huo's bright blue eyes followed them as he nonchalantly wove his way through the lobby guests, keeping a respectful distance behind them. He had no trouble in spotting Trent. The resident MSS agent at the Ottawa Embassy had quickly and easily put together a photo file on Trent, culled from legal articles he had written and photos of social functions he had attended. MSS's mole in the White House had passed on intelligence that Trent had appeared at the UN in disguise, and confirmed that he and his woman were staying at the Plaza, but didn't know under what name or room number. He cautioned that they were also believed to be under the protection of two diplomatic security men.

Janice linked her arm in Trent's. She suddenly felt sophisticated, very feminine and possessive. She studied their reflection in the court's mirrors, pleased how her peach- colored dress accented her blonde hair and quietly complimented his Hugo Boss suit and tie.

Huo had watched them enter the Palm Court and be greeted by the Maître d'. The fat little man swayed back and forth like a penguin as he scanned his domain for a table. Suddenly he made a flourishing gesture and led Trent and Janice through the tables. Huo's eyes followed the little procession winding its way past a gigantic floral arrangement and leafy palms to disappear into a sea of nibbling lunchers. He waited for the dapper Maître d' to emerge, satisfied that his prey had settled in that part of the Palm Court. He knew the area where they were seated, but it was difficult to pick them out, what with the reflecting mirrors multiplying the diners and their actions many times over. He waited several minutes, then satisfied that his prey had settled in, he moved through the lobby facing Fifth Avenue and hurried out and down the red carpeted stairs to exchange a few curt words with the capped driver of the silver-gray Cadillac parked in front of the Fountain of Abundance.

"What are you going to say when we get home." asked Janice, sipping on a glass of ice- cold water.

"Nothing. When you were busy in the bathroom putting on that pretty face of yours, I called the office and spoke to Jonathan. Seems they got a call from the PM's office telling them that I was suddenly called upon to handle a vital legal matter of national security, and that I would return home shortly. Oh, and not to ask questions. They also added that the government would pay for my services at my hourly fee basis, plus a handsome bonus. As somebody once said – 'All's well that ends well.'"

She threw him a sunny smile, "That's wonderful, you know —"

"What the hell are you staring at?" Trent asked in sudden surprise.

"You." replied Janice, titling her head toward the man and woman seated nearest one of the Court's regal mirrors. "He looks exactly like you, even in profile. Same build, same thinning hair, same taste in clothes. I'd swear he's in the same blue suit you're wearing and he got the same maroon tie. Even French cuffs. It's uncanny."

Trent turned to glance in the direction of her staring. "Well he hasn't the same taste in woman." Irritated at the coincidence, and annoyed at the almost perfect duplication of his wardrobe, Trent dismissed the incident with a grunt. "Never mind looking at my carbon copy, turn those inquisitive blue eyes in search of our waiter."

Huo had returned to the lobby and taken up a position that allowed him to watch the area where he knew Trent and Janice were seated. An aging matron vacated a lobby chair and he settled into it, popping a root beer lifesaver into his mouth and waited. He objectively weighed the situation. He and his brother Tong couldn't grab and snatch them in the lobby. If they went back to their room, he could ride the same elevator and watch them enter their room. The girl presented a problem. They always scream, but could be dealt with. There was also the question of any security guards. Still, he believed he and Tong could handle them. They'd done it before. But if they didn't go back to their room and instead went outside, he'd have to tail them. And their security guards would be sure to tag along. They couldn't mess this one up. Feng had said it was the most important operation they had ever been given. They knew he would accept no failure.

Vladimir Baryshnikov was having trouble with his English. The Black Russians had imposed a slight slur on his heavy accent. Worse still, his bladder was now pushing an irritating pain into his side and groin. He had to relieve himself. He faked a look at his watch and excused himself from a very mellow Aurolyn with the explanation that he had to call the consulate on a matter that had slipped his mind. He teetered to attention and cautiously picked his way around the tables. The FBI surveillance team rightly assumed that he was going to the men's washroom, and decided not to follow him but stay with their prime target, Aurolyn Turner.

Janice saw him stand up and was again impressed by his resemblance to Trent. He had the same lanky frame and the suit was an identical color and cut to Trent's. As he walked away from her, his loose body movements mimicked Trent's free and easy gait. Her eyes dropped to study the girl he had left, and she thought her quite attractive and fresh looking.

As Baryshnikov came out from the Palm Court and entered the lobby, Huo watched him walk down the hall. He waited to see if he was being followed, then trailed after him at a safe distance, positive he was tailing Trent Marshall.

Baryshnikov went into the men's wash room just as a man was coming out. Huo hesitated, and then decided to go in. The room was empty except for the two of them. Huo took the urinal stall next to Baryshnikov. The Russian stood with his legs slightly apart, one hand against the wall to steady himself while the other hand directed a steady stream into the urinal. Relief spread through his body and he relaxed his stance until the Black Russians, now a pale yellow, had been purged from his system. He stepped back, zipped up his fly and pivoted around unsteadily to face the mirror and water basin. As Huo watched Baryshnikov leaning over the basin, it was quite obvious that he was drunk. Huo took out a small barrel-shaped cartridge from his pocket and fired it into the rump of the Russian.

The movement was practiced and fast: a single fluid action that returned the cartridge to his pocket. It was an air-cartridge gun and the soft plump of its discharge was muffled by the running of the tap water. A small surgical dart had punctured Baryshnikov's gluteus maximus with a power and a pressure that pumped ten c.c.'s of souped-up sodium thiopental into his system. In his drunken state he hardly felt it, and his wet and soapy hands stopped him from probing for the sudden prickly irritation. A fast-acting anesthetic, this version would put him out in about forty-five seconds, and he would remain unconscious for about twenty-five minutes. An inhaled anesthetic agent would be given to him later to induce a twenty-four-hour "traveling" coma. Huo stepped up behind him, smiling at him in the mirror as he put his arms around him. Baryshnikov returned his smile, the last smile he would ever give. Forty seconds later, his body slumped forward, knocking hid head against the mirror and dropping both his hands<SEP>– up to his cuffs – into the soapy water. Huo moved quickly to steady him, pulling him upright to take his sagging body with both strong arms. Holding him with one arm, he pulled the dart out of his rump and dropped it into his pocket.

At that moment an elderly gentleman entered the washroom. Huo gave him a look of boyish embarrassment. "My mate here, I'm afraid he's had a liquid lunch. Too much to drink. He never knows when to stop. He's out like a light. Could you hold the door open? I'll get him through the lobby and into a cab."

The obliging gentleman, turned and held the door open, and in a tone of stuffy disapproval, remarked, "Unfortunately, these things happen. Too bad it happened here."

Huo responded with a weak smile, and took the limp Russian out into the corridor. Huo wore a mask of tender concern as he held him upright and half-dragged and half-steered him through the lobby toward the Fifth Avenue doors. Several people stopped to stare. As he came outside, the doorman helped him take Baryshnikov down the steps and over to the waiting silver-gray Cadillac parked in front of the Fountain of Abundance.

A knot of people watched the actions as Huo and the doorman gently slid the flaccid figure into the rear seat. Huo rewarded the doorman's compassionate assistance with a crisp ten-dollar note, sliding in beside Baryshnikov as the doorman closed the car door. The limousine rolled quietly away from the fountain and into the traffic on Fifth Avenue.

The doorman had noticed that the limousine had diplomatic license plates. UN diplomats get away with murder, he thought, pocketing the ten-dollar tip and returning to take his place on the steps of the hotel.

The capped chauffeur behind the wheel was Huo's brother Tong, and he spoke quickly to Huo, the speed of his Mandarin betraying his nervousness. Both brothers sat calmly but talked excitedly, kindled by the adrenaline rush that flowed through their bodies and heightened their senses. They had worked out several scenarios for the abduction, never expecting such luck, such ease and simplicity when it actually happened. Who knew that their target would be drunk? Abandoning caution, Huo had seized upon the opportunity of the moment, and they had been successful.

Baryshnikov was propped in the back seat, his body against the window frame, his head resting on his chest. with his face turned away from Huo as if looking out the window. His breathing was regular but shallow as his body succumbed to the effects of the drug

The silver-gray Cadillac had now been swallowed up in the stop-and-start traffic flow of New York. The drive took exactly nineteen minutes before they arrived at the entrance to the underground garage on West 45th Street. The limo slid quietly into its reserved space on the second level, pulling up alongside a white Volkswagen van. They turned off the lights, the sudden extinguishing of the car's beams plunging them into a gray dimness. They went to work quickly. Huo got out of the Cadillac. He found the van's keys taped to the underside of the rear bumper and quickly opened the back door to transfer the limp Baryshnikov from one vehicle to the other. Baryshnikov passed through the darkness in a series of lifts and bumps to end being shoved along the van's floor against a rectangular metal container about the size of a large office filing cabinet. The sharp edge of the van's open door scraped his back, pulling his coat and shirt up around his upper torso, temporarily cutting off the circulation in both his arms.

Tong moved quickly around the limo to squeeze himself between the grill of the car and the concrete wall. He bent down into the shadows. There was a ripping sound of tearing as the double-faced masking tape reluctantly surrendered the fake red-white-and-blue Diplomatic license plate to reveal a New Jersey plate underneath. He squeezed out and moved to the back of the car to repeat the tape surgery on the rear plate. Huo was now performing the same operation on the Volkswagen, peeling away the front and back faked New York plates to reveal Washington DC plates underneath. The brothers then got into the back of the van. In the dark interior, they removed the top of the container. Inside it had been padded in key places with foam rubber. A wooden board – that would serve as a bench – was secured to the inside walls. Carefully lifting up Baryshnikov, they folded the lanky Russian into the box so that his rump sat on the narrow bench. Placed around the inside were strong leather belts attached to the container walls. Huo and Tong fished into the container for the loose tongues of the belts. It took ten minutes to securely strap and buckle the comatose frame of Baryshnikov into a permanent praying- mantis position. Tong tucked the forged license plates behind the Russian's trussed legs.

From the container, Huo had removed a gas cartridge attached to a plastic mask that would cover Baryshnikov's nose and mouth. Huo put it in place, forcing the senseless Russian to inhale a strong anesthetic agent that would put him in a coma for up to nine hours. After that time, it wouldn't matter. They put the container top on and screwed it securely in place.

The container top presented the false fronts of four filing drawers. The backs of the 3-inch by 2-inch index tabs above each false drawer handle had been carefully cut away and replaced with a fine white gauze to allow ventilation. In addition, a series of small ventilation holes had been drilled through the back and base. The Russian would not suffocate, but the combination of the drugs, his body heat, and the insulating properties of the foam rubber could conspire – over a long time – to gradually raise the false filing cabinet's temperature to a dangerous level.

The two brothers locked the limo, taped its car keys under the rear chrome bumper, and then drove the van down to the third parking level and parked it, locked it, and taped its keys under the van's rear bumper. Smiling and sure of themselves, they took the garage elevator up to street level and walked several blocks along West 45th Street before Huo called a New York resident Chinese agent to tell him in Mandarin "That his suit was ready whenever he wished to pick it up."

This short innocuous call would trigger the operation to get their captive out of America. Supporting "shallow water" Chinese agents would go to the second level of the garage, "sanitize" the Cadillac limo and return it to the car rental agency in New Jersey. A second team of similar agents would go to the third level of the garage, pick up the Volkswagen van and drive it to a secure parking area on 12th Street, leaving the keys in the van. The moment they left, two "shallow water" agents took possession of the van. As one drove out to the JF Kennedy International Airport, the other one in the back of the van, applied official Chinese Embassy tamper-evident seals on all sides of the false filing drawers, giving the filing cabinet diplomatic immunity from U.S. Customs' search or seizure. Both men had counterfeit diplomatic passports. This entire Department 2 operation was undertaken without the knowledge of either the Chinese Consulate in New York or the Chinese Embassy in Washington.

Air China, the nation's international flag carrier, now flew eighteen flights a week between New York and Beijing and Shanghai. Their fleet consisted of Boeing 747-400 and the Airbus A 340, and the nonstop flight time was between fourteen to eighteen hours, depending on destination.

Both aircraft had been modified to have pressurized and climate-conditioned cargo hold sections for transporting live cargo. An Air

China flight to Shanghai was due to take off that evening, and the two Chinese, posing Consulate officials, shepherded and supervised the loading of the "filing cabinet" into the aft cargo section two hours before takeoff. They returned to New York, turning the van over to another "shallow water" agent to drive it back to Washington and return it to the car rental agency.

Huo and Tong checked out of their New York hotel and took an American Airlines flight to Los Angeles, where they would board an Air China flight to Shanghai the next day.

Arriving in LA in late afternoon, they booked into the Hyatt Regency Hotel, and after deciding that they should reward themselves for their daring achievement, checked out the Chinese restaurant reviews in the LA area. They picked a Szechuan restaurant that sounded good, and after a few drinks in the hotel bar, took a taxi to it. It was a long cab drive but, unlike New York, nothing is ever close in Los Angeles. It was not a fancy restaurant and most of its patrons were Chinese, including several large family groups: a reassuring sign that the food was good and the menu authentic.

They ordered ten dishes to be shared. The waiter was amazed that two white men would have such a knowledge of spicy Hunan cuisine, and so was the chef, for their selection of dishes was an epicurean balance of textures and tastes that few of the restaurant's Chinese patrons would know enough to order.

The two brothers washed their meal down with several Chinese beers, saying very little as they eavesdropped on the gossip and small talk – a mixture of Cantonese and Mandarin – that filled the restaurant. More than satisfied with their meal, and looking forward to returning home, Huo and Tong took a taxi back to their hotel to enjoy a good night's rest before their flight the next day. They did not know that the evening's sumptuous meal would be the last to ever touch their tongues.

"Trent Marshall" would arrive in Shanghai a full thirty-six hours before them and it wouldn't take Major Feng long – after finding a green Russian diplomatic passport in the coat and comparing intelligence photographs – to discover to his horror that his two top agents had made a disastrous, inexcusable mistake that would bring great disgrace to Department 2 of MSS, and a dishonor that might end his career.

They had grabbed the wrong man – a diplomat, a Russian diplomat – and he had not survived the flight. Feng would have to clean up this mess. He would have to make this dead Russian "disappear" permanently, and in due course, also Huo and Tong.

In New York, on the day Baryshnikov vanished, Trent and Janice left the Palm Court and ambled through the entrance facing Fifth Avenue to cross over to 58th Street. At four o'clock, Trent had an appointment at the hospital on 1st. Street for a PET/CAT brain scan. It would only take an hour, then they would be free for the evening. It took over two hours, but Trent found Dr. Himstein interesting and humorous, especially when he said, among other things, that most politicians were brain-dead and didn't know it.

It would be a week later at the Mayo Clinic – after meticulous examination of Trent's scanned images – that Dr. Himstein, an intrepid explorer of the human brain, mapping and navigating its unknown world – would be disappointed to find that Trent's brain was annoyingly normal, fully functioning in all regions, both on the right side and the left side.

Chapter 21

The Garden Ring is a circular ring road around central Moscow. It varies from six lanes to eighteen lanes at it widest. For hundreds of thousands of *Moskvich* commuters, driving on it is a daily run of life and death in the fast lane.

Overlooking the Garden Ring – at the corner of Orlikov and Pereulok Street – sits a massive bunker-like building, wrapped in monotonous ribbons of sightless windows. Built during the Soviet era and red-rust in color, it is a brutish reminder of a Stalinist architectural style designed to serve communism's social purposes. It opened in 1933 as the Peoples Commissariat of Agriculture. Today it is the Ministry of Agriculture of the Russian Federation.

On its fourth floor an enormous office takes up one corner of the building. It is a room frozen in time. Paneled in dark oak, it's sixteen-foot walls are anchored to the ceiling by a border of carved hammers and sickles that march around the room in dusty monotony. A large floor-to-ceiling window – framed by dreary maroon velvet drapes – overlooks the Garden Ring traffic. On one wall a larger than life painting looms over the room: an iconic socialist realism canvas painted by Alexander Gerasimov, Stalin's favorite painter. It portrays two young flaxen-haired farm youths standing bare chested in a wheat field with sickles in hand as they stare stoically into the future. At their feet, a Georgian Tbilisi carpet runner crosses the oak wood floor from the room's double-door entrance to stop in front of a massive green marble-topped desk.

Sergei Barinov sat behind the marble desk and stared at the two people seated before him. Sergei Barinov was Russia's Minister of Agriculture. A graduate of the London School of Economics, he was a protégé of former President Putin, and had climbed the slippery ladder to Kremlin power through political savvy and a brilliant analytical mind.

"Irina, what do our people at Sergiyev say?"

"It's too early. They're flying there as we speak. And live birds are in the air on their way to Sergiyev for examination," she answered.

Irina Oborkin was the Deputy Head of the Federal Service for Veterinary and Phytosanitary Supervision. Sergiyev Posad – a city just outside of Moscow – was the home of the All-Russia Research and Technological Institute of Poultry Breeding.

Barinov stared at the opened files on his desk before looking back at Irina. "We will have to wait. But wait for what? What secrets did Baryshnikov know before he disappeared?"

Gregory Shepkin, Acting Head of the Veterinarian Department, spoke up. "Sir, we've gone through every report from Baryshnikov. Every word. There's not a clue of what he might have known. Our intelligence people tell us that they believe he learned something on the day he vanished. They say that the FBI turned New York and Washington upside down looking for him. Our people believe that his disappearance was the work of the CIA."

Barinov noticed Irina bite her lip and her eyes suddenly watered up, for Baryshnikov had been a close professional colleague, and years ago in university days, much more than that.

It was a grim meeting for the three of them, brought about by the sudden poultry crisis in the Southern Urals: thousands of Russian chickens were refusing to eat, drink or lay eggs and the poultry factory farms there were now in a stage of panic. What was happening in America and other parts of the world was now happening in Russia.

Irina looked at Barinov, hesitated, and then said, "Sir, you should know that I've been told that there's great activity on VK. Panicky farmers are scared to death. They don't know what's happening. They're exchanging messages and sharing images and videos."

"VK will only increase their panic," said Barinov.

An older version of Facebook, VK (VKontakte) was the most popular social network in Russia and Eastern Europe, with over 250 million accounts and more than fifty-eight million daily users. Russian-speaking users around the world, but especially in Ukraine,

Azerbaijan, Kazakhstan, Moldovia, Belarus, and Israel would now learn that Russia had caught the "American chicken disease."

In all of the reports flooding in to Barinov's office, none mentioned the numerous murmurations of thousands of Stumus Vulgaris Poltaratskyi – the Russian starlings that inhabited the Urals.

Next to the Belgorod region near the Ukrainian border, the Southern Urals were the second largest producer of poultry meat, supplying over eighteen percent of the nation's broiler chickens.

When Putin first became President of the Russian Federation in 2000, he vowed to make Russia's agricultural industries equal or superior to those of the West. At that time, poultry disease was an ongoing problem throughout Russia, with over thirty percent of chickens infected with bacteria.

Putin set out to change that. The Russian parliament passed stringent new laws and inspection systems to fight against the spread of salmonella in poultry. Under his orders – executed with relentless efficiency by Barinov – new factory farms, using European poultry technology and processing methods – gradually increased domestic production by over seventy percent, drastically cutting back on poultry imports from the US.

Barinov recently boasted that Russia had now become self-sufficient in its poultry needs, and that by 2025 Russia would be a major exporter of poultry, grandly predicting between 700,000 to 800,000 tons of Russian poultry products for export per year.

Barinov was now looking at the monitor screen on his desk that was feeding him the latest poultry and egg statistics from the Federal State Statistics Service. "As of yesterday, we have enough chickens in the system to fill our national needs for three weeks. After that, who knows? If the chickens refuse to eat or lay eggs, there will be nothing coming down the line."

"Without eggs or poultry meat, other food products will soon be in serious trouble," said Irina, before adding, "No eggs. No bread. Russians can't live without their bread. And then there's Kolbasa. Many of our cheaper sausages contain up to forty percent chicken filler."

"We could always find another filler," replied Shepkin. "Fish or potato," said Irina. "We could make all Kolbasa all-meat. We could freeze the prices and subsidize the food producers". "Let us stick to the chickens," said Barinov. "If these birds refuse to eat they will waste away to skin and bones. We cannot allow that. Their disease is obviously a neurological one – a disease of the brain, not the body. We should slaughter and process them now. Russians are a hardy people. Believe me, no matter what chicken nonsense is being posted on web sites, Russians will eat these chickens."

. . .

In the fall of 2013, then President Putin appeared on the celebrated TV news program "Vesti Nedeli" hosted by Yuri Sodoyov, a popular news personality. During a one-hour interview, Putin discussed a wide-ranging series of national goals. He was relaxed and congenial, answering predetermined questions in simple direct terms, but always with an undertone of "Motherland" nationalism.

In speaking about Russian agriculture, Putin said that no great nation – or nation that wants to be great – can afford to allow others to feed its citizens. In this part of the interview, Sodoyov suggested that Russian cuisine is as much a part of Russian culture as the Hermitage Museum, and that the great dishes of Russia are traditional tastes that should never be debased with foreign food ingredients. Putin agreed.

These casual comments did not go unnoticed by the restauranteurs in Moscow and St. Petersburg. Within a week of Putin's television interview, the menus of restaurants featuring Chicken Kiev or Chicken Kotleti proclaimed that these national dishes were made only with the finest Orloff or Yurlov chickens. One Moscow restaurant went so far as to assert that Chicken Kiev was created by the chef of the Moscow Merchants Club in the early 20th century, and was later given the name "Kiev" by a wandering cook from Ukraine. In the light of this newly unearthed culinary history, the restaurant had now renamed their version "Chicken Moscow".

. . .

Irina nervously wetted her lips with her tongue before speaking. "Mr. Minister, this is Dmitry Volodin, Deputy Supervisor of all Federal egg production."

"So what is our egg situation?" asked Barinov.

The three of them had moved from Barinov's desk to a large conference table at the other end of his spacious office. Volodin had been summoned to report on the state of the egg crisis. This was the first time he was in the Minister's office and he was in awe of its size.

"The chickens are not laying eggs in any of our eleven time zones."

"So how long can we last?"

"My people tell me a month, six weeks at the most." For a country of 143 million people, there were only 450 egg-laying farms, and of those, only 150 operated at full capacity. The state had invested over 300-million rubles in more than 400 poultry factories to modernize and upgrade their production, but they had done so at the expense of the egg-laying farms, most of which were built during the Soviet era.

Unlike the old days, many of the farmers were now in debt, unable to afford feed or electricity that in the last three years had nearly doubled in price. Unable to afford hatching eggs from Western Europe, waves of bankruptcy swept across the smaller egg-laying farms in Northern Russia, causing egg production to drop.

Fearing the inevitable shortages of eggs – and unknown to the Russian public – the government had been importing eggs from Poland and Ukraine and repackaging them in Russian cartons.

In the following two hours, Barinov called in two Deputy Agricultural Ministers, the Deputy Minister responsible for Federal poultry and egg inspection, and four other senior poultry bureaucrats. They sat upright around the conference table, reading out their troubling reports on command, often interrupted by Barinov's sharp and penetrating questions. When he became convinced that he could learn no more from this worried group, he got up from his chair and walked back to his marble desk He stood there for over a minute, weighing what he would say. Then he picked up the redline security phone and called President Kozlov. He would have to explain the unexplainable.

Outside of Barinov's office window on the Garden Ring, it was the peak of the evening rush hour, except nobody was rushing anywhere. It seemed like all of Moscow's four-million cars were bumper-to-bumper, moving slowly under the highway lamps like a shimmering sequined serpent. It would take most drivers more than two hours to get home. Dinner would be at 8:00 pm earliest. And for many of them, the main course would be chicken.

Chapter 22

Upon arriving at Pudong International Airport, Huo and Tong were quickly cleared through Customs and led to a small VIP room. They entered smiling to be met by Major Feng and six burly Ministry of Public Security policemen. Bewildered by this reception and Feng's icy silence, they were suddenly handcuffed. They screamed and yelled, but Feng said nothing, turned away, and left the room for his limousine parked outside. As his chauffeur drove the long trip back to his headquarters, he felt a deep sense of sadness and profound disappointment. It was the last time he would see his two creations: creations that had failed him.

The brothers were put into a black unmarked police van and driven a secret Department 2 prison. Here they were shown the body of Vladimir Baryshnikov and his Russian passport. It was at that dreadful moment of truth that they realized their unforgivable mistake. For the first time in their lives, fear choked their throat and was mirrored in the terrified look they gave each other. Then they were separated and taken to individual interrogation rooms to recall and record every single detail of Baryshnikov's Plaza Hotel abduction.

The interrogation lasted throughout the night into the next day. They were allowed no food, no sleep, no water. On the night of the second day, still separated from each other, they were each given a small bowl of rice noodles in chicken broth and a cup of hot tea, infused with a toxic tasteless mixture of aconite and thallium sulfate.

Within a half hour, both had slipped into a coma, and before the hour was up their hearts had stopped beating.

Wrapped in prison blankets, the bodies of Baryshnikov and the two brothers were taken to the far west corner of the inner prison wall. There they were dumped one on top of the other into a grave dug earlier that day. First in was Tong, then Baryshnikov and finally, Huo. The earth was quickly shoveled back in and tamped down, and in less than forty minutes, all three had "disappeared" from the face of the earth by being put under it.

. . .

Four days after the appearance of the chicken at the UN General Assembly, the Russian Ambassador tabled a formal note to the Secretary of State Brandon on the sudden disappearance in New York of Vladimir Baryshnikov, their Counselor-Agricultural Attaché at the Russian Embassy. The note was diplomatic but stern, and called on the American Government to use all of its national powers to find Baryshnikov and return him safely to their embassy. This unexpected incident took the Secretary of State and the President by surprise, as there had been no Russian defections to America for many years. Secretary Brandon sensed that the Russians suspected that somehow the Americans were involved in Baryshnikov's disappearance, and that it was related to the chicken crisis.

After Baryshnikov failed to turn up at the embassy on Monday morning, the Russian embassy's security people had spent three days searching for him before the Russian Ambassador went to the State Department. They had visited all his known haunts in Washington, discreetly checked out his American friends and the many ladies in his social life, and took apart his two-room apartment in the embassy's residence building. In New York, the Russian Consulate tracked down his last known movements at the UN.

His professional file was spotless; he was a staunchly committed nationalist with a career path that could eventually lead him out of the diplomatic service into the central government. They ruled out any possibility of a defection.

Their final conclusion was that in his sanctioned affair with Aurolyn Turner, she had given him secret information on the chicken crisis that the Americans did not want the Russians or the UN Assembly to know. Whatever it was, they reasoned, it must have been told or given to him at the Plaza Hotel, for he had mentioned – with a wink to a fellow delegate who knew of his many amorous affairs – that he was off to the Plaza to "harvest an American goddess of Agriculture."

The Russians concluded that Aurolyn Turner was "burnt": no longer an intelligence asset. The disappearance of the Russian agricultural diplomat was a troubling concern to both Secretary Brandon and the President. With all that was happening, the President didn't want the Russians – who were always skeptical and distrusting at the best of times – to think that the American government played any part in the Russian diplomat's disappearance.

The White House ordered the FBI to find Baryshnikov. They already had a standard file on him, and assigned forty agents who backtracked his movements. His relationship with Aurolyn Turner had been under scrutiny for some time, since she had access to classified agricultural documents of national security importance.

For the past three months she had been under intense FBI surveillance, and the agents shadowing her at the Plaza Hotel had reported that Baryshnikov had met her for lunch, left the table, and never returned. She had waited for over thirty minutes, was observed to become increasingly distressed, and then left, returning to the Helmsley Hotel.

The FBI began be interviewing the Palm Court staff. When shown photographs, the maître d' could vaguely remember them, stating that they arrived separately. The waiter that served them proved to be a keener observer of the Court's clientele, and said that they appeared happy and intimate, though the man hit the drinks – Black Russians – a little too hard for lunch.

It was the doorman that gave them the first hard clue. He remembered the man who was drunk. He had helped another younger man with blond hair put him in a waiting limo. He was sure it was a gray Cadillac. The young man had tipped him ten dollars. The limo had diplomatic license plates, but it had happened so fast that he never noticed the license plate number.

There are over 2,600 diplomatic license-plated cars in New York City. Most of the cars are black, though some of the African delegates like red and yellow sports cars. There were only three silver-gray cars sporting diplomatic license plate: two of them Cadillacs. All three were tracked down and two of them were not in New York City on the day of the UN Assembly meeting, and the third was in a Brooklyn garage for an engine tune-up. It would take weeks to check out all the registered silver-gray Cadillacs in the greater New York area, assuming the doorman was correct in his identification in the make of the car.

Aurolyn Turner was brought in for questioning, but could provide no information as to the whereabouts of Baryshnikov. She said he just excused himself from their table to make a phone call and never came back. She was told he was a Russian agent and was threatened with charges of treason, fifteen year's imprisonment and a fine of fifty-thousand dollars for collaborating with him.

Under intensive questioning she soon broke down, confessing that she had given her lover highly sensitive agricultural files dealing with economic analysis of food security, long term international crop outlooks and highly classified research on gluten proteins and South American Amaranth crops. She was ordered to hand in her immediate resignation from the Department of Agriculture and that she may have to go to trial. In reality, the government had no desire for an agricultural spy-and-sex story in the media. For the moment, the FBI's search for Baryshnikov had gone cold.

When the Director of the FBI presented the agency's initial report to the President, the President and Secretary of State Brandon decided that the President should call President Kozlov with what they knew, or more tellingly, what they didn't know. The conversation between the two presidents lasted twenty-minutes.

The American President was open and frank, stating that he could offer no explanation for the disappearance of Baryshnikov, or any reasons why he should just vanish. Both Presidents were more than aware of Baryshnikov's relationship with Aurolyn Turner, but it was never brought into their conversation. President Kozlov said very little during their interchange and ended by coldly thanking the President for his call.

Secretary Brandon then turned their attention to a preliminary report from the State Department's Office of Global Food Security. It was not good news. Preliminary figures indicated that the loss of poultry in a nation's food chain would vary from country to country. It was the nations that were the most vital in getting the world back from the brink of another deep recession that would be hit the hardest by the poultry crisis.

America, Russia, China, Brazil, Turkey and India would suffer the greatest economic setback and social disruption by virtue of their population size and consumption of chicken. Many of the smaller countries, where chicken was not a central part of their sustenance pyramid, could turn to fished-out oceans for an immediate food alternative.

Adding to the President's worries, was a growing public anxiety and uncertainty, and an underlying fear that their government was helpless. Secretary Brandon wondered where was the World Council of Chickens, and when and where would their next representative appear? What country would it be, and who would be the new human interpreter? UN Ambassador Skillet, in a closed video conference, reported that delegates were divided in how the UN should respond to the World Council of Chickens' ultimatum. The smaller nations feared that if were left to the Security Council – the permanent Council of China, France, Russia, the United Kingdom and the United States – these powerful nations would put their own interests ahead of other members.

Two days after the President's telephone call to President Kozlov, the Russian Foreign Office declared Winston E. Price, the American Embassy's Minister-Counselor for Agricultural Services, *persona non grata* and he was given forty-eight hours to leave Moscow.

The Undersecretary-General for UN Legal Affairs and UN Council brought together twenty-four of the world's leading professors and lawyers of International and World Law for an emergency meeting at the International Court of Justice, the UN's primary judicial branch at the Peace Palace in The Hague in the Netherlands.

The UN Secretary-General implored them to find a fast legal path to what was quickly becoming a world chicken time-bomb. They had less than one month. They were divided up into three groups of eight, each tasked to consider how to amend the UN Charter to meet the demands of the World Council of Chickens, including the creation of a UN High Commissioner of Animal Rights. This would give the UN three legal draft opinions from which it was hoped a final document could be presented to the UN General Assembly within the one-month deadline.

It was a monumental task for the world's best legal brains to solve under such pressure. The issues of existing treaties and state sovereignty, official legal procedures, precise amendment wording, signature, UN assembly ratification and finally, entry into force, were of staggering complexity. It demanded a creative reinterpretation of the Charter. The added word "species" set an unknown precedent, that in turn, brought about intricate legal arguments whether it should be two and four-footed species only, so as to exclude insects, fish and what one cynical legal mind referred to as the future prospect of "talking trees or a goldfish in a bowl" appearing before the UN General Assembly.

Some argued that a separate but parallel Charter be drawn up which kept the species issue legally restricted to chickens only. This special agreement between human and chicken would be added to *Jus Inter Gentes*, the body of treaties, UN conventions and international agreements that binds nations and states together. This, some counter-argued, meant that national laws to conform would have to be legislated by each UN nation.

One group advocated the creation of a "Supranational Law" patterned like the UN Security Council, that transcends national boundaries and governments, is globally accepted, and could be immediately enforced by a two-thirds majority vote by the General Assembly. Try as lawyers might, the law professors became more and more entangled up in legal jargon and abstract arguments that was doing little to find a definitive solution.

Since the General Assembly meeting, the poultry crisis was spreading worldwide. In China, Africa, Australia, parts of northern Europe and throughout South America, flocks of chickens were refusing to eat, breed or lay eggs. Patterns of chicken rebellion were becoming discernible; they started on the coasts of these continents and then moved quickly inland in successful waves. At the same time, long distance migratory birds were sighted outside their natural migration routes, normal ranges and seasonal movement. In particular, spectacular murmurations of starlings were seen coursing through the sky. Their appearance was not in great numbers, still this unnatural phenomenon was puzzling to ornithologists.

It was Professor Fiona Smyth-Hastings at the Center of Ornithology, at England's University of Stanhope, who believed she might have an answer. In an article written for *The Times of London*, she put forward a thesis that these unnatural long distance migratory patterns and the spreading patterns of the chicken crisis inland might be related. She reasoned that in some manner which man can't comprehend, these birds were carrying messages or instructions to chickens beyond the North American continent. If this were the case, then the concept that birds only communicated to each other by song, sight or body movements had to be rethought. What gave more credence to her theory was that these long distance migratory birds, after resting and feeding, flew back from where they had come. She reasoned that they had been on a mission and this could mean that they would migrate naturally again in season.

If chickens could transmit thoughts to the human brain, Smyth-Hastings postulated it was possible that birds of different species could transmit thoughts to one another through a similar process. She speculated that the avian world might have a sixth sense which man has yet to discover. She cited the cognitive intelligence of starlings and their ability to communicate with each other and possibly with other birds.

Her theory was given more credibility when ACIAR, the Australian Center for International Agricultural Research, reported that a team in the Solomon Islands – on a mission to improve village-based poultry production – witnessed the sudden and odd arrival of large murmurations of Polynesian starlings. The next day not a single village hen laid an egg.

Two weeks after the extraordinary UN General Assembly meeting, Sebastian Heron, a well-known gourmet and food critic in the San Francisco Bay Area, published an article in *The San Francisco Weekly* extolling the virtues of mock chicken that's primary ingredient is soybeans. He reported that he couldn't taste the difference from the real thing and that it looked like the real thing. In his article he claimed that the mock chicken he sampled was tender, juicy and meaty. His article went viral on the internet, and in less than two days there wasn't a single mock or vegan chicken product to be found in any of America's health stores or upscale supermarkets.

Mock chicken was a product made for vegetarians, people with chicken allergies, and for those who had animal ethical concerns, or seeking a healthy alternative. In America's food industry of over one trillion dollars annually, chicken and meats made mainly from soybeans was a mere four-billion-dollar market. After decades of research and development – some of it pioneered by the University of Missouri – vegan chicken could now be made as chicken breasts, grilled strips, nuggets, wings, drum sticks and patties. It could be grilled, pan fried, barbecued, in fact cooked in any way as real chicken. There was even mock chicken soup. High in protein, vegan chicken had zero steroids and no hormones or antibodies that were pumped into real poultry.

Eggs presented another problem. If there were no chickens, there were no eggs. There were already various egg substitutes and replacements on American grocery shelves that could be used in baked goods, and Tofu products were good replacements for scrambled eggs and omelets, but it looked like hard-boiled eggs might go the way of the Dodo egg. However, one company claimed it was working on a substitute hard-boiled egg modeled on the method of the confectionary production of chocolate-covered Easter eggs with their imitation candy yolk and white filling.

The Soybean futures suddenly soared and America's competitive process food companies just as suddenly saw a profitable future in producing vegan chicken and meat products if they could gear up in time to grab their share of a new, unexpected market.

Fortunately, America's soybean crop was second only in size to its corn crop. Along with Argentina and Brazil, America was one of the three largest soybean growers in the world, and the leading exporter of soybeans globally. At present, eighty percent of world's soybean crops was fed to livestock, and especially chickens. If the chickens refused humanity their flesh and their eggs, or reduced their numbers, soybean for chicken feed could be used to produce vegan chicken.

With over 21,000 soybean producers, The American Soybean Association and the Soy Foods Association of America saw a bright new future. Industry gurus predicted that vegan chicken, once mass produced, would be cheaper than real chicken. Environmentalists claimed that switching from animal meat products to plant-based products would be better for the health of the individual and definitely better for the health of the planet. In a poultry crisis of global proportions, soybeans were touted by some as the long-term answer, regardless of the World Council of Chickens.

Other ways of finding a potentially cheap supply of protein were being explored that could help reduce hunger around the world, improve animal welfare and be environmentally friendly. In 2013, lab-grown beef had been developed at Maastricht University in Holland. From stem cells extracted painlessly from a living animal, "cultured beef" had been grown that was close to meat in flavor and texture.

Professor Mark Post, who lead the research, claimed it could eventually replace ordinary beef in the diets of millions of people. Funded by the Dutch government and Google entrepreneur Sergey Brin, the technology was at an early stage, but Professor Post predicted that the meat could be on supermarket shelves in ten to twenty years.

In *Japanese Poultry Today*, an article by Professor AIkioi Tanaka of Niwatori University, predicted that the scientific principles of lab-grown beef could be applied to the growing of eggs on a factory basis from mass cloned chicken embryos. His early research leads him to believe that this could be possible within the next fifteen years.

The chicken crisis was the dominate economic story in *Bloomberg Businessweek*, with reporters covering every aspect of its impact on American business. One small item reported that Sunnyhen Food Inc. and Ling Jiro Poultry Co. Ltd. had halted their negotiations for the sale of Sunnyhen to the Chinese poultry company. The five-billion-dollar deal – the largest foreign purchase of any American company – was not dead, said Sunnyhen President and CEO Harold Dempsy, it was just "sleeping". Washington lawyers for Ling Jiro Poultry had no comment.

Around the world, animal rights activists viewed the chicken rebellion as a vindication of their movement. While made up of different groups with different and sometimes conflicting perspectives, they were united in their fundamental belief that all animals are entitled to the possession of their own lives, and should be afforded the same consideration as the similar interest of human beings.

Rising up together under the banner of Animal Fairness International, they launched a global broadcast, print and social media campaign directed to their national governments and the United Nations. In the America. there were marches on the UN building, the White House and Capitol building. Demonstrators paraded carrying banners and signs reading, "Black Liberation, Woman's Liberation,

Gay Liberation," and below it the larger letters "Animal Liberation Now!"

In Augusta, animal activist demonstrators were picketing in front of the Dempsy Building with placards of the Sunnyhen cartoon logo shackled with a ball and chain around its leg with a word below it reading "Slavery!" as they chanted "Sunnyhens equal Carcinogens!" over and over again.

In Africa, the Chinese Ambassador delivered a formal note to the President of Tumpawie from the Chinese Minister of Agriculture informing him that the joint soybean "plantation" project in his nation was in temporary abeyance due to unfolding chicken events.

In Brussels, European Union politicians and bureaucrats were on the verge of a collective nervous breakdown. Poultry was the second most important source of meat protein on the continent, employing over 673,000 workers. Chickens across the continent were not breeding, eating or laying eggs. The leading poultry producers, France, UK, Germany and Poland, were reporting total industry collapse. To make matters worse, Brazil's poultry industry – Europe's largest supplier of imported chicken – was in free-fall. In Russia things were getting worse. Factory farms were in panic. Russia's largest, the Novorossiysk Poultry Farm, producing over one billion eggs a year, suddenly stopped as its egg-laying chickens sat in their cages refusing to eat. Bird watchers in Russia and across the continent reported murmurations of starlings making unusual patterns in the sky.

The poultry crisis crowded every other world event off the world's television screens, dominated the world's newspapers and magazines, and blared through radio receivers in dozens of languages. It swamped the social media as tens of millions of people reacted to rumors, made predictions, accusations, arguments and suggested dark multinational conspiracies. Worldwide, over nine billion e-mails were being sent every day.

Thousands of people around the globe claimed they could talk to chickens or that chickens had talked to them, but it was all copycat nonsense. Ever since the appearance of the unknown chicken translator at the UN Assembly, investigative reporters, journalists and private detectives were on the hunt for this elusive man.

In New York and Washington, they contacted their usually reliable sources, scrutinized video footage frame-by-frame and interviewed anybody and everybody who had even remotely been near him. They pried, probed, poked around and came up with nothing. For one of the few times in modern memory, Washington was leak-proof.

At the Vatican, the new Pope came out of the kitchen closet to announce that he was a vegetarian, and had secretly been one for over forty years. He prayed for the chickens of the world, citing St. Francis of Assisi's example of treating every living thing with kindness.

Three weeks later, in the leafy Chicago suburb of Palos Park, Janice and Trent got married in her parent's garden. It was a small family wedding. Senator Andrew Morriston was the best man. The wedding reception was a culinary cornucopia of vegetarian dishes.

Chapter 23

"Now doesn't that look handsome. She's a real looker." Buck Travis stood back to admire the Dickert long rifle, a graceful, long barreled weapon that he had just mounted in the glass-fronted cabinet. His wife, Bucky, agreed with a pleasant nod of her head, "I done told you it would look good in there." Pleased with himself and his wife's approval, Buck closed the cabinet door and locked it. They were both standing in a large stucco room that Buck had added to the ranch house twelve years ago when times were good and they were flush with money.

It was bigger than any one room in the ranch house, so much so that from the outside it almost looked as if the house was an addition to this room. And in many ways it was, and all because of Buck's last name and the stories his granddaddy told him when he was a boy.

The room had whitewashed stucco walls with eight large glass-fronted mesquite hardwood cabinets, four on each side wall. The end wall had a library case and bar, also fashioned out of mesquite hardwood. On the wall above the bar, a large Lone Star Flag hung next to a smaller American Stars and Stripes. Below the two flags, in a gilded frame, was a photo enlargement of a sketch of William "Buck" Travis by Wyly Martin. It was the only known portrait of this Texas legend that was drawn during his lifetime, and it held a special place of pride in this room. His image was not alone. In-between the cabinets and at either end of the room, black-and-white archive photos of The Alamo and early Texas scenes of pioneer settlers filled in the white spaces on the stuccoed walls.

The Alamo is the heart and soul of Texas history and the birth of many myths. As a boy, Buck had sat at the feet of his granddaddy, and listened to the legends and lore of how – from February 23 to March 6, 1836 – less than 260 brave Texans had fought to the death against a Mexican army of more than 2,400 soldiers, led by the cruel President General Santa Anna.

Granddaddy Elwood Travis was a great storyteller who had a yarn spinner's tendency to stretch and bend historical truths if it added to the telling of his tales. Among the Texas legends that died at the Alamo were Davy Crockett, James Bowie and the co-commander of the fort, Lt. Colonel William B. Travis. He filled Buck's young mind with imaginary achievements and adventures of William Travis, and that the Travis of Alamo history lived on in young Buck's blood, since their family were direct descendants. Aside from their name and generations on the land, there was nothing to prove this, but there could have been some truth to old man's tall tales, for while Travis was a popular first name in Texas, less than 900 Texans had Travis as a surname in a state with a population of over twenty-six million.

For over 157 years, Buck's family had cattle ranched in Southern Texas on 61,000 acres between what is now Corpus Christi and Brownsville, and he was the fifth generation of Travis's to raise Texas Longhorns on this land. A lot had happened in his lifetime: Houston had mushroomed in size and he hated its skyscrapers and its new smart city ways. He never went there. San Antonio had also grown, but it was his spiritual home and the Alamo was still solidly the same as when his granddaddy used to take him there once a year before the old man got feeble and "funny". He still went with Bucky on an annual pilgrimage to the Alamo, never tiring of looking at the paintings and weapons in the Long Barracks.

Buck was fifty-five years old, a big man with a full head of graying hair topping a tanned face weathered from the Texas sun. He was a good man, a no-nonsense man, a plain-speaking man with a set of values that were straight up black-and white. Bucky was one year younger. Her first name was really Chloe, but they'd been called Buck and Bucky ever since their sweetheart days in high school.

"Will the boys be over this weekend? asked Bucky.

"Saturday," replied Buck. "I was fixin to go over to Isabella's. Is that still all right with you?"

"Well you do that. Me and the boys will sizzle up some steaks." They were both now sitting at the large square table in the middle of their "Alamo" room where the boys would drink their beer, eat their steaks and end the night into the early morning playing "Hold'em", a popular form of poker in Texas.

Most of the boys were also gun lovers, and would spend part of the night admiring Buck's collection and reverently fondling and hefting them. Buck's collection was impressive. All of them were made before 1835 and were as varied as the men that had once fired them. Five of the cabinets contained Dickert long rifles, Pennsylvania and Kentucky long rifles, mountain rifles and two 1817 U.S. Common rifles. There was also a collection of the shorter and plainer Trade rifles, fowlers, and three double-barreled shotguns, any one of which could have been in the hands of Colonel Travis if Buck willed it. It was possible, but not probable, that some of these guns could have been Alamo guns.

The other three cabinets contained paper cartridges and musket balls of the period, two Kentucky pistols, three British horse pistols and a Harper's ferry pistol. The Mexican side of the armory was a collection of foreign-made arms, represented by Brown Bess, a British- made standard arm of the Mexican army, Tower flintlock carbines, a Mexican cavalry favorite, one French long-barreled Tulle, several Baker rifles, a French Charleville military musket and an Escopeta, a Spanish short, smoothbore musket. Three of the rifles had fine Mexican inlaid silver work on the gun stocks. Altogether he had eighty-four antique fire arms.

Buck's collection of "Alamo" guns was for showing, not shooting. He had never fired any one of them, and never would. They were too sacred, and besides, they might blow up in his face.

His shooting guns and live ammo he kept locked in a metal cabinet in their bedroom. That room was home to a Ruger shotgun, two Smith and Wesson revolvers, an M1 Carbine, an AK-47 rifle and a Glock 19 pistol. Lately, he'd had little time to go out on the local shooting range. He was a member of the NRA and a sworn supporter of the Second Amendment Foundation.

Buck knew that he shouldn't have bought the Dickert long rifle, but he had to have it to add to his collection. He knew that Bucky had wished he hadn't, times being what they are and what with the ranch being tight on money, but she didn't say anything and he loved her for that. Even though his surname gave his guns' extra weight, he never wanted real gun experts to come and see his collection, for he feared what they might find. He was right about that. Two of his long rifles were fakes, in the sense that someone had taken parts from partial real guns and put them together to make two whole guns.

They sat there looking at the Dickert long rifle, when Bucky suddenly said, "Isabella said that their clucks weren't giving eggs."

"I didn't know they had any."

"They keep about twenty, pecking about at the rear of the house. Just enough for breakfasts and baking."

"I guess they've got that thing you keep hearing about on radio and TV. Beats me how all the clucks in America could suddenly sit on their ass and not pop an egg. They must be dumber than dirt."

Bucky stared at him and her face took on a little look of sympathy. "All those chicken farmers are facing ruin. They'll lose everything if this chicken thing goes on forever. It's horrible. They'll be wiped out."

Buck looked at her and reflected in a somber tone of voice, "Well, I don't know, and it's all bad – but the Lord never closes one door without opening another one."

"What do you mean by that?" asked Bucky.

"Well the boys are saying that if there's no clucks then everyone will be wanting to eat beef. That means it's the old story of supply and demand. And that should oughta raise the price of our cattle."

"I don't think it's right to think such things. We're all Americans."

Buck sensed that she did not go for what he had just said by the little frown that crossed her face: a sure sign of her disapproval that he'd learned to recognize over the years.

"I should oughta truck up to the bunkhouse and give Eduardo his grub money." She nodded, then gave him a little understanding smile. Buck left the ranch house by the back door and climbed into his Ford pickup truck. He bought it in 2010 and it was faster and easier to get around on his land than on horseback, especially in this hot Texas heat wave. In the cab he always had a .22 caliber "varmint" rifle to protect his livestock from the damn coyotes that seemed to be growing bigger every year. The other gun that was always with him was his nickel-plated holstered Glock, which only left his waist when he was either showering or sleeping.

It was about a five-minute drive up to the bunkhouse on a dirt road running along barbed wire fencing, the Ford pickup leaving a trail of swirling clouds of red dust from the sunbaked, crackled earth road. This was the third year of drought. Some said it was the worst since the Dust Bowl Years of the 1930s. Wildfires and drought had caused the Governor to declare a State of Emergency in 138 of the state's 254 counties. Others said it was part of the man-made Climate Change around the world. Buck didn't know about that. What he did know was that it was costing him more and more to truck in quality hay, water, supplementary protein feed, salt and mineral licks.

As he drove along the barbed wire fence, he noticed that there were about sixty longhorn cows standing in the heat watching the pickup as it passed them. Most of them were dark tan or brown. Over the years, he'd never had a problem with any of them. They were direct descendants of the first cattle brought over by the Spanish between 1493 and 1512, and had an innate gentle disposition that made them easy to handle and herd. They were hardy and self-sufficient, and they were good mothers, productive and protective of their calves.

He parked the pickup and trudged up the dusty path to the large bunkhouse that was partly shaded by a small grove of trees. This year it housed and fed twelve Texas-Mexican cowpunchers, second and third generation single males who moved from ranch to ranch as needed. Their forefathers were *Vaqueros*, cattle herders from northern Mexico, and ranching was in their blood. These days they called themselves *Tejanos*, which was now a name of pride in their Texas heritage.

"Anyone home?" said Buck as he entered the bunkhouse. "In the kitchen," piped up Eduardo. Eduardo was short, overweight and always happy. He was nearing sixty-two and was a permanent part of Buck's family. He was like a father to the young Tejanos, feeding them, looking after their minor cuts and scrapes, and generally keeping the peace in the bunkhouse. He was one hell of a cook and could stretch a food dollar further than any man Buck ever knew when it came to feeding a group of healthy, hungry men. Buck and Eduardo talked ranch-talk for a time before Buck gave Eduardo the grub money to go into town.

"The boys are out in the grasslands doing what you asked them to do."

"Grasslands, That's a laugh. Everything's burned black as the bottom of a frying pan." Eduardo shrugged and then added, "Carolos took one team fixin up fences. Hilberto is doing chamuscando in the sixth divide." Chamuscando was a 17th century Spanish process of burning off the spines of prickly pear cactus so Buck's cattle could eat the cacti pads for fiber and water where there was no grass. After about twenty minutes with Eduardo, Buck stepped out of the bunkhouse to walk down the path back to his pickup. As he did so, the longhorns moved toward the barbed wire fence, lining up along the fence all the way down the path to the pickup. They did it in almost a military manner that Buck had never seen before.

As he approached the first of the lineup along the path, the strangest thing happened. All of them, in perfect unison, began to lift their left front leg and slam it down so that the hoof made a dull thud on the parched ground, raising small clouds of red dust. Together, they began drumming a slow steady muffled beat on the hard earth: a synchronized beat drummed by a chorus of stamping hoofs. Buck stopped dead in his tracks. He'd never seen this before. As he stood there they began to moo. It was a deep-toned repeating raspy mooing ending in a short grunt. It was not loud, but it was beginning to resonate inside his head.

Then something impossible happened. Pushing through their mooing, his inner brain was receiving patterns of words. "Murderer! Murderer! Bloody Beef Murderer! Murderer! Murderer! Bloody Beef Murderer!"

The words were being chanted to the beat of their drumming hooves. It was frightening. The words were exploding inside his head. The shock of it paralyzed him. There was a fire in their eyes of sheer hatred. He could no longer stand it and ran and half-stumbled down the path past them to his pickup. Tearing open the door and jumping in, he started the engine and wheeled around, racing back to the ranch house. In the rear mirror he could see that they had broken their ranks and were now turning away from the fence to lie down on the bleached grasslands.

When he pulled up at the back of the ranch house, he sat just sat there, his heart racing and his hands shaking. Slowly he calmed down, telling himself that it was the heat; that the mind can do terrible tricks on you when you're under stress. He had a dull thumping headache when he got out of the pickup and entered the house. What Buck couldn't know was that across Texas, thousands of longhorns were drumming their hoofs, mooing their strange chant, lying down where they stood – and refusing to budge.

"Is that you?" chirped Bucky from the kitchen.

"Yup," answered Buck.

"How's Eduardo?" There was no reply. "Honey, did you hear me? How's Eduardo?"

"He's fine, just fine."

Bucky came out of the kitchen just as Buck was sitting down at the dining table. "The girls called, they're coming home from university next weekend."

"Good," replied Buck.

"You look tired sugar. Why don't you have a rest before dinner."

"What's for dinner?"

"Steak, with hash browns."

"I don't fancy steak tonight." There was a firmness in his tone. "What else ya got?"

"Well there's beef chili, and I have some frozen lamb chops. You could have those with that hot chili mustard of yours."

Buck looked up at her and said with no great enthusiasm, "I'll have the lamb chops."

. . .

Over 7,000 miles away from where Buck sat, in a land called *Aotearoa* by its indigenous Maori people, more than thirty-one million sheep stood their ground and refused to budge.

New Zealand farmers stared in shock and their sheep dogs circled in confusion as these docile animals formed thousands of tightly packed concentric circles, pounding in unison on the soft green pastoral land with their left front hooves. Their muted drumming resonated through the hills and could be heard as far away as downtown Christchurch. From the air they looked like great white empty dinner plates laid out on an immense green tablecloth.

. . .

Buck could hear the sizzle of the lamb chops frying in the pan. The green-blue earth continued to orbit around the sun.

* * *

189

POSTSCRIPT
Notes to the reader

STATISTICS

Statistics are facts, but facts change with the times. While many of the facts in the story are true, most of the story's statistics are imagined, some based on numbers that have long been out of date since the time of writing.

TUMPAWIE

Tumpawie is an East African country of fiction. It is an imagined Bantu-speaking country patterned after several East African countries that have an Indian Ocean coastline.

SUNNYHEN FARMS

Sunnyhen Foods Inc. is a fictional poultry factory farm patterned after the large poultry factory farms that dominate the American poultry industry.

AUTHOR'S NOTES

THANK YOU

Thank you for reading this book. I hope you enjoyed it. If you did, please recommend it to other readers and friends that you think might also enjoy the story. Unlike the story, no chickens were injured in the writing of this book.

I'D LIKE TO HEAR FROM YOU

A writer should always be interested in what readers think of his work. To that end, I'd like to hear from you. Please reader-rate this novel on a 1 to 5-star scale. I always appreciate constructive literary criticism, questions, comments or picking me up on historical and/or factual errors. You can contact me at *bahawkins33@gmail.com*. I promise to reply. Thanks.

ABOUT THE AUTHOR

Brian Hawkins is a Canadian writer-producer who has enjoyed an international career working and living in London, Paris, New York, Tokyo and Sydney. Television and advertising assignments have taken him to over 18 countries and he is the recipient of numerous international awards and recognition. A graduate of the Ontario College of Art who was banned from Life Classes for tracing, he is also a figurative painter who has had four one-man gallery shows, and his work hangs in attics and behind furnaces in England, France, North America and as far away as New Zealand. He is still married to his first wife and has two sons whose wives made them fathers. A lover of all things Art Deco, he is hoping that a merciful French government will forgive that unfortunate incident in the Musée d'Orsay and allow him back into France.